BEYOND REASON LIES . . .
GRIM

"Let me just say it," Melanie said with tired irritation. "Captain Bender, I saw him out there. He looked exactly the way he did in the dreams. The same dreams I've had *every single night since my husband was murdered*!"

Bender shook his head, chastised. "Sorry, Mrs. Merrick. It's just kind of hard to accept, you know?"

"Captain," said Melanie patiently, "you have a man who looks like death warmed over, walking around, twisting heads off pushers and pimps. Don't you find that hard to accept?"

Bender nodded.

"Now my dreams are different, Captain. He's on the move. He's seen something else. He has to do something about it."

"Stay out of it, Mrs. Merrick," Bender suggested. "Go home. Leave him to us. We'll stop the dreams."

"That's what I'm afraid of."

LIVING HELL

Ric Meyers

A DELL BOOK

Published by
Dell Publishing
a division of
Bantam Doubleday Dell Publishing Group, Inc.
666 Fifth Avenue
New York, New York 10103

The trademark Dell® is registered in the U.S. Patent and Trademark Office.

ISBN: 0-440-20856-4

Printed in the United States of America

Published simultaneously in Canada

October 1991

10 9 8 7 6 5 4 3 2 1

OPM

DEDICATION

To Ann and Vera
Curse you, bless you . . .
you know who you are.

ACKNOWLEDGMENTS

Thanks to C. Dean, Kurt, Tom, and Whit
for comments, suggestions, and inspirations.

PROLOGUE

Some men wish evil and accomplish it
But most men, when they work in the machine,
Just let it happen somewhere in the wheels.

The fault is no decisive villainous knife
But the dull saw that is the routine mind.

—Stephen Vincent Benet

As he slammed against the door of the patrol car, Detective Wade remembered why he had never moved into this city. Captain Bender was in the driver's seat, spinning the wheel as if he were a sea captain in rough seas.

The brown sedan sailed over a bump and landed heavily back on the rutted roadway, propelling Wade's head into the ceiling. The shock absorbers squealed and the undercarriage scraped the asphalt, sending sparks as high as the windows.

Wade looked at Bender, wondering if the NYPD captain had gone completely bonkers.

"Who has time," Bender muttered. "Drive until it falls apart." His voice was low and guttural. He didn't care whether the Connecticut cop heard him or not.

Wade didn't comment. He kept his hands on the side window and dashboard, waiting for his senses to clear. He couldn't see the street clearly. The road and buildings seemed to streak, like a watercolor picture dropped in a toilet. He got an impression of Munch-like faces that loomed in the windshield before they swept by.

His ears were filled with the crackling spit of the police radio. The dispatcher's words were calm, but very fast and brittle—constantly interrupted by tense barking from the other cars. After the first few minutes, Wade had lost the ability to distinguish words. It was now just a symphony of tightly controlled hysteria.

He had never driven so fast in the city. He was used to lurching along, taking advantage of sudden clearances, only to be slowed and stopped by a gridlock of delivery trucks and yellow cabs a few yards later. Manhattan was choked with congestion, on the streets and below them—even in the skies.

But Bender knew the shortcuts and had the siren. He weaved through the midtown traffic as if the car were jointed between the front and rear seats, his alarm shrieking. He turned, waved, and cursed. It was quite a performance.

Then they got out of midtown, and Wade held on for dear life. Bender tramped down on the accelerator. Wade could imagine the car turning into a beast that ate the road as it went, leaving jagged ditches and potholes in its wake.

The car roared up Amsterdam Avenue, Wade wedged in place. He started to glimpse the flashing lights of the other squad cars, winking between buildings on parallel streets. Red, blue, and white emergency lights chopped through the blocks like laser beams.

Bender grabbed the radio's hand mike. "We're getting close," he said after identifying himself. "What's open?"

"The Henry Hudson is clear," replied dispatch after acknowledging rank. "Straight up on Waldo."

Christ, Wade thought. This was as bad as he had suspected. Even at this time of night, clearing the Henry Hudson Bridge was no easy matter. As they drew nearer, Wade spotted frustrated travelers forced to pull over and park. Their cars looked like dead husks. He saw traffic cops pointing and spinning their arms.

Bender barely slowed down. The patrolmen recognized his vehicle and signaled it ahead. They sped across the bridge like medicine through a syringe. They streaked into Riverdale.

The mood was entirely different here. While Manhattan was dark gray, Riverdale was dark green. While the buildings on the island were like bone erupting from brittle skin, the houses here were mold-covered fungus. The place stank of greenery mixed with garbage. The dense trees, foliage, and ivy covered everything, almost completely disguising the crumbling brick, wood, and stone.

Wade knew he wasn't quite back in suburbia. Riverdale was where the city and the suburbs met, mingled . . . and mutated.

Waldo Avenue was also clear. That wasn't surprising. It was late. Most of the apartment buildings' lamps were out, but the night was infused with an unusual light that billowed on the horizon like a frozen explosion of red, blue, yellow, and white. The sky was a dome of light, made up of many illuminated circles.

"Van Cortlandt Park straight ahead," Bender said under his breath. "Mosholu Parkway and Woodlawn Cemetery to the east. Kingsbridge to the south. Hudson River to the west. What do we have here?"

The radio noise had escalated into a constant babble. Bender turned down the volume, finally slowing. Now that they were almost there, Wade felt the captain's dread like a third man in the car. Then it was gone. Bender couldn't afford to have his doubts along. Whatever was happening was big, but Bender had to control it.

"Talk to me," he said to Wade. "Tell me something. Tell me anything."

Wade still said nothing. He stared through the windshield as Waldo met Broadway and the Henry Hudson Parkway. They were close to Van Cortlandt, and the buildings and other structures seemed to leap out at them from the thick bushes and trees as they passed.

Suddenly the captain's car came upon it, the site yawning before them. One moment they had been on a quiet street. The next, they were at Groundbase Alpha, the far side of the moon.

There were lights atop every city vehicle. There were as many cars as trucks. Wade saw city parking, housing, fire, water, rescue, medical, special weapons, and tactics. Their back doors were all open, people jumping out like performers in a big circus act, alight with rainbow strobes.

The captain and the detective got out of Bender's car. The Manhattan cop was tall, with a jaw wider than his forehead, close-set gray eyes, and dark red stubble. He wore a black felt baseball jacket and coarse wool slacks. Wade was the shorter and heavier of the two. He wore the regulation blue suit under a dark tan raincoat.

They stood on either side of the car, trying to take it all in. Fire hoses were everywhere. The ground was slick, as if it was bleeding. Firemen and firewomen in their yellow and brown slickers marched by as fast as their rubber boots would let them.

City, county, and state cops were also there in

force. They appeared in every opening like surprise targets on a shooting range. Something big was definitely going on, but everyone seemed to be wandering around trying to figure out just what it was.

Bender plunged ahead, heading for the center of the hurricane. Wade had to trot to keep up with him. As they got closer to whatever it was, the crowd grew thicker. Faces slipped by Wade's vision, their expressions mingling conviction and confusion.

"Too many cooks," Bender grumbled. "Too many people giving orders around here."

The chaos was just barely contained at the perimeter. Riverdale and Kingsbridge cops were struggling to keep most of the neighborhood residents away from the site. Everyone had rushed here to see what had happened. The nearby homeowners had thought it was the end of the world. The police on duty had heard the explosion from miles away.

"What is it?" Wade asked them as Bender pushed through the circle of people. "What happened?"

None answered. Their tired faces looked straight ahead. Some stared as if hypnotized. Some were crying, but without showing any emotion. It was an automatic reaction to any change.

He followed their gaze as he and Bender broke through. The captain looked in amazement at the gaping, smoking hole where the block had once been.

A fireman walked by Wade, looking down, shaking his head. The detective stopped him and showed him his badge. Even though it was a Connecticut shield, the fireman talked.

"Damnedest thing I've ever seen," he said. "Look." He pointed up. Above the shallow crater were trees, their thickly leafed branches waving in the night wind. "Not a scorch on them," marveled the fireman. He looked down into the hole. "Whatever was on this block went up so fast there's hardly any rubble left." He looked up at the trees again with something close to wonder. "Yet not a burn mark on them."

The fireman walked away. Wade looked at the multicolored leaves carefully. The explosion . . . or whatever it was . . . *hadn't even knocked the autumn leaves off the trees.*

Wade felt a chill. He looked back down at the strangely empty block. Except for the mob, it looked as if city wreckers had just left. (Coming Soon to This Spot: another convenience center or a parking garage.) He noticed that the captain was moving deeper into the devastation, leaving Wade behind with the audience.

"What used to be there?" he asked the cop behind him.

The man shrugged. "I'm from Kingsbridge," he said.

Wade asked a passing light-and-power-department man. "I don't know," the man said irritably. He continued to mutter while moving away. "God, no leaks. But there's got to be leaks. Not our fault this time . . ."

Wade turned, frowning. No leaves burned, no trees aflame, no gas leaks, liquid or otherwise. He turned to an old woman in a housecoat next to him. "What used to be there?"

"Here?" said the woman. "Well, it was . . . a block, you know?" She suddenly turned away from him. "Isn't that funny?" she said in a distant voice. "I've lived here all my life. Isn't that funny? What *was* here?"

She didn't turn back to him. Wade stepped away from her. He looked at all their faces. They looked at the missing section of their town as if watching a less than riveting lecture. Wade took another step back.

Suddenly he noticed a flash of white out of the corner of his eye.

He turned in that direction. The white had vanished behind a squat copper water truck. Wade started to walk away from the site, parallel to the white.

There it was again. As he moved past the front of an ambulance, he saw the whiteness moving behind fire and police people. It disappeared behind a fire truck.

Wade kept dogging it, trying to remember what it was reminding him of. *A person . . . wearing billowing white, moving in a jerking slow motion.* Actually, the white he was looking at now was moving almost between speeds, its limbs shaking in a strangely frightening rhythm.

Wade remembered a nightmare he had had as a child. No images, just shapes. Shapes and movements. He remembered it was almost as if time itself had been taunting him. *Someday he would get old. Someday he would fall apart. Someday he would die. . . .*

Wade snapped his fingers, the sound popping the memory like a balloon. *That's it,* he thought. *Curse of the Mummy.* That movie. That had scared the crap out of him when he was a kid. That's what the figure in white reminded him of.

Wade kept going, not wanting this irrational fear to make him lose his grip now. He would confront it and defeat it. *Probably just a doctor or a nurse,* he thought, *wearing a long lab coat.* Then he could laugh at himself and get back to Bender and find out what had happened here.

The detective took a shortcut between vans. He just missed the figure in white, who moved behind a police truck. Wade started to trot. He jogged to the other side of the truck, just missing the white again.

He brushed past milling officials, mumbling apologies. The figure had moved between hose-carrying trucks. Wade started to run. He raced to the other end of the trucks, almost colliding with an ambulance that was parked in front of the fire engines.

Wade slipped and nearly fell, coming to a stop with bent knees, one hand on the cement, the other on the ambulance door.

"You okay?" he heard. He looked up into the face of a paramedic. "You need any help, mister?"

"Fine," Wade said breathlessly, standing. "Just slipped."

"Just our luck," said another paramedic, sitting on the ambulance's bumper. "Called out this time of night, to this ruin, and there's not one injury!"

"Thanks," Wade said hastily, already moving. "Did you see . . ."

"What?" asked the first paramedic in confusion as Wade swept by him, heading around the ambulance.

Wade heard other words, but he was already turning his head, calling back to the paramedics. "Somebody . . . in white . . ."

He nearly ran into her. He stopped short, both feet sliding on the slick pavement. This time he did fall, at her feet. Her face was in his sight for a second, but before his memory could latch on, the image smeared as he fell.

He landed on his rear, the wind knocked out of him. His eyes teared, clouding his vision. He heard her speak, but the blood thundering in his head drowned out the words.

"Wait," he gasped, but she was already past.

The paramedics were on him, their hands on his sleeves, their bodies blocking his sight. He tried to pull away. He tried to point. He tried to tell them to leave him alone, but he couldn't find the strength. Finally when he could breathe, he roughly pulled himself free. "If you want a . . . a *victim,*" he said angrily, pointing between them, "there!"

They blinked and turned. "Where?" they said. "Who?"

Wade was already shouldering between them, running toward the figure in white.

It was a woman. That much was painfully evident by her shape and long blond hair falling across her shoulder blades. It was a fairly young woman.

She was wearing a white dress. As Wade got closer, he could make it out in more detail. Not white, really —bone-colored. Tight, satiny, with lace and pearl trim.

It was a wedding dress, he realized. The skirt was torn, ripped up her legs in tatters. He could see her dirty, blood-streaked calves and bare, blackened feet.

How could they have missed this? he wondered. *How could the fire, police, and medical personnel have missed her? She must have come from the explosion site. How did she get past everyone?*

He saw her head was moving. He heard quiet words, but couldn't make them out. He saw her arms at her sides, hands in front, fingers seemingly feeling the air. She walked slowly but purposefully, like a blind person refusing to acknowledge her handicap.

Wade had trouble reaching her. His mind was making him stumble. It was as if his brain was trying to get a message to him through a brick wall. He couldn't think, but he didn't let that stop him.

He got his hands on her shoulders. He turned her around. He looked into the face of someone he knew. Someone he had come to Manhattan to find. The wall collapsed. The spell was broken.

"Melanie!"

Melanie Merrick stared up at him with empty eyes. She didn't recognize him.

"Melanie," he repeated, gripping her shoulders harder. "It's me. Detective Wade. Westport Police? Remember?" Her eyes remained hollow and unseeing. "Are you all right? Where have you been? We've been looking everywhere for you."

The paramedics were back, trying to push past Wade to get to her. They had finally found a customer and they weren't going to let her get away.

"Wait a minute!" Wade yelled angrily. "Wait a minute! Back off! Let her talk!"

Suddenly all three men backed up, giving her room. They stared at her, confused. All had suddenly became aware of how muddled their thinking was, as if looking at her had given them a cue. But, try as they might, they couldn't clear the mist from their minds. The closer they had gotten to the site, the more constipated their thought processes had become.

They were all gripped by it, this cone of confusion that hovered over Van Cortlandt Park. A block had been razed to the ground and not one of the dozens who stood there knew why, how, or by what.

Her lips moved. The words were tiny but certain. She said them like a little girl, not like a drunk. Her words cut through the men's skulls, nestling in the center of their pulpy brains.

"Let me tell you what evil is," she said. "I want you to know what evil is. . . ."

PART ONE

I am! yet what I am who cares, or knows?
My friends forsake me like a memory lost.

—John Clare
(written in Northampton
County Asylum)

1

The only thing he was certain of was that his name was Grim. The rest was lost in his mind. He searched through it the way he searched the streets. He walked slowly, carefully, feeling pain in every step. He had no preconceptions and no hopes. He simply tried to be ready for whatever he found. He didn't know what he was looking for but had faith he'd recognize it when he saw it.

He kept his head down, but his eyes were always moving. He studied the sidewalks, the streets, the buildings that he passed. He used the other pedestrians as beacons. He dared not let them see his face. He instinctively knew he was not like them. He trudged from one to the next, getting as close as he could. They all reacted the same way.

He knew he was getting too close when they began to move away like opposing magnets. Only then did he straighten his feet and keep his distance. He could feel them relax. That was when he would look at them.

They never looked back. They dared not make eye contact, as if afraid they would turn to stone. He was just a bum, they probably thought. Who knew what he'd do if they returned his gaze?

Their features burned into Grim's mind. He was starting a collection. Every face. Every nuance. Every reaction their features elicited in him. What was beauty? What was ugliness? How did the minute movements of the brows, eyes, nose, and mouth mingle to create meaning?

The face was the closest thing to the brain. It was the soul's signpost, the heart's diplomat and translator. Grim wanted to learn. He *had* to learn, or he would never find what he was looking for.

Consciousness. It was gone. He had lost the connection to his god. He had no guidance, no direction, no control. Every waking moment was a wonder. His thoughts weren't a jumble the way those around him were. There wasn't foreground thinking against background noise. His every sensation was distinct.

He heard the requests going into his brain, like letters sinking in tar. *Please let me walk.* He felt the orders from his brain moving to his limbs like electric shocks. *Make him walk.* They were reluctant pronouncements from a dictator he couldn't see.

He felt the pain with every movement. It came from every limb, but mostly from his stomach. His right hand pressed at the spot, as if it had been grafted there. He was stopping up a slit, a hole that was barely covered with a spider's web of skin.

He felt the blood sloshing in the barely repaired veins. He felt a curtain on the inside of his flesh, like a single coat of fresh paint. The battle raged there and the dictator up top was barely keeping it under control.

Unlike all the people around him, Grim was not fooled. He was the one who knew that the brain controlled him—he did not control his brain. It was more powerful than he, and smarter. It knew things he would never know, and it would always keep secrets from him.

But that was all Grim knew. He didn't even remember where his name had come from. He had awakened on a subway platform and gone in search of his consciousness. So he moved from person to person like a moth to flames. He looked at them, and he remembered them. He swore he would never forget anything again.

Every brick in the walls, every crack on the sidewalks, every sight, every name, and every sign he would bury in his memory. One Hundred and Tenth Street, he read. Cathedral Parkway. He looked around. There were no more people. He was safe. He could raise his head.

The large, seemingly lidless black eyes glowed dimly, reflecting moonlight. The still-tattered skin was riffled by the wind. Some bits flaked and fell off. The nose was torn, almost flat, the nostrils protected by the thinnest layer of almost translucent flesh. The lips were torn and pulled back. The teeth were ivory-white, burned clean, the color of skulls.

He walked until the asphalt turned to glass-covered grass of yellow, green, and brown. It sparkled beneath his feet, but each crystal had a bite. He tried to place his feet in between the bits of colored glass.

The cars sped by him on his right, six lanes thick, going in the opposite direction. Their headlight beams moved across him in curtains of white. They slapped his right eye, keeping him awake. He used the strobing to study his clothing. He wore black high-top sneakers, denim pants, a black T-shirt, and an olive-colored army jacket. He did not know where they had come from. He knew they had once felt good, but now they were dirty and torn. The grit inside them rubbed like sandpaper.

On his left was the river, held in by the wharves nearby and the cliffs across the way. Grim turned and contemplated the water. Despite the oil, tires, cans, and planks floating in it, it continued moving inexorably to the sea. It looked so deep and so cold. Perhaps he could find solace there. Perhaps he could join with it and find peace.

He took a step toward the river's edge. At that moment, the surface of the water seemed to separate. Grim looked up, mouth agape, as pieces of the water seemed to rise from the river. He stepped back. As he watched, the drops took new shapes of their own. Grim realized they weren't exploding water. They were undulating crystals. They were gem-worms.

Grim recoiled, snarling. The wound at his waist seemed to flare. He grimaced and almost went down. He silently shouted at his brain to give him strength. He could imagine the dictator up there studying the charts. Gem-worms. Living impulses. Something Grim could see but no one else could. Evidence that another sort of creature was nearby. Something beyond the natural.

The pain covered him before he could name the threat he knew he had faced once before. The pain picked him up and threw him away from the water. He ran north, hunched over. He tried to think, but the dictator was pounding him with sensations. The lightning filled him, threatening to explode, tearing him apart.

Grim begged. He begged to know why the swirling, sparkling gems made him feel so ill. He begged to know what he was looking for and why he was running. He begged to know who and where he was.

It was too much for his wounded, battered body. His need had overwhelmed everything. His final connection to his senses snapped. The dictator immediately cut off all communication.

But the body kept moving. Freed from pain, the mind made it walk quickly, stopping only when it had to—resting by leaning on fences and trees. Grim did not see the buildings give way to forest and structures that looked like giant brick headstones. He did not see that just a few blocks from places dense with people were empty monuments to corruption and decay. In these huge squares of rubble, the war was over. Everyone had lost.

The dictator was alone in his bunker. One by one, his army had collapsed. He was holding on by sheer force of will. He *was* Grim's will. And he knew it was time to retreat. He had to get to a place of safety, then regroup. He could no longer ask the neural system to report. That unit had deserted. Instead, the dictator searched for a mausoleum in which to fall.

He directed the limbs toward the closest structure, lightning flashing all around him. The empty slum building grew larger and larger until it almost completely filled his vision. The dictator looked around wildly, trying to secure the location. The signs sped past, but he could read them.

One Hundred and Eighty-third Street. High Bridge Park. The Harlem River to one side, the Hudson River way on the other.

Grim slammed into a wall. He nearly toppled over backward.

"No!" bellowed a voice inside his head. "You're here now. You're safe. Let nothing stop you!"

Grim heard him. The words were distant, but distinct. He still couldn't see or feel, but he heard him. He smiled, wasting valuable muscle energy. But he couldn't help it. His god was back. His god would not desert him. His god loved him.

Grim's hands found the weak spot. In the huge expanse of brick, there was a portion of steel and wood. Grim's entire body surged forward. He would not be denied, or he would die. The partition sprang inward, swinging, accompanied by a sharp cracking sound.

For a second, Grim stood framed in the doorway, his form in silhouette against the moonlight. Emptiness yawned behind him. Darkness pulled at his front. Finally he fell and was swallowed by the black.

He was a handsome man. He had brown hair and brown eyes. He was six feet one inch tall. He was muscular, with broad shoulders and a slim, hard waist. He was a good man. Fair, reasonable, certain, educated. He was moral. He didn't smoke, drink, or take drugs. He was an insatiable explorer. He always wanted to know more, do more, be more.

He was a brilliant man. He appreciated beauty in all things, but knew beauty was a side effect of love. Beauty came from love of oneself and of life. He wanted to revel in the possibilities of living. He prided himself in excellence. He wanted to be the best, knowing that human perfection was the understanding and acceptance of good and bad, as well as the repudiation of evil.

He could dance, he could cook, he could make love without guilt or fear. He was magnificent. His name was Geoffrey Robert Merrick. His initials were monogrammed on his tailor-made shirts. G.R.M.

He could fly.

He flew through the puffy white clouds and the bright blue skies. He could catch falling planes and smash apart storms. His smile lit the heavens. He winked once and sped off.

Beneath him was the railroad station.

The clouds disappeared and the sky turned a deep dark blue. He slowly floated down to the parking lot and landed. The sky turned purple, then black. All the cars disappeared in the darkness, save one.

Its keys were in his hand. He opened the door. He sat in the driver's seat. He put the key in the ignition.

"No, no, no, no, no!" his wife screamed, sitting bolt upright in bed.

The dream was immediately gone, its only evidence the rattle of the bedroom window pane. Melanie Merrick looked toward it. She knew she had screamed in her sleep again, even though she hadn't heard the words. She knew she had had the same nightmare, even though she couldn't remember it now.

She reached yearningly with her mind, hoping to capture some part of it, but it was completely gone. She was alone again. She thought about crying, but knew she couldn't. She had already seen too much. She was alone now even in crowds. The only time she hadn't been alone was when she was asleep. But now even that was over. Her dream monster was lost.

She looked around the room. It was much the same as it had been when Geoffrey was alive. Clean, soft, light, and warm. He had known the colors and textures that would soothe. Even though he was gone, they worked their magic on her.

Melanie got up and went to the adjoining bathroom. She drank a glass of water, then splashed some on her face. She put her hands on the counter and stared at herself as the drops ran down her features. Blond and blue-eyed as ever. Skin smooth and pale. Nose straight, lips neither too thin nor too thick. The only difference between the time Geoffrey was alive and dead was how she clothed and carried herself.

The blue eyes were now never as bright. But what she lost in color, she had gained in depth. Her hair was rarely loose now. It was either in a tight tail or as it was now, in a bun.

She wondered how it would look if she cut her hair. Would a short hairstyle perk up her face? Would others notice the sweep of her neck and the strength of her chin? Would it enhance the swell of her chest, the sweep of her hips? Would it make others notice her more?

Melanie didn't want that. Her gaze flitted down the mirror to settle on her body. She didn't wear the tights and lace T-shirt to bed anymore. Now it was his T-shirts and pajama bottoms. She liked them loose. She didn't want to see her shape.

She wasn't about to ruin her body purposely by drinking or eating heavily, but she refused to enhance it knowingly anymore either. She didn't want people attracted to her just because of her face and figure. Even so, she'd be damned if that was going to force her to punish herself.

Damned, she thought. *That's what I am.* Ever since Geoffrey got into his car that night and turned on the ignition. The bomb had been so powerful it tore open the vehicle. The fire was so intense it cremated everything inside. Even the tires were ripped apart and scattered.

That was when the dreams started. Melanie had always had dreams, but after Geoffrey died, they were no longer hers. *That's it,* she realized. She had been having someone else's dreams. They were dreams of death, destruction, evil, and resurrection. They were dreams she flew through, as if she were part of a cosmic wind.

Melanie toweled off her face and went back into

the bedroom. The clock read 4:56. Good, she thought, nodding. *The Avengers* would be on the local New York station. By the time the exercise and news programs came on, she might be tired enough to try sleeping again.

At least she didn't have to worry about being late for work. Geoffrey had seen to that. Even in death he was protecting her. He had had insurance policies with independent brokers and through his corporate holdings.

Melanie propped up the pillows and grabbed the TV remote control. She sat waiting for five o'clock— her back straight, her legs straight out and crossed at the ankle. Her mind began to wander. Geoffrey had been murdered. The police had no suspects—not even a man assigned to the case any longer.

Geoffrey had died because he didn't want drug money corrupting the corporation he worked for. Just before he was taken off the case, Detective Wade of the Westport Police Department had told her that the key to Geoffrey's killer was at Dice-Corp —the company he had lived and died for. And if his murderer was going to be caught, it was up to her.

And so, Melanie investigated. But she wasn't alone. The dream monster was with her. She had been able to see him whenever she slept. She even thought she had seen him on the streets of New York, but she couldn't be sure. There had been too much death. There were men, and blood, and sliced skin, and guts spilling into the gutter. . . .

The Saigon syndrome, her doctor had called it. It was a particularly virulent form of shock that shuts part of the consciousness down when events become too horrifying. A side effect could be certain symptoms of amnesia. The mind couldn't remember what it wouldn't allow itself to.

But it might give hints. . . .

Melanie shook her head, holding the TV remote control in front of her like a protective weapon. Geoffrey was dead. The dream monster was gone. She was alone. Totally alone.

The television on the console at the opposite wall came to vivid life. She had timed it perfectly. Across the twenty-five-inch screen was the image of a chessboard with life-size pieces. A man fell dead with a knife in his back.

Oh good, she thought. *An Emma Peel episode.*

"Extraordinary crimes against the people and the state have to be avenged by agents extraordinary. . . ."

Melanie tried to blank out her mind during the commercials, but instead she saw the face of Valentino DiCenzo, the head of Dice-Corp and her guardian angel. She still had the keys to his New Jersey estate in Cape May, and could use it anytime, with the blessings of his wife, Louise.

She saw the face of Keith Sullivan, a contemporary of Geoffrey's—another vice-president at the company, as well as an ardent admirer of hers. He had tried to offer comfort and consolation after her husband's death, but never really had a chance. Visions of the dream monster had kept intruding. Maybe now that the dream monster was gone . . .

Melanie snapped out of her reverie when the commercials finally ended. She saw Christopher Lee walking beside an English country road. She saw him wander into the middle of the street. She saw a car hit him. She saw the driver examine the body. She saw Lee pronounced dead. She saw him get up and walk away. The music swelled as the title came on the screen.

"Never, Never Say Die."

The music faded as the subtitle appeared.

"In which Steed meets a dead man, and Emma fights the corpse."

Melanie Merrick stared in disbelief. Then she started to laugh. Her laughter pealed through the house like falling crystal.

2

He saw the flames. Fire meant more to him than just licking tongues of yellow-orange. Like everything in his existence, Grim considered them in terms of pain. Beyond those tongues were teeth, which bit at him—trying to eat him whole.

He saw them cover him. He saw himself swirling inside them. He saw them spit him out, ash-covered and smoking. He saw them erupt from his prone body, as if his limbs were mined. Flame exploded from his joints: from his knees, from his elbows, from his shoulders, and finally from his forehead.

The fire covered his vision, then just as suddenly winked out. There was still fire, but not in him. This time the flames came in streams, flowing from the hands of four young men. He took a step toward them, but the fire did his work for him.

The young men were smiling, feeling the power of the flames that shot from their arms. But the fire had a surprise. The young men were not controlling the conflagration. It was using them. As they laughed, the flames began to crawl back, over their wrists.

As they watched, the fire crossed over their forearms. It began sweeping over them like an oil slick. Their expressions changed from those of sadistic pleasure to ones of pain-wracked terror. Grim had started forward to fight . . . but now he sought to save them.

Too late. He was always too late. The flames leaped from their arms into their mouths. Fire covered their faces. It surged into their hair, lighting them like matches. Grim had to move back because the heat was too great.

The young men stood as if rooted, fire replacing their flesh. They twitched as the flames crackled with loud laughter. Grim stepped back until he could see them all, standing beside one another, consumed in fire. The flames' crackling grew in volume until Grim had to cover his ears.

At that moment the four men erupted as if made of napalm. The fire swept across the landscape, burning it clean. The inferno swept Grim back, tumbling. It hurled him into a mountain of corpses.

He stood at the base of the mountain of prone dead. All their feet faced outward. All their heads faced inward. All their faces were up, all their eyes were open. Their skin was mottled, discolored in tones of dark purple and green.

Many lips were pulled back across clenched teeth, as if these bodies were doing vicious impersonations of Grim's appearance. Many others' mouths were open, their pulpy tongues lolling out. Their stench was almost worse than the sight.

Grim stood in the center, at the base of the pile. He did not blink. He did not flinch. He searched among their intertwined limbs for a way out. As far as he could tell, the base was as wide as the hill was tall. Pushing through to freedom in either direction would take as long.

Grim accepted his situation. He saw no other option. He pushed his hands forward and started to move through the bodies.

They were all rotting. The skin was like wet paper. Every time he pulled or pushed, whatever he touched ripped off.

An arm came off, dropping to his feet. Blood flowed out from the shoulder stump. A head tore off, falling slowly. When it hit the ground, it cracked open. The brain oozed at the opening, as if trying to escape.

Grim backed away, too quickly. His hand hit a torso and sank in. He pulled it out, seeing intestines flop to the ground like so many crimson-coated tubes.

Grim stood completely still. His eyes narrowed as his mind adjusted. What were they, he asked himself. Blood, guts, and bone. They were dead. What was he? Somehow, someway, alive. So be it.

Grim continued to dig through while blood splattered him. Even when the faces started to blink and scream at him, he kept going. He concentrated only on his goal.

He could see the open air just a few yards beyond. When the limbs started to multiply, he only dug through them faster. When the added corpses tried to keep pace with him, he became a human drill, his arms windmilling.

When he couldn't see anything but blood and bodies anymore, he finally burst through, taking limbs and flesh with him.

Grim was on his hands and knees, panting. He was covered in guts. He got his breath back and started to wipe himself off. He stood and looked back at the mountain.

The bodies were like a wall, with just the smallest of openings to show where Grim had come from. Their limbs were interlocked like a giant jigsaw puzzle. Grim looked up to see that they were no longer a mountain. All the corpses were part of a huge limb. Grim had come from the ankle of a giant leg.

Grim backed away until he could see the entire figure. His shriveled lips came off his teeth.

Grim ran back the way he had come. He raced between the creature's legs. He stood there, holding himself in the same position as the corpse giant.

The corpses began to disintegrate. They turned to dust from the feet on up. Grim watched the faces melt, the limbs dissolve. He recognized them all. They were the faces of the people he had killed.

As the dissolution went faster and faster, the giant seemed to crack, come apart, and completely shatter. It turned to red dust, which rained down on Grim the Undead.

He stood up to his knees in a red desert, covered in a coat of scarlet sand.

He raised his arms to the sky. He had won. He was still alive!

That was when Melanie Merrick woke up. She stared at the canopy of her bed with a mixture of relief and loathing. Her dream monster was back. And her husband's murderer was still out there, waiting.

Grim allowed himself a smile. He had faced evil and not given in. He wasn't happy, but he was satisfied.

That was a mistake. He was betrayed by his own body. He felt the pain from inside, digging from his stomach outward. His grin turned to grimace, his knees buckling. He looked down in time to see the skin on his torso rip open. He saw the steel snake emerge. It stopped halfway out and turned its sharpened head toward him. It smiled, then slithered all the way out, smacking the ground in a coil.

Grim's body began to collapse. His heart dropped, hitting his stomach, which smashed into his liver, taking out his spleen, all colliding with his intestines. They all streamed out of the gash in him, sloshing on the ground.

Grim folded up, his bones clacking against one another. He felt his brain falling, the images streaking, the mind wiped clean. His identity was once again gone.

The handsome man was back in the realm between life and death. There was no tunnel of blue lasers, no great white light to follow. He did not float or fly. He merely existed and perceived.

"Hello," said the Imp.

He finally recognized it. The creature with the evolving shape, surrounded by the gem-worms it created. Its minions were impulses, which fed on weaknesses of the mind. The greater the human temptation, the stronger the impulse. He remembered it all.

"Nearly had you that time," said the Imp. He felt its smile inside his mind.

"Not quite," he said.

"Oh? Why do you think you're back here? You're very close to joining me. You'll soon be mine."

Grim was not impressed. "So take me."

The Imp became angry, its shape darkening. Gem-worms shot from it, swirling through the air like drill bits. They slammed into him, shattering like glass. He bore down with his mind, sending out a shock wave that burst the impulses in midair.

The Imp became clear. The gem-worms disappeared.

"That all you have?" Grim asked derisively.

"Don't gloat," said the Imp. "If I'm here for a reason, so are you."

Grim shrugged. "I'm healing. This is the only place I can go." His mind had opened upon death, and he had fallen into the Imp's realm. He had rejected both the Imp and death. He had returned to the human body . . . such as it was.

"Undead," the Imp taunted.

"Unknown," he replied.

"But with you, I can become known," the Imp insisted. "With your power, we can bridge between my world and yours. It *has* to be. Why else would you be sent here?"

For a moment he saw the logic of the Imp's reasoning. At that moment, it took all the Imp's willpower not to bombard him with impulses. But that would have surely put him on his guard.

"I *fell* in here," he said. "It was not predestined. It was a mistake! I'm here when there is nowhere else for me to go."

The Imp grew dark and threatening again. "Liar," it said. "There *is* somewhere else for you to go. The place you escaped from. The place that traps you . . . that frightens you." The Imp started to grow. "If you will not help me, I will not have you here. Get out. Return to the walls of your mind."

The Imp was gigantic now, filled with gem-worms. He could see millions of them coiling inside the frustrated, angry creature.

"Get out!" it screamed, about to burst. "Get out, *now*!"

Grim's eyes snapped open. He felt his body start. The black, glistening orbs adjusted to the dark immediately. He was in a cellar. He was alone, except for the rats. They kept their distance, smelling the death of one of their own on him.

Grim dimly remembered finding dead rats around him the very first time he had awakened. He must have killed them in his sleep.

He lay on hard mounds of dirt; rotted boards and rusted metal surrounded him. The walls were made of cement blocks covered in dust. Above his head were dark brown beams of different widths and lengths, covered by a network of wet iron and copper pipes.

Out of the corner of his eye he could see a doorway set a few feet up in the far wall. It was slightly open. It must have swung shut after he fell through it, although he didn't recall the incident.

Grim closed his eyes. He felt better but was still exhausted. He didn't know how long he had been here, but he wanted more sleep. He had to continue sleeping. . . .

"Get up."

Grim did not open his eyes, but he came to full awareness.

"Get up," he heard.

Grim tensed his muscles. They complained, but responded without mind-numbing pain.

"Get up," his god repeated.

Grim's god was handsome, with brown hair and brown eyes. He was muscular. He was a fair, moral god. He gave Grim direction and guidance. He made Grim do what had to be done.

He was reconnected. Knowledge and memory flowed back into him. He saw the teenage gang who had called themselves the Firebeaters. They had killed derelicts. He had killed them. He saw the Avenue A pushers. They sold poison. He had killed them. He saw the man who called himself Cryst, the

King of Killers. He saw the man's knife, with its wicked grin, burying its teeth in his stomach. Grim had killed him too.

Grim saw the blood, heard the bones crack and break, felt the living flecks hitting his face. . . .

"Get up," said his god again.

Grim did not move. He did not want to fight. He was too exhausted.

"Listen," his god said.

Grim listened. High above him, he heard the sound of movement, the vibration of words, and the noise of struggle. Down here, far below, the ceiling planks quivered, sending a shower of dirt across Grim's prone form.

Let them be, Grim thought tiredly. *Let them go.*

"Listen!" his god insisted.

Grim started to breathe more deeply. His body grew heavier, sinking in the dirt. His mind cleared, as if a skull light had gone on.

The sounds were louder now, sharper. His brain cross-referenced them with the sounds he had heard on the streets. The deeper-toned noises were strident, tense, and fast. A higher-pitched sound was breathless and desperate. Heavier vibrations were certain and solid. The lighter vibrations seemed to fly, then fall.

Grim finally heard a faraway shriek, muffled at the end, then cut off.

Grim recognized bravado, anger, and fear.

"Get up," his god insisted.

Grim got his elbows under him. His back came off the dirt. He sat up. His stomach rumbled, then actually seemed to squeal. Grim ignored the pain from his wound. It really wasn't that bad. But he realized he was starving.

He looked around. Nothing but rats. And they might be poison.

They scattered when he stood. He stood slowly, like a growing tree. He looked at the door and turned away from it. The noise was coming from up above, not from outside.

There was a rotting stairway against the wall behind him. Grim drew in breath through his loosely clenched teeth and trudged toward the steps.

As he climbed higher, the sounds grew louder. As he slid his feet across the first-floor landing, he could make out one constantly repeated word.

"Bitch."

It was being used almost as punctuation, said more sharply and loudly than any other word. It was being said with effort, like little explosions.

Grim continued to climb the stairs, his head down, his shoulders hunched. He had to go carefully. He had to put his feet on the most solid stairs, often skipping two at a time. If he wasn't careful, he would plunge through a rotting step.

Grim stopped for a moment on the second floor. The sounds came from here, but he could see no doorway. The place used to be an apartment house, with a center staircase that emptied onto tall, narrow halls. The black-and-white fleur-de-lis wallpaper was rent and peeling.

Grim walked slowly but smoothly along the hall, listening.

"You can't play games with us, *bitch*; we're not your usual scum, *bitch*; charging three for the price of one, *bitch*; now you're going to get it like you've never gotten it before, *bitch*."

The apartment door had been plastered over, Grim realized. There used to be two entrances to the apartment, but now there was only one, from the front. Grim had entered the building from the back.

He kept moving, raising and lowering his head to look through the small holes in the wall. He looked through a foot-wide gap filled with balsa wood slats, crumbling mortar, metal cords, and plaster chips.

"You think anybody cares about you, bitch?" The man had grabbed the kneeling bleached-blond girl by the hair, then pulled her head back so she had to look at him. "You think your pimp is going to save your sorry white ass?"

Another man laughed, looking on. "Yeah, you can't treat us like your usual johns, bitch. We're special."

The man holding her hair gave it another yank. She cried out again. "Yeah, bitch. We paid your little pimp plenty, so there's nothing you can do about it."

A third man stood away from the others, his arms folded, his face calm. "He said we could do whatever we wanted with you. So we are. We will."

The hair puller did it one more time. "So no 'that'll be twenty bucks more,' bitch," he said. "We're going to do the sex encyclopedia on you, bitch, for free!"

The second one laughed. "Yeah, Ike, let's do all the 'linguses' on her."

The hair puller threw her down. She just barely got her hands under her in time. Her face was red and covered in sweat. Her hair hung, limp and dripping, across her eyes.

The man's hands went to his pants. "Yeah. Hold her down, Shel."

Grim sagged heavily against the banister. It almost gave way under his weight. The men did not hear it. They were too busy trying to get their anger to its fever pitch.

"Come on, hold her down, will you, Shel?"

"I'm holding her down, I'm holding her down! Stop wiggling, will you, bitch?"

"Hey, no sweat there, Shel, I kinda like it."

Both men laughed. "Hey, Phil, aren't you going to help?"

Phil didn't answer. He just kept standing off to the side, watching calmly.

"Let's go, Shel, let's go. I can't hold on forever."

"Damn, damn, just so close to the wall. Can't you get her back from the wall?"

"Sure, Shel." Ike got up from his crouch, still holding the girl's arms, and dragged her, kicking, to the center of the room.

"That's better," said Shel, starting to walk after them.

He stopped suddenly, two and a half feet away from the wall. His head snapped back and he made a strange gurgling sound. Then he dived backward, head first, into the wall itself.

The two other men gasped and shouted. The girl was able to raise herself up on one elbow, the back of her hand across her mouth. They watched as Shel burrowed backward into the wall.

Grim kept his fingers tightly gripped in the man's hair and kept yanking, as if hauling a boat in by its anchor line. He had taken off his jacket and reached through a hole in the wall only big enough for his arm. Then he had slammed the man back.

Grim felt the head coming through the balsa wood and plaster. He felt the slats and metal tearing at the man's scalp and skin. But he kept pulling. He "sawed" the man through. Whenever the movement stopped, Grim put slack in his arms, then yanked again. He made the man a pile driver.

He slammed the man's head through, making a bigger hole. He got hold of his chin and slammed his shoulders through, making an even bigger hole. Grim grabbed the man's lapels and dragged his torso through.

"Remember what it was like being born?" Grim heard inside his mind.

Then the overworked wall gave way. A man-shaped doorway was ripped out of it, creating a rain cloud of white dust.

Ike had gotten to his feet. Both men and the girl stared in wonder at the hole. When the dust settled they saw a completely different man standing there.

He was thin and looked short, but that was because he was hunched over. His black T-shirt was streaked with white. His arms were amazing. They looked like long coiled bands of wet steel hemp. They were dark amber, almost black gold. His head was down, but they could see his long, matted hair, barely covering his livid skull.

"Who . . . who the fuck are you, man?" Ike stammered.

"Who cares who he is, stupid," Phil shouted. "Get rid of him!"

Phil ran forward and grabbed the girl by the hair again, dragging her back. Ike's head twisted that way and then back. Grim had not moved or spoken.

"Get out of here, man!" Ike yelled. "What the hell did you do to Shel?"

Grim did not move or speak.

"I've got a knife, man!" Ike announced, pulling it from his pocket. It was a long switchblade. He clicked it open and the blade caught the moonlight.

Grim remembered the steel snake chewing through him. It smiled up at him from the patched hole in his torso. He almost stepped back.

"Don't," said his god.

"I'll stick you, man!" shouted Ike. "I'll stick you good!"

"Don't say it," shouted Phil, holding the girl as a shield. "Do it!"

Ike charged forward. Grim didn't move. He watched the knife.

When Ike was three feet away, Grim jumped to his left. He grabbed Ike's wrist as he went, twisting it with both hands. He twisted up, back and around, keeping the grinning silver blade as far away from him as possible.

Ike grimaced and grunted, feeling his muscles pulling and bone joints locking. He stopped short, trying to move back. Grim stepped in front of him, still holding on to his wrist with one hand.

Ike saw his face. He opened his mouth to shout in surprise, warning, and fear, but then Grim's palm filled his vision. Afterward all he saw was black.

Grim let go and stepped back, lowering his head. Ike fell like a cut tree, his nose pressed inside his face, the one bone lanced into the underside of his brain. He smashed, back first, into the floor—his arms wide.

They heard the floor crunch and saw another cloud of dust rise. When it settled, Grim was still there.

Phil had his own knife and it was pressed against the girl's throat. "Back off, man," he said. Grim didn't move. "I'll stick her," he warned.

Grim's shoulders slumped even further. *Let him go*, he thought.

"No," said his god.

What will he do? Grim thought. *He won't hurt her now. He just wants to get away.*

"No," said his god.

She's a prostitute, Grim thought. *She let them pay for her.*

"Look at her," said his god.

She wasn't really pretty. Her face was round, her nose flat, her chin weak, and her lips too thin. She was underfed, but had a solid bone structure. Her tear-filled eyes were hazel, and her hair roots were mousy brown.

No, not really pretty, Grim thought. *Beautiful*.

"Victim," said his god.

Grim took a step forward.

"I'll cut her," Phil said. "I swear!" He shook her, pressing the knife tighter against her throat.

Ike's body was the only thing between them. Grim purposely took another step, putting his foot squarely on Ike's chest.

The floor gave way when he put his full weight on it.

Phil and the girl watched as the two bodies disappeared through the floor.

Grim dropped twelve feet in a torrent of spinning wood and plaster. Ike's body crashed to the floor below. He had turned slowly during the drop and landed face first.

Grim used Ike's back as a cushion. He felt the skin around his wound tearing as he slid sideways. He landed on his own back, groaning.

The dust hadn't even settled when he heard his god shouting.

"Get up, get up! Don't let him get away!"

Grim saw the girl's face. He knew she didn't want to be a prostitute. Nobody *wanted* to be a prostitute. But he had to do this quickly, before the dictator overrode his god and cut off all power again.

His eyes opened. He snapped to his feet. He saw a collapsed table and some chairs at the side of the room. He grabbed a chair. He put it in the center of the room. Over his head, some feet to the side, Phil peered through the ceiling hole, still holding the girl, still holding the knife to her throat. All he saw was Ike.

Grim stepped on the chair, then onto the chair back. He stood straight, with perfect balance, grabbing at the hanging, broken light fixture. He hoped it was strong enough.

He grabbed the thick cord attaching the fixture to the ceiling. He pulled himself up.

The girl tried to pull her hair out of the man's grip. He pushed the knife as tight against her throat as it could go without breaking skin. He was trying to look through the big hole in the floor. She was looking behind him. She saw a small hole behind him start to grow.

It was no bigger than a mouse hole, and it broke open like a tiny volcano. Grim's fingers emerged. Then his arm. His arm grew. He reached, grabbing at the air.

The girl pushed herself against Phil. He started cursing, trying to move her toward the door. He stepped near the center of the floor. Grim's fingers grabbed his pant leg.

Phil screamed. Grim yanked, pulling the man's leg over to the hole.

Phil kept on screaming, the girl screaming with him. Grim yanked again.

The floor around the hole was like thin ice. As Phil's weight hit it, it cracked. The hole grew. Phil tried to say he'd kill the girl, but she punched her elbow into his ribs. She scraped her fingernails across his face. She twisted away from him, falling heavily to the floor out of his reach.

Phil tried to grab the air. He tried to stab his pant leg. Grim let go of the hanging light fixture and hung just by Phil's pants. The entire leg plunged through the ceiling.

The man slammed to the floor on his crotch. His other leg was straight out, as if he were a sitting one-legged man. His arms continued to wave, as if he were drowning, and his head lolled on his neck as if his neck had snapped. His mouth was frozen in a wide "O." His eyes shot around their sockets like pinballs.

The floor gave way again. Phil was pulled through it.

Grim landed on his feet, still holding Phil's leg. The man slammed into the floor tile, which cracked in dozens of places. Grim stood there, in the torrent of dust, looking as though he had used the man as a sledgehammer.

Grim looked down at the two dead or dying men, his lips squeezed tight. *Just johns,* he thought. *Men who paid for sex.*

"No," said his god.

Grim turned away. He stopped when he saw the girl in the doorway.

She had smoothed her skirt down. Her clothes were tight pink cotton: a sleeveless T-shirt that exposed her midriff, and a frilly, three-tiered miniskirt. She wore white, studded, high-heeled boots.

"Who are you?" she asked with childlike wonder.

He looked again at the broken men around him, and didn't answer.

"Th-thank you," she stammered.

It looked to her as if he might have nodded, but he might have just lowered his head farther.

"My name is Betty," she said, trying to smile.

He didn't move.

"Please," she began, but couldn't say any more.

Finally Grim walked toward her. Her eyes widened as he came near. But he just turned his head so she couldn't see his face and brushed by her.

She watched him go to the stairs and start slowly down. She tried to understand what had happened. It was almost too much for her, but not quite. Her expression cleared like the rising sun. She very carefully, very purposefully, followed him.

3

"Nightmares come true," she said. "But if you wait long enough, so do dreams." She grew quiet and wistful for a few minutes. Finally she said, "You just have to be able to tell the dreams and nightmares apart."

Betty curled over onto her side and cuddled up to him. Grim continued to rest. They lay side by side on the floor of a first-story rear apartment.

"So if the floor caves in, we won't have to fall so far," Betty had said.

The place had only a little light, coming in from a hole high up in the otherwise windowless back wall. Betty liked to lie in the warm pool it made on the floor. It made her feel blessed, she said.

She had followed Grim down to the cellar. She sat on the stairs while he returned to his previous spot. She called to him while he tried to find sleep.

"Vincent?" she said in a small hopeful voice.

He hadn't answered.

"What's your name?" she asked. "You have to be called something. I don't just want to call you . . . beast."

He finally told her, his voice a rusted creak.

"Grim," she said from the darkness. "Thank you, Grim."

When he woke up, she was lying beside him.

He had not moved. He looked down at her peaceful, sleeping face without expression. He looked at her clothes and skin, which were now as dirty as his, and went back to a dreamless, recuperating sleep.

"Those men didn't just want to screw me," he woke up hearing. "They wanted to hurt me. I think they wanted to kill me."

He had not moved. He lay in the dark, listening.

"When I first saw you," she said, "I thought you were my living thoughts. I thought you were my worst dreams, taken form. I knew those men were bad . . . were evil. I knew you would kill them."

Then she started to cry, silently, the tears running down her face, her body shaking. "But," she said, "but I thought you were going to kill me too." She waited until the tears stopped. She lay against him a few minutes more. "I thought I was bad. Evil. When you didn't kill me, I knew . . . I knew . . . maybe I wasn't."

She fell asleep again, before he did. He looked upon her miserable, beautiful face, resting in the dirt. He carefully put his arm under her head.

When he awakened again, he felt something on his stomach. It had felt good, not like the steel snake, so he had not lashed out. His shirt was pulled up. She washed and bandaged his wound.

"I can't keep it clean down here," she said. "It's too dirty. We'll have to move."

That was when they found the rear apartment and a worn mattress. When she came back the second time, she was wearing black denim jeans and a fake fur jacket. She held a plastic canister of disinfectant baby wipes.

"You can do it if you want," she said, making cleaning motions, "but I still think you're too weak. Besides"—she finally smiled self-consciously—"I'm pretty good at it."

He had fallen asleep again before she even finished his chest. During the night, he found himself naked under a single, newly bought sheet. When she came back the next night, she brought new clothes . . . and food.

"Chinatown," she said. "That's where my doctor is. He takes care of me when . . . well, when I need him. I do all my shopping down there. It's really cheap, but pretty good quality—if you know where to look."

Grim chewed on the roast pork, chicken, and peanuts before attempting to stand. He drank the lychee juice and soybean milk. Finally he had the strength to try on the clothes.

"I'm a pretty good judge of men's sizes," she said as he pulled the stuff on. "I checked your torn things before I went, but still, I've got a pretty good eye. I used . . . to get . . . my little brother . . . and father . . . stuff . . . before I left home."

Grim stopped and looked at her. Her eyes were glassy, her face turned away. She became aware of him and quickly shook her head, trying to smile. "Let's see how I did."

Grim carefully stood. The black, long-sleeved T-shirt and thick, soft-cotton, olive-colored fatigue pants settled across his body. The black athletic socks felt good on his lower legs, and the black sneakers were better designed and padded than his previous high-tops.

"Perfect," she said happily, jumping up. "Only

you don't get the full effect without the belt." With studied nonchalance, she tucked the shirt into the waistband and slipped the black belt through the loops. She clipped the oval belt buckle tight, and stood back.

"There," she said. "Look at the belt buckle." On it was a jade-colored circle. "Chinese symbol for life," she said. "If you look close, you can see the yin-yang symbol inside it. I thought . . . I thought it was really beautiful."

She broke the spell by hopping around and chattering about the other accessories she had bought him.

"Try on the jacket," she said. "It matches the pants."

It was also olive-colored, thick, soft cotton, which zipped up the front, had two low pockets, and a narrow lapel.

"I got you a hat," she continued, handing it to him. "Took me hours to find one without a symbol. I just didn't think a blue Yankees or Mets cap was . . . you."

He pulled it on, keeping the rim just above his eyes. It felt warm and comfortable.

"Black," she said. "To match the shirt and shoes. And no plastic thing in the back. No mesh backing. It's one of the real caps—with elastic and cloth. It'll cover your hair for when . . . if you go outside."

Grim smiled. She almost gasped and stepped back. He quickly lowered his head and waited for the pleasure to pass. When he looked up again, she tried to make believe nothing had happened, but then her eyes filled with tears.

"I'm sorry," she said. "It's just that your eyes . . ." She turned away. "So black and deep. So hurt. You make me feel like . . . I have no troubles at all."

When she turned back, she held out a final item.

He took it, confused. "They're sunglasses," she said. "But not really. Visors, almost." Instead of glass, they were made of malleable plastic, black on one side, mirrored silver on the other. Instead of stems that reached behind the ears, they had a band of elastic.

"The great thing is that they don't make it darker," she told him. "They're like one-way glass. You can wear them at night. So . . . so when you go out, nobody can see your . . ."

She started to cry again. Grim just stood there, holding the glasses, seeing the moonlight reflect off the painted jade on the belt buckle. Then he carefully took off the hat and jacket, put them beside the mattress, and lay down.

She lay down next to him, on her back.

She came from Iowa. Her mother was an alcoholic, she said. That wasn't so bad, not really. She'd get drunk every day, and it was like she wasn't even there, unless you said something or she saw you. Sometimes she'd go crazy and break things, but she rarely came into the kids' room. It was just that you couldn't depend on her for anything. And you couldn't bring friends over and nobody would visit and you were afraid to let your teachers meet her.

"It was like she wasn't there, but she was, you know?" Betty said. "It was like you didn't have a mother, but some sort of monster instead." Just some sort of animal in the house you couldn't train, but you had to be nice to, and defer to, and obey.

"But nothing we did was ever right," she said. "She called us names."

That was okay, though. That really wasn't so bad. It was just that their dad was as frustrated as they were about it. He worked in a factory. He was a man, and he had a man's needs, but he couldn't get anything from his wife either. He worked hard all day, he really did, and when he came home he wanted what any husband and father wanted.

Betty had tried to take care of her little brother and do her schoolwork and housework and cook. She hadn't been anything special. Boys liked her because she was funny. Maybe she spent too much time with them because she didn't want to go home, but every time she finally got in, things were worse. Everybody was mad at her.

But that wasn't so bad, really. Every family had fights. Everybody had problems. It's just that her father needed some sort of release too. Mom had the bottle, but what did Dad have? She wasn't surprised when he started hitting.

That was bad, but not really bad. He was just punishing them when they did stuff wrong. Pretty soon, whenever she went to her room, her little brother was crying about something else he got a whipping for. She tried to make him understand that he had to be extra careful, but he was so young. He couldn't distinguish between having fun and doing stuff that would make Dad mad.

She was too old for spanking, but he'd slap her sometimes. Like when she came home late, or couldn't do her chores, or upset her mother, or got bad grades, or talked back. Then she'd run to her room and he'd try to stop her and explain, but he'd always be yelling and he didn't know his own strength, you know?

Then her mom got on his case. She and her little brother would lie awake, listening to her scream at their father about abusing the children.

"I could understand it," Betty said. "Dad wasn't really smart or anything. He didn't go to college. But he wanted to make amends. I know that."

So he would come into their room, mad and sad at the same time. He would sit on the side of her bed and try to explain, stroking her hair. He would kiss her, trying to make the boo-boo better. Pretty soon he was coming in every night.

Betty was crying again. "I tried to stop him. I did. I was a good girl. I didn't do the stuff they said. . . ."

Her mom had told her dad that she was becoming a slut because of him. Because he didn't control her, she was spending too much time with the boys. She needed a father figure, but he was too busy to discipline her. It was always his fault.

He explained this all to his daughter as he stroked her hair and kissed her.

"He was choking me. I tried to fight. But he was my father. He kept telling me that. 'I'm your father and I know what's right.' "

Betty thought she could live with it, but she couldn't. Every time she looked at him, she wanted to cry and scream. She tried to stay away from the house as much as possible, because every time she came home, they accused her of more things. Things she never did.

She didn't like being touched anymore. Things just kept getting worse. She thought of her town as a prison. She imagined that maybe her real parents were aliens who put her there to be punished. She promised she'd be good, if only they'd come back for her. . . .

But still, she could live with that. She did live with it, for years. She might have kept on living with it, if one thing hadn't happened.

It was just another night, like so many others. Her little brother was fitfully asleep in the top bunk, while her father was with her in the bottom. He was doing it slowly, like he always did, not to alert her mom. His hands were on her shoulders, holding her down. She was biting her lower lip, trying to find some biological comfort. This was sex, after all. It was supposed to feel good.

"Daddy, please," she whispered.

"Sssh," he said, head up, not looking at her. "Doesn't that feel good?"

"It's pulling. It hurts."

He slowed even more, but didn't stop. "You're growing fast, baby," he said. "You're becoming a woman." He proved it by showing her how big her breasts were getting. "I'm very proud of you."

"Daddy," she begged.

Their eyes met, by accident. But they locked and he stopped completely. Nothing happened for at least five seconds.

Then his lips started to curl off his teeth and his eyes turned red. His hands came off her chest and he started slapping her across the face. Back and forth, back and forth, with both hands, while she screamed.

"What do you think?" he snarled, grabbing her by the shoulders so hard it hurt. "That I'm some sort of child molester? God damn it, girl, I waited. You don't know how long I waited. I waited until you were sixteen!"

Although he warned her not to run away, and threatened to come after her if she did, Betty left home the next day—before her father could tell her what might happen to her little brother and her mother if she did go.

"I was afraid of that," Betty said. "I was afraid if he told me that, I'd never leave. . . ."

"You have to be able to tell them apart," Betty repeated that fourth night. "I mean, look at you." She stroked his chest lightly. "Your skin is so dark, so tough. Your face is so . . . I don't know, it's not re-

ally scarred, is it? It's like . . . ripped open." When
he didn't react, she kept going.

"I can say anything to you. You don't care about
looks. You care who a person is. But a year ago, I
wouldn't have been able to look at you. I wouldn't
have been able to get close to you. I wouldn't have
been able to . . . touch you." Her hand stopped in
the middle of his chest. She could feel his heart beat
—like a fist pounding inside him.

"A year ago, I'd say you were the nightmare." She
looked away from him. "But *you're* the dream,
aren't you? Aren't you?"

As always, Grim said nothing. He lay beside her,
knowing she was using him like a fireplace: for
warmth and comfort only. She would not get too
close or she would burn.

"Street is the nightmare," she said, her voice suddenly hard and bitter.

He didn't question her. In his quiet, recuperating
mind, he assumed she meant "the street." He was, in
his own way, pleased that he was helping her by just
existing, and grateful for her company and consider-
ation.

He drifted between awareness and sleep, thinking
of his angel.

She was real. He had seen her; blond hair flowing
in the night wind, her face aglow with halo light, her
body as perfect as an angel's had to be. She was
suprahuman perfection. She was warmth and hope.
His god gave him direction. His angel gave him control.

He saw her now, in his mind's eye, flying above his
battlefield like a piece of white satin. She inspired
him to go forward, not to let the pain and horror stop
him. She was his star, leading the way to his fate—a
destiny he knew was as wondrous as she. She would

not direct him to doom. Gods gave the quests. Angels gave the reward.

Grim felt his fists hitting his god's enemies. He felt their flesh split. He felt their bones lock and shatter. He felt their brains slam against their skulls and their hearts crash against their ribs.

His angel would not speak; his angel looked away. She would suffer with him. He knew she would tell him when to stop. She was his solace.

He knew when she was in pain. He knew when she was threatened. He would do anything for her . . . even defy his god.

"No!"

The word was huge, filling his head. Grim sat up, his eyes wide, his heart pounding.

He felt sweat on his face. He touched it, feeling the healing slickness. He felt that his clothes were damp. He looked down, gripping the new black-and-olive cloth. He saw the jacket, cap, and glasses by the side of the mattress.

He looked the other way. Sunlight made a pool of white on the dusty wooden floor. There was no one there. The girl, Betty, was gone.

4

She didn't come back that night, or the next, or the one after that. Grim became hungry again. He started wandering through the tenement's rooms, hoping to find her. All he found were the rotting, chewed corpses of the men he had killed. It seemed that the rats were not averse to dining on them.

Grim dragged the bodies to the cellar, placing them close to the wall. Now the vermin wouldn't have so far to go for their meals.

Grim put on the shades. He put on the jacket and hat. It was time to go out.

The night was cool, and heavy with moisture. Grim could hear the water all around him, although he couldn't see it. The harvest moon hung heavily over the city, illuminating the peninsula Grim stood on. The street itself was dark and empty.

Grim walked away from the water, to the corner. He read the street signs. One Hundred and Sixty-

eighth Street and Broadway. He looked back the
way he had come, at the small triangle of slums nestled in the shadow of High Bridge Park.

Without the woman there to help him, the building was useless. Grim walked away without looking
back.

He didn't study faces anymore. He had his fill of
faces. He kept his head down, his black eyes moving
behind the silver shield. The farther south he went,
the more people were on the sidewalks. He saw
young lovers, holding hands or with their arms
around each other. He saw groups of friends—little
gangs of fun-seekers.

He kept his distance. It was different, now that he
was relatively clean and had new clothes. They
didn't openly avoid him anymore. They glanced at
him, judged his threat, then went back to what they
had been doing so quickly any other person might
not be aware of the split-second confrontation.

Grim didn't care. Some were dressed provoca-
tively, but none had the stance or attitude of Betty.
Grim kept moving south, looking.

At One Hundred and Fortieth Street, things
started to change. The trees and bushes died out as if
strangled. Taking their place were new plants, made
of aluminum, tin, paper, and glass. The sidewalk
cracked and broke. The streets became bulbous and
smoked. Grim was riding a dragon into Harlem.

The buildings loomed, dark and ominous—their
eyes and teeth made of iron bars and sheet metal.
The people smelled of fear. The streets reeked of
desperation, alcohol, and urine.

Street and car headlights swept across him. He
stopped near the curb and risked raising his head.
No one paid any attention to him. There were no
judgmental gazes. Here, people kept their distance

and only reacted if you invaded their space. Then each invasion was a declaration of war.

The glass here was like grass anywhere else. Dark green and clear shards seemed to grow in the sidewalk cracks. The store signs were garish, offering everything from alfalfa to voodoo goods.

He lucked out. He passed a Jamaican restaurant just as it was closing. He waited until they locked up, then went around to the garbage cans in the alley. When he finished eating, he turned to see ten glowing marbles floating in the darkness. Five scrawny cats looked at him accusingly. Grim left them to the scraps that remained.

He moved back onto the main street. He took his time. He followed people who looked and smelled the way the three johns had. They had a definite attitude that was both brash and furtive.

Grim followed their confusion: a trail of conflicting emotions as clear as dropped bread crumbs. Their body language said, "So what? Want to make something of it?" They were black and white, straight and stooped, thin and fat. They all seemed to be heading in the same direction.

Grim turned the corner of One Hundred and Twenty-seventh, between Powell Boulevard and Lenox Avenue. The block was made of neon, and there was little doubt what they were selling. It said so in every window. Some signs on the first floors offered palm reading and future casting, but everything on street level was spelled out in three letters.

Grim took a step forward. He stopped when a man offered him a piece of paper. Grim didn't move. The man offered it again, then dropped the paper with impatience. He walked away, muttering obscenities. The paper blew against Grim's leg. He read it without bending down.

A Dozen Girls. White, Black, Red, Yellow. Live

Nudes. Booths. Videos. Peep Shows. Magazines. Books. All Categories, All Day, All Night, All Year!

Grim moved his leg. The sheet of paper flew down the street. He looked at the busy, crowded sidewalk. He wondered where those girls were. There was not a single one on the block.

Grim walked deeper into the neighborhood. He looked up, over the storefronts. Young men lounged on the stoops, smoking. As others walked by, they turned their heads and whispered. Grim did not get close. He stayed in the middle of the sidewalk.

"Drugs," said his god.

Grim acknowledged it, but did nothing. He was looking for the girl.

Someone grabbed his elbow. Grim pulled his arm up and immediately backed toward the street.

"Hey, hey," said the old man, laughing and grabbing for his elbow again. "No need to do that, my man. I'm not going to hurt you. I'm going to help you. Come here, come here, I won't bite." He got close and stage-whispered, one hand beside his mouth. "Though I can't make that guarantee for the girls inside. You want the best? Go no further. It's right here. Legs, ass, tits, faces, they're all here. What's your pleasure, gentleman, what's your pleasure? You like to watch? Golden showers, bronze showers? It's all in there to see. S/M? B/D? Take a look, take a look, but no touching, please."

Grim stood and listened, letting the man hold his arm. "Betty?" he croaked.

"Why, sure!" said the man, his gray-and-black hair glistening, his teeth ivory and gold. "Betty, Becky, Bertha, Bella, Bernice, Beryl, Bessie, Betsy, Beulah, Barbie, Billie, Bonnie, Beverly, and Babette! Take your pick, my good man, take your pick!"

Grim was about to take a step toward the door, but his way was blocked. He suddenly became aware that an appreciative crowd had grown. Grim saw them all smiling at him. Young faces, old faces, white and black. He lowered his head and quickly moved away.

"Hey, don't go away mad," said the man. "Come on back! Five dollars off. Seven fifty. What do you say?"

Grim got near the end of the block without further incident. He realized that they were all the same here—all united in guilt. They all wanted to know that what they were doing wasn't wrong.

"Hey, buddy, got a match?"

Grim turned his lowered head. A young, muscular, dark-skinned man was standing beside him, his head also down.

Grim moved away. The man kept pace with him. "I said, you got a match, mister?"

Grim shook his head, continuing to move away. The man continued to move with him. "What's a matter, mute or something? Do you have a match or don't you?"

Grim said, "No." He continued walking, but didn't pick up speed.

"What's a matter? You not from around here? How about the time? You got the time?"

Grim saw them coming from two sides. One was coming across the street at them. The other was coming across the sidewalk from a stoop. The man nearest saw Grim had gotten wise. His hand shot out toward Grim's torso.

Grim grabbed his fingers, plucking them out in midair. His own fingers bent tight, wrapping around the man's pinky. Grim quickly bent it back and heard it snap.

Grim danced away, starting to turn so he could face the man. Incredibly, the young man grunted, pulled his hand close to his chest, and swung his other arm in a vicious arc at Grim's head. Grim was just able to duck in time, the man's flat palm barely touching his cap.

Grim put space between them, his movements light. By then the other men had him sandwiched between them. Grim's left leg came up, his knee bending. As he and the man crossing the street came level, Grim's foot went deep into the man's stomach. He doubled and went down.

The man coming across the sidewalk tried to clip him with a fast left, straight from the shoulder. Grim pulled his head back, letting the fist go by, then swung the side of his right hand into the man's throat. Grim skipped back, along the sidewalk, as that man stumbled and went to his knees.

But the first man kept coming, snarling, as Grim backed away from him. Grim was amazed. The pain must've been incredible, but this guy was acting as if it were a sprain.

Grim readied himself. *Go for the nose or neck, foot or knee. When he's blind or crippled, disconnect his thinking.*

The dictator gave the order to his body. Grim's feet anchored. Grim's hand shot forward. It was just about to slam into his enemy's face, when the man's head snapped back. Grim's fist stopped with a millimeter between it and the man's nose.

To Grim's eyes, it looked as if the man's torso grew a half dozen more arms and hands. They grabbed, pulling him back. From them grew heads, shoulders, and torsos.

"What the hell you doing, man?" said one, and then more people appeared between Grim and his quarry.

The man nearest put both his hands on Grim's chest and pushed. "Keep it cool," he said. "Chill out, baby, chill out."

Suddenly everyone stopped. There was a small group surrounding each of the four men involved. The man in front of Grim seemed to be the leader. He was the one speaking, and making sense.

"We don't need this kind of thing here, gentlemen. If you got some fighting to do, take it into an alley." He pointed at the man who had started it. "Alexi, I told you to stay off my street unless you're horny."

The young, dark-skinned man looked up, clutching his hand. "He broke my fucking finger, man!"

"Man, maybe you should use that finger for fucking instead of plucking," said the leader. His friends and helpers laughed. "Don't think I don't know what you do," he continued. "You wouldn't want me to tell the Acid Lords you're peeling on their turf, would you?"

"Christ, no!" said Alexi, suddenly showing his age. "I'm sorry, Classy. I just thought . . . I won't do it again."

The man turned back to Grim. "I've been watching you too, son. You just walked down the street, doing nothing, buying nothing. You sight-seeing, son?"

Grim shook his head, looking the man square in the eye from behind the glasses.

"My name is Classy Jack," he said. "I run this street. I don't like trouble and I don't like mirrored shades." He paused to let Grim talk if he chose to. He continued when Grim didn't. "Maybe you had just better move along, son." He let Grim go and turned to walk away.

"Betty," said Grim.

Classy Jack turned back as the others got the muggers to their feet. He studied Grim carefully from head to toe. Then he talked fast and angrily, as if ordering a commoner from his sight. "You want hookers, man. We don't have no hookers here. Go to Lenox Terminal, near the river."

There were all shapes and sizes here as well, but packed in spandex and leather. They hung out everywhere but the terminal itself. The area was industrial, and closed. The motorways and walkways were traveled by people interested in only one thing.

Grim saw them on street corners, under bridges, on medians, and in doorways. Their skin colors were black, white, and yellow—and everything in between. Their clothes were bright red, yellow, black, white, or animal prints. They wore boots that went up to their knees or thighs. They wore shiny shoes with stiletto heels as long as Grim's middle finger.

They were round and bulging. They threatened to spill out or over. There was more skin than cloth, and Grim got close enough to see them covered in goose bumps—as if their flesh were coated with sandpaper.

They accepted Grim immediately. They didn't blanch or panic when he approached. It was all a new experience for him. They couldn't see his eyes, but he could see theirs. In them he saw that he was not the worst-looking person they had ever been nice to.

He first walked all around the area, keeping his distance. Then he repeated the circuit, getting close. They had noticed him on his first lap, so were prepared for his silent advances.

They called him Cap or Specs or Handsome or Good-looking. They all asked him the same thing, with different words. "Want to party?" "Want to have fun?" "Want to feel good?" "Want a date?" "Want to fly to the moon on gossamer wings?"

He said the same thing to all of them. "Betty."

"You can call me anything you want," they said.

Grim stood facing the Harlem River. He was more

frustrated than ever. What good was he? He wanted
to find someone, not kill them. His god was no help
at all. It was as if his deity was purposely keeping
silent, giving no direction, lest it distract him from
his lord's quest . . . whatever that was.

Grim looked across the river, to the Bronx. She
could be anywhere, he thought. He remembered
her face and all its tragic expressions. He remembered the clouds of hope that passed by—the ones
she told herself not to feel. She dared not hope, she
said.

He remembered her words. Her last words to him.

Grim turned to look at a girl in a white spandex
top and black leather miniskirt. Her skin was the
color of milk chocolate. She looked back with indif-
ference. "What do you got in there?" she asked, motioning at his mouth with her head. "A whole
melon?"

Grim moved up close and smiled.

"Jesus!" she said. "Get a load of those chicklets,
honey. You one of the Osmond family or something?
Is your tongue as good as that, baby? If it is, we might
be able to cut my rates, you know what I mean?
Sixty-nine cents sound all right to you, honeychile?"

For the first time, Grim really wanted to talk. He
wanted to tell her to can the tourist crap. He wanted
her to be real.

Instead, he said one word, still smiling.

"Street."

Grim was back in Classy Jack's territory. He came
around the other side, so he stood in the alley in back
of the stores and clubs. He knew he couldn't get in
the front way. He didn't have any money.

He had stood there for nearly a half hour. He respected this street. He had broken Alexi's finger.
That would have paralyzed anyone else. But on this

street, they swallowed that and just kept coming. The young man nearly laid a fist on him. Grim didn't like that. It didn't make him comfortable.

"Oh, you want the Wise Man," the milk chocolate prostitute had said. "He'll be around here later."

"Now," Grim had said.

"Keep your pants on, big teeth. You so hot to trot, go on over to the K Club. That's his shack. You can find him there." He had started walking away. "Hey," she called after him. "You think I'm flapping my gums for free?"

He had shown her the inside of his pockets. "Asshole," she said. He tipped his cap to her.

Grim saw people moving behind curtains, blinds, and shades. He remembered where the K Club was. He had memorized the signs on his first go-round without thinking about it. He got shapely silhouettes and glimpses of flesh. He moved quickly into the shadows beneath the windows. He pressed himself into the wall, to the side of the rear door.

He waited hours more before the back door of the K Club opened and an old woman came out. She was carrying a plastic garbage bag. When she went to throw it into a nearby Dumpster, Grim slipped through the door behind her.

He stood in a narrow hallway, lit only by a naked red light bulb in the ceiling. There was another door just inside, to his right. He opened it and stepped into a tiny bathroom.

He waited there until he heard the old lady return, close the back door, and walk down the hall. When he heard another door close, he went back out into the corridor.

He stood, listening carefully. The hall thumped with a loud bass beat. He could hear music coming from the other end. He could hear footsteps above him. When he pressed his ear to the wall, he could hear women's voices.

Grim moved silently to the door at the other end of the hall. The music was louder now, the bass beat rattling the hinges. Grim turned the knob, opened the door a crack, and slipped through to the other side.

The noise was as good as a smoke screen. The people on the other side would see him only if they were looking straight at him. And because they didn't hear him, they didn't look. They were concentrating on something else.

Grim was standing against the back wall of a strip club. Recessed into the wall beside and above him was a narrow stage, lined with flashing lights. It had a ramp that went through the center of the room. It, in turn, was surrounded by a horseshoe-shaped bar. Two bartenders and the old woman worked in the channel between the stage and the stools.

The bar was lined with men. More men sat at tables near the front door. There was only one other female in the room. She was on stage, taking off her clothes and dancing.

Grim was immediately struck by how much the stripper looked like Betty. It wasn't she, but she had the same slight build, the same off-center face, and the same intense expression that said: "I'm enjoying this . . . I *really*, really am." She was doing a cowgirl number. She had just dropped her cheap chaps.

"You wanna drink?"

Grim lowered his sights. A bartender was leaning across the counter, looking straight at him. Grim moved closer to him.

"Betty."

"She's not here tonight," the bartender shouted above the music. "You want a drink?"

Grim moved close so he didn't have to shout.
"When?"

"How the hell should I know? They come and go.
Plenty of girls. You want a drink or what? Just a
minute." A paying customer had caught his attention. Grim took the time to study the room.

The hall behind him had only three doors: two
exits and the bathroom. But there had to be a dressing room. Then he saw another door, on the other
side of the stage. That had to be the connecting door.
There was probably another exit door to the alley,
which was used exclusively by the dancers.

"Hey," he heard. Grim looked back at the bar,
where the old woman was this time. "You going to
drink? You can't stay in here unless you buy a drink."

"Street," said Grim.

"You a friend of his?" the old woman asked. He
nodded. She looked him up and down. "I can believe
that. Sit down. I'll tell you when he gets in. First
drink on the house. What'll ya have?"

Grim shook his head and moved away from the
bar. He saw a nook where the wall angled out, just
beneath a Schlitz Malt Liquor Bull sign. Grim put his
back against it and folded his arms. From here he
could watch the entire room, except for the front
door.

He saw the old woman go under the bar in the far
corner and come up by the second rear door. He
watched her open it and go in. He waited. He marveled at how the music was the only sound in the
room. It swallowed up the noise the bartenders
made. And nobody talked. The men sat, swigging
their beers, and stared at the stage. Nobody was smiling. They all looked as if they wanted to be alone.

The dancer concentrated on her routine. This
wasn't a place where they stuffed money in her
G-string. This was a take-it-all-off-and-get-out joint.

This was a six-girls-an-hour showplace for people who liked their lust distant.

The music pounded and pulsed and pounced. This was a place where the music did everything for everybody.

Grim lowered his arms when the back door reopened and two burly men came out. Both were wearing gym T-shirts and jeans. Grim noticed that both bartenders were standing at the base of the horseshoe, their hands below the counter. All four men were looking at him.

"Get out," said his god.

Grim didn't move.

The two burly men stood on either side of him. The one to his right made his chest muscles dance by tensing them. The one to his left did the talking. The rest of the room ignored them. Grim kept his head down.

"What do you want, old man?"

"Betty," said Grim.

"Betty?" the man to his left said with mock concern. "Hmmm, I don't remember anybody by that name. You know anybody named Betty, Cliff?"

The other man shook his head, grunting.

"Nobody named Betty, old man."

"Street," said Grim.

"Mr. Wise is busy, old man," the one to his left said without a pause. "But I'll be happy to take a message for you. What do you want, old . . ."

But Grim had already heard what he wanted to hear. He was already moving. He snapped a bottle of beer out of the hand of the man sitting closest to him. In the same motion, Grim smashed it across the talking man's face. He finished the move by kicking the other man between the legs.

The two musclemen were strong. They thought they were fast. They thought they were prepared for

anything. But they had never seen Grim the Undead
when he respected a street.

The one to his right started to double over. Grim
dropped the bottle neck, grabbing the first man by
his shirt and belt. He pushed and ran forward.

Grim's lips were off his teeth. The muscleman's
face was smeared with blood, his eyes blinking like
little stars in a red sky.

Grim heard the explosion above the music. He saw
the smoke, seemingly coming out of the muscleman's head. He felt him shake. Pieces of the
man's shirt and back flew off. The man's expression
turned from surprise to pain. Grim didn't slow.

He smashed the man into the bar. The counter
shook and broke, the force hurling the bartender
who was holding the sawed-off shotgun into the
stage. The bartender smashed into it back first and
dropped.

The other bartender leaped onto the counter, his
right hand gripping a black nightstick. Grim ran to
the man's right, slapping his hand on the man's left
knee and gripping.

Grim swept the second bartender's legs out from
under him and kept going. The man slammed onto
the countertop. Grim ducked under the man's flailing arms.

The first bartender was up, trying to get the shotgun aimed, but Grim was already close to the stage
door. The old woman came at him, her hands up and
clawed.

Grim stopped short, as if he hadn't been running
at all, and tripped her. She went headfirst into the
wall. The man at the table nearest him laughed in
spite of himself.

Grim threw open the door and plunged through.

He was amid women almost immediately. They
were running through the hall, clutching their street

clothes. They screamed when they saw him and tried to dodge. He kept moving fast, letting their features freeze in his mind's eye. None of them was Betty.

He slipped quickly into their dressing room. It was long and narrow, with one wall taken up by a low makeup table and a mirror. The other wall was lined with worn, overstuffed sofas and chairs. The remaining few girls screamed as he ran through, checking every corner.

No Betty.

He charged back toward the one door, finally aware that his god was also screaming at him. What was he doing? He was hunting for a hooker. What for? What was he going to do? Ask for her hand in marriage?

Grim tried to ignore his god. He hammered a sentence up there. He painted it on a huge banner and used spikes to secure it in his brain.

I'm looking for a nightmare.

He collided with the first bartender as he came out the door. He didn't slow. He let his momentum carry him over the falling man. Directly in front of him now was the silent muscleman, his shoulders hunched and his face mottled. The angry, wounded man reached for his attacker.

Grim knew a few broken fingers would not slow him down. Something more drastic was called for. His god told him what.

Grim tried to find another way out, but the man's legs were too thick to slip through. Grim saw the man's muscular hands fill his vision. He saw his own hands coming up.

Grim moved in close, turning so that his back was against the man's chest. He got one of the muscleman's arms under one of his own and wrapped the fingers of both his hands around one of the muscleman's.

Grim's right hand held the muscleman's first and middle fingers. His left hand held the man's fourth finger and pinky.

"There are no bones between the two sets of fingers," his god told him.

Grim ripped open the man's hand almost to the wrist.

Grim let go and ran up a narrow, winding stairway facing him on the left wall. He took the steps two at a time, leaving behind the women's high-pitched screams and one man's.

He heard the bartender with the shotgun coming after him. He saw a closed door, painted black, before him. He heard noises from inside.

"The gun!" his god bellowed.

Grim stopped dead in his tracks and flattened himself against the wall. When the barrels of the shotgun appeared from around the curve, Grim grabbed them, pointed it away from him, and pulled.

The bartender came quickly after. Grim hit him on the front of his head, using his arm like a hammer. He just wanted to stun him. Grim then got his free arm around the bartender's shoulders and hustled him up the remaining few steps.

Grim put the bartender in front of him. He put his hand on the back of the bartender's head. He rammed the man's face into the door.

"Knock, knock," said his god.

Bullets ripped open holes in the door, several plunging into the bartender's body. Grim had already dropped, and he let the newly made corpse roll over him.

The bartender with the nightstick wasn't so lucky. He had been following. He had stopped, but not ducked when the bullets slapped into the wall in front of him. The corpse knocked him over like a bowling ball.

Grim dived at the door, hitting it low. It sprang open and Grim landed on the floor.

He was in a small, square office. A foldout bed was to his right. A large metal desk was in front of him. Papers were blowing across it. The window behind it was open. The room was otherwise empty.

Grim slammed the door behind him and raced to the window. He vaulted out to the fire escape. He watched as a well-dressed man stopped running down the alley, turned, and pointed a revolver at him.

Just before he ducked, Grim got his first look at Street Wise . . . every hooker's nightmare.

5

Everybody wanted to know what the others were doing there.

"Bad enough," Sergeant Cahill muttered to his partner. "Bad enough we got a wholesale slaughter at a meat market. Bad enough it gets me out this time of night. But we have to have an officers' convention?" He surveyed the congregation of brass who hovered near the front door of the K Club.

There were Lieutenants Connolly and McMurray. There was Assistant Chief Collins. Practically everyone who was upstairs at Manhattan North was at the scene of the crime.

Officer Peters smiled up at his partner. "Look on the bright side, Mitch. You could be mopping up addicts on St. Nick Ave." He stood, looking back toward the dressing room, his eyes alight. "How're the witnesses?"

"Blind, deaf, and dumb," Cahill grumbled.

"Yeah," Peters said with a leer, "but they got all their parts, right?"

"Look sharp if you ever want to make detective," Cahill replied. "The eyes of plainclothes are upon you."

Peters returned his attention to separating the refuse from the clues. It wasn't long before he heard his partner swear. He looked up in time to see, through the open front door, two vehicles converge, grill to grill.

Out of one came Captain Frank Bender of Central Division. Out of the other came the night camera crew from Channel Six *U. R. There News.* Alan Ross, the evening producer, was already shouting.

"Captain, Captain, this way! Over here! Captain!"

Bender didn't even look at the man. Instead he looked right at the video lens—which was already being hefted to the cameraman's shoulder.

"Make me look good, Jonathan," he said without stopping. "This time of night."

"Captain, Captain," said Ross stridently. "How does this investigation tie in with your work at Central Division?"

Bender slowed, turned, and walked backward toward the door. "You in focus, Jonathan? Sound rolling, Mark? Everything ready? Good. Listen carefully. I'm only going to say this once. No comment." The captain turned and marched through the door of the K Club. "Keep them back," he advised the patrolmen on either side of the entrance.

Alan Ross stopped within five feet of the door, trying to see inside. "I wonder what he's doing here," he mused.

Jonathan Gavey lowered his camera, smirking without humor. "Probably just wants a late-night glimpse of tits and ass, mate. Wouldn't you?"

Mark Williams turned off the tape recorder. "I'm

surprised the entire division isn't down here doing strip searches."

Inside, Bender went directly over to the assistant chief. "Jesus H. Christ, Bill, I like skin as much as the next guy, but what the hell are you calling me for?"

Collins flipped open the small notebook he carried. Old habits died hard after twenty years on the front line. "Various A.P. descriptions," he read— "A.P." was shorthand for alleged perpetrator. "Tough skin, leathery skin, torn skin. Burnt skin." Collins looked up. "Still like skin, Frank?"

Bender's attitude changed for the serious. "Long hair? Livid scalp?"

"He was wearing a hat."

Bender surveyed the damage. The place was a wreck. Broken glass was strewn everywhere. The wall panels were cracked in several places. The cash register was rifled. The bar itself was broken. Paramedics were scooping bodies into stretchers and gingerly rolling them toward the door. Klieg lights were already set up outside so the television cameras could get every inch of agony.

"He did all this?" Bender wondered.

"They didn't need his help," said Collins. "Most of it they did to each other." The assistant chief turned and pointed. "One of the bartenders shot a bouncer. The other bartender and bouncers are in pretty bad shape."

"What happened to them?"

"Second bartender, name of Max Brady, practically had his jaw removed from his skull. Major concussion too. Second bouncer, Cliff Hidleberg, had his right hand opened, between the middle and fourth finger, almost all the way to his wrist."

Bender hissed in sympathy. "Sounds like my boy, all right."

"That's not all, Frank," said Collins. "The first bar-

tender is dead. Shot. And probably not by your boy."
That got Bender's attention. "Seems he was caught
in a crossfire. Our best guess is that the owner accidentally blew his own boy away."

Bender's expression cleared. "Will this stick?"

"Maybe," said Collins.

Before they could discuss the situation further, the
policemen were distracted by unusually loud activity from outside.

"What the hell is going on out there, Lieutenant?"
Collins shouted over the noise.

"Another news truck," said McMurray. "Channel
Ten. And another car . . . holy Mother of God, it's
the Ice Pick herself."

"Ashley Smith?" Collins said in wonder. "What's
she doing here?"

"And she's not alone," added Connolly. "Sam
Niven is with her."

"Christ Almighty," said Collins in genuine alarm,
heading for the door, forgetting Bender completely.
"Keep them out. For heaven's sake, keep them out
of here!"

The assistant chief was out on the sidewalk almost
immediately. Bender watched him go. The captain
saw the area flooded with light. Beneath the spots, it
was dueling newscasts. Channel Ten was heavily
outnumbered, however. The Channel Ten cameraman was going crazy trying to keep Channel Six
personnel out of his no-doubt-soon-to-be-exclusive
shots.

All he had was a film unit. Channel Six had their
top gun—the city's number one newsperson. Ashley
was resplendent, as usual, wearing a black suit and a
red silk shirt. She was already hard at work, asking
questions of the various people strapped down on
gurneys as they rolled by. New to the scene, she kept
the questions simple.

"What happened in there? How did you feel?"

Collins threw open his arms as he approached. "Ms. Smith! What a pleasant surprise seeing you here! To what do we owe this honor?"

"Can it," said Ashley under her breath, irritated at the interruption. Assistant chiefs she could corner in their lair downtown. She knew she'd get the same quotes either place. But this was heart-wrenching, stomach-tugging news!

Sam Niven, news director, cut in front of her, his expression diplomatic. "Chief Collins," he said, "we might ask you the same thing."

Bender chose that moment to turn away. "What *are* they doing here?" he wondered aloud. Channel Ten's anchor, Kelly Browne, was conspicuous by her absence. "Shouldn't the Ice Pick be getting her beauty sleep?"

"Desperate," said McMurray absently. "Ever since the Firebeaters and Jeremy Bancroft slipped through their fingers, they've been going around the clock."

Bender knew it well. The group of middle-class teens who had been immolating derelicts had been killed, and the public's interest had died. Then the nauseating, frightening story of Manhattan's supposedly most prolific serial killer had been taken over by the national press corps—who soundly rejected Channel Ten's offer of assistance and contributions.

They even ignored the florid name Channel Ten had tried to make famous: Cryst, the King of Killers. Having been cheated of the limelight, Sam Niven and Ashley Smith were flailing around for something new to sink their teeth into.

Bender walked away, leaving the politics and camouflage to Collins. After all, that was the man's job. His job was to find the man who had killed both the

Firebeaters and Jeremy Bancroft. The man who may have been here tonight.

But if they could nail Street Wise in the process, they'd make a lot of influential people happy. Bender shook his head. Both he and Collins really had their work cut out for them. But even though his own investigation was going to be time-consuming, the captain didn't envy the assistant chief. If Collins didn't keep a lid on it, the case might be blown sky high. Anyone could evade the cops if their every move was broadcast on TV.

Bender headed for the club's dressing room and office.

". . . Naturally Central was concerned that this might be the start of a new gang war in the area," Collins was saying outside. "We're now convinced that it was merely an isolated incident. But, since we're here, we thought it best to assist the Sixty-eighth Precinct with their inquiries."

Niven was not impressed. "This isn't *news,* Bill," he said flatly. Ashley wasn't concerned. She was still trying to talk to the wounded while the paramedics tried to get them into the ambulances.

"I don't know what you want me to say, Sam," Collins complained. "All I can tell you is the truth."

Niven looked as if he had swallowed a particularly sour grape. "Bill, what are you doing here? What is Captain Bender doing here? And I thought I saw Lieutenant McMurray. What is he doing here? And there's *more* brass in there. I saw their shiny blue suits. What's going on, Bill?"

"McMurray is the officer on duty, Sam," Collins said patiently. "This is the biggest thing that went down tonight. We had to make sure the lid was still on up here, Sam. Surely you can understand that."

The news director made a dissatisfied face. "Listen

to yourself, Bill. You're telling me something happened, but nothing happened. What am I going to do with that?"

Collins swallowed his anger. He hadn't gotten to where he was by blowing up. He learned long ago to turn the tables. Whenever he felt rage, he rechanneled it into pity. "Not everything's news, Sam," he said sadly.

Niven didn't blink. "Yes, it is, Bill," he replied.

"I've got it," interrupted Ashley Smith breathlessly, coming up behind her news director. "Slaughter on Seventh Avenue. Perverted lust explodes into violence. What do you think sounds better, Sam? Forty-second Street North, or Combat Zone West?"

Only Collins could see Niven's grimace. "There," said the assistant chief. "There's your story, Sam. I'll be happy to do an on-the-scene interview."

Ashley looked uninterested. "We'll set up an appointment with your office," she said kindly.

"Fine. I have to make sure things are in control here." Collins checked his watch. "Then I better get some sleep. Will you excuse me?" Niven nodded. "Look forward to hearing from you," said Collins as he walked away.

The last ambulance pulled out. Channel Ten's crew turned off its lights and started packing up. The Channel Six team remained near the K Club entrance in a huddle.

"I can get some mileage out of this, Sam," Ashley promised. "Do it from the woman's angle. A week-long report. Something like 'Porn: Freedom or Bondage?' We'll pour on the dramatizations. We'll get great ratings."

"We always do with naked birds," Jonathan said drily.

"Something's going on here," said Sam, still preoccupied. "Something more."

"What do you mean?" Ashley said, disconcerted. She didn't like anything that disrupted her thoughts.

"He was so busy telling me this was an isolated incident . . ."

Alan Ross was tired. "Maybe it is, Sam."

"Use your brain, will you?" the news director replied irritably. "Isolated incident? McMurray calls Collins. Then Collins calls Bender? The lieutenant would only call the assistant chief if he was afraid it wasn't. The A.C. would only call the captain if he was *sure* it wasn't."

Ross was duly chastised. "What do you want to do, Sam?"

Niven stared at the entrance of the K Club. "Stay on it. Alert everyone. I smell a story. A big one."

It had been a very bad night for Classy Jack Watkins. First that damn fool Alexi tried more garbage on his street. Then the K Club got done over. He had been closeted with the cops for hours. He was just as eager as they were to know if this was the start of new class action between the Acid Lords and the Black Rules.

Right now, all he wanted to do was run some water, get the salts, and soothe his aching feet. He turned on the little reading lamp beside his chair and went into the kitchen. He didn't turn on any other lamp. He liked his apartment to be illuminated by the neon of his street. He liked the way the red and blue washed over him through the caged windows.

He filled the pan three-quarters full with hot water, took the box of baking soda and rock salt from the cupboard, and headed back to the living room. From there he could look out the bay window and watch the block from corner to corner. He could sit in the semidarkness and see that all was right in his world.

He sat down with a deep sigh. He realized he'd be able to see the sunrise tonight. He leaned over to start taking off his shoes. He stopped when he saw his guns lying on the Persian rug.

He liked them big, solid, clunky, and old. There was the .45 automatic from the kitchen, the .38 revolver from the bathroom, and the P-25 automatic from his bedroom. They were all lying on the floor ten feet away from him.

Classy Jack froze, one shoe half off, his eyes flitting this way and that. They settled on a shadow between the door and the front foyer. With exaggerated calm, he continued taking off his shoes.

"I got big feet," he said. "Too big. I should get a pair of those super ultra kickback sneakers, but they don't have them in my size. Thirteen, double wide." He displayed one of the worn, battered limbs before picking up the box of powder and pouring it into the water. "Better come out, son. I think we should talk."

Grim stepped just far enough into the room so his left side was traced with soft red light. He had his hat off—in respect. But his shades were still on.

Classy Jack Watkins carefully put his feet into the water, clenching his teeth and hissing. Finally he relaxed and went "Aah."

"The salt gets to you," he said. "But it cleans you out. Takes care of all the impurities that might have slipped into the cracks while you weren't looking. Then the soda softens them up. Makes them nice and smooth." He looked directly at the intruder. "Looks like you could use a salt bath over your entire body. What should I call you, son?"

Grim didn't answer. It didn't faze Classy Jack.

"I'll call you Ace, then," he continued. "That's

how I got my nickname, too. I didn't say nothing, just did what I had to do. And somebody else, bigger than me, he gave me the name and the job. 'I like you,' the man said. 'You're a class act, Jack.' So here I am." He paused. "And there you are. I told you, Ace. I don't like mirrored shades."

Grim took them off, gingerly. Classy Jack gave a low whistle. "I knew you were something the moment I laid eyes on you. I surely did. How did you get in here, Ace?"

Grim said nothing.

"I said, let's talk, Ace," Classy Jack said with anger. "I'm not going to just sit here, flapping my gums. I ain't gonna do no monologue for you, boy. I spent thousands of dollars sealing this place up tight. Now I'm gonna ask you again, Ace. How did you get in here?"

Grim looked outside. He looked back and shrugged. "Air, water gets in."

Classy Jack stared at him for a few seconds, then nodded. "I can tell from your tone of voice it's no great pleasure for you to talk. I shall keep that in mind. What did you do, Ace? Come through the toilet?"

Grim smiled at the thought.

"She-it," said Classy Jack. "I can see it's no pleasure for you to do anything. You must've come in through the air ducts, then."

Grim nodded once.

"I didn't think they were big enough for more than a boy," Classy Jack mused. "But there it is, and here you are. Gonna have to wire them ducts. Should've done that before." He slapped his knees. "So. What can I do for you, Ace?"

"Betty," said Grim.

Classy Jack leaned back. "You've got to understand some things, my boy. First, I'm talking to you out of respect. I don't like it, but you gotta respect a man who did what you did tonight. You're a force, Ace, and I'm going to treat you like one. I'm not going to lie to you, boy. All I ask is that you return the favor. You're not going to get in trouble because of me, and I'm not going to get in trouble because of you. Do we have an understanding?"

Grim nodded.

Classy Jack nodded back. "Okay. The first thing you've got to understand is that I don't know no Betty. Dozens of girls, sometimes hundreds, come through here every week. I'm not exaggerating, Ace. They come from all over the city and all over the country. They come here because they get the word. The lucky ones come here, Ace, you understand me? The unlucky ones I think you've already met. They're up on Lenox and down on Park Avenue South. Look out the window, Ace. You're looking at Shangri-la for these people."

Grim shook his head sharply. This was not what he had come to hear.

"Okay, okay," said Classy Jack. "Long story short. I don't know no Betty. And I get the distinct impression you're not going to rattle off no detailed description."

Grim retreated into the shadows.

Classy Jack just sat there for a few minutes, then started to get nervous. "Hey, Ace," he called. "What are you going to do? Where are you, boy?"

Grim reappeared in the neon light. In his hands was the pad and pencil that had been sitting on the foyer table, next to the phone. Grim flipped him the small pad.

Classy Jack snapped it out of the air. On the first two-by-three-inch page was a pencil drawing. It was basic but informative. Small, wide-set eyes, flat nose, thin lips, weak chin, lifeless hair.

"Betty, huh?" Classy Jack said with sadness. "No, son, I'm sorry. I don't know her. I haven't seen her. She's not on this street." His subtext was clear. If she wasn't here, bumping and grinding for a buck, she was on her back somewhere—where the stakes and money were higher.

Grim broke the pencil. "Street," he said.

Both men could feel the mood change. The room got darker. The air got thicker.

"Now there," said Classy Jack. "Now there we have a little problem, Ace. No one knows his real name, unless that was a cruel joke played by his parents. And considering the parents I know, that isn't out of the question. No one knows where he lives and only the crazy ones want to know. He's bad news, Ace, and we don't like bad news around here."

"Street," said Grim.

"He's a pimp. That's not a hard guess. But he sees his name as a divine calling, you know what I mean? It was like he was raised for it. Control and power. That's what he wants. That's what he *is*." Classy Jack watched Grim carefully. "Like you. A little like you."

Grim's lips came off his teeth. They shone red.

"The K Club was his shack," Classy Jack went on. "But he doesn't keep paperwork. He's more of a hands-on man. If you want him, it'll have to be on the streets."

"Where?" said Grim.

"You know, man," Classy Jack said tightly. "I sent you there. You must've seen the whores. They must've told you. Nobody's gonna lie to you, man. Not you."

Grim took a step into the room. Classy Jack dived for the floor, his hands scrambling for his guns.

The water splashed everywhere, dousing Classy Jack and the carpet. He gagged and choked with the effort, falling heavily on his stomach, the air knocked out of him.

His fingers grabbed frantically, wrapping around the steel and plastic. The weapons seemed to slip through his fingers, as if made of mercury. His vision clouded and the blood roared in his ears.

Finally he felt the .45. He wrenched himself onto his back, gasping for breath. He pushed the gun out in front of him with both hands.

Grim stood above him, two feet away. Classy Jack Watkins aimed the barrel at Grim's chest and tightened his finger on the trigger.

Suddenly he fell back, letting the gun fall beside him. He sucked in air for a few seconds, then finally talked.

"It's not loaded, is it?"

Grim just stood there.

"None of them are loaded, are they?" Classy Jack looked at the two other handguns with resignation.

Grim kicked the underside of Classy Jack's right foot.

"Okay, okay," he said. "I heard what you done. Ripping a man's hand open. That's not right."

Grim kicked again.

"All right!" Classy Jack exclaimed. "But we still got a deal, right? I know nothing, you know nothing. Right?"

Grim could see that the outwardly assured man was deathly afraid. But not of the undead man who stood before him.

Grim didn't nod. Instead, he turned and walked back into the shadow. He turned only when he reached the foyer.

"Okay," said Classy Jack. "The K Club was his shack. But I know where his crib is." He gave Grim the address. Grim turned to go out the door as Classy Jack climbed back into his chair.

"Go the way you came," the old man said. "I don't want anybody seeing you leave here."

Grim stopped and looked at him. He was sitting as if he had just had a heart attack. But he was strong enough to look back at Grim and smile.

"Sure, I might turn on the furnace while you're climbing down," Classy Jack Watkins said, "but we're just gonna have to trust each other. Aren't we?"

6

Even in the city that never sleeps, there seems to be a pocket of time when peace descends on the troubled streets like a warm winter blanket. Between the time all the night people decide to go home and the day people start waking up, the neighborhoods are quiet and empty. This was true of Dyckman Street in Washington Heights, on the very northern edge of the Manhattan island—an oasis of relative calm between the Washington and University Heights bridges.

The house Grim looked at was on the northernmost tip of High Bridge Park. It was a handsome four-story brownstone. Unlike Classy Jack Watkins's residence, it was clearly fortified. Alarm stickers were on every window, and even the tiny basement panes were protected by iron bars.

Grim looked from the purple, orange, and pale blue horizon to the quiet cobblestone street lined with small, well-tended trees and shrubs. He looked

at the brownstone windows, seeing the thin strip of
light green that ran around the edges of every single
one. Even if he could tear or bend the protecting
bars, breaking any window would set off the alarm.

Grim saw the alarm box set midway up the side of
the brownstone, in the middle of the wall—far away
from the drainpipes. Someone would have to be a
human fly to reach it. Grim realized he would not be
able to enter this vault as easily as he had Classy Jack
Watkins's.

He knelt to peer through a basement window.
Sure enough, the heating system was modern. There
was no furnace door, no matter how small, to
squeeze through. No rectangular ducts to climb up
or slither through. Only a mouse could travel
through these new plastic heating pipes—and a
small mouse at that.

Grim was not upset. He remembered what he had
said to the Combat Zone West boss—his longest sentence to date. "Air, water get in." If he couldn't get
in by going up, he would get in by coming down.

Even in this upper-middle-class neighborhood,
yard space was at a premium. The brownstones were
separated, if only by a space of a few feet. There
were narrow alleys between them. Although the alleys around this place were carefully fenced in and
locked, that was not the case for most of the other
buildings.

Grim walked to the back of the second house to
the brownstone's right. It was a more traditional
two-family dwelling, with sloped roofs and New En-
gland architecture. Grim went to the very edge of
the small backyard and placed himself against the
high wooden fence. Then he ran toward the covered
basement stairs.

He ran up that incline, leaped, stepped onto the
base of a first-story window, and grabbed the ledge

of the second story. Without pausing, he pulled himself up, lightly climbed across the shingles, and
grabbed the ceiling lip of the small third-story section. Grim paused ever so slightly in order to swing
up without any other part of his body touching the
windowpanes or walls. He stood on the very apex of
the house, looking across to the next building. The
entire climb had taken less than a half minute.

Grim ran across the crest of the roof and leaped
the twelve feet between structures. He soared
through the air, landed, rolled, and came up on his
feet—all without making any noise. He was hardly
winded. He walked on the balls of his feet to the
edge of this building and gauged the distance between it and the brownstone in question.

He stopped, marveling at the strangely beautiful
greenhouse on the roof of Street Wise's "crib." It
glowed aqua in the dark dawn light. It was made
entirely of thick opaque glass blocks, bracketed by
firm silver framing. The design was modern, but still
somehow ancient in appearance.

"Mayan," his god whispered.

Grim could make out dark, smudged shapes inside. He turned abruptly and walked back to the
other side of the building. Grim turned the way he
had come once more, then ran. He jumped again.
He flew between buildings, crossed over onto
Street's property, and landed on his feet.

He looked at the door to the main building, then at
the glass structure. Finally he walked away from the
four-story crib.

He carefully checked the greenhouse for any
alarm system. Unlike the rest of the building, it
seemed to be unprotected. The only obstruction was
a small lock on the glass blockhouse's one door. Grim
stood before the door, carefully pressing each glass
square. Finally he decided on one close to the

ground. He knelt, his feet anchored slightly behind him, placed both hands flat on the square, and pushed.

He started with short pressure alternating with long pushes. When he felt the cement on the inside of the silver framing giving way, he began a series of short, concentrated pushes. He wasn't worried about the thick, solid glass breaking under his assault. It was too strong for that. Instead the block began to move inward.

Grim pushed until it popped out of place. He lay down to look inside.

It was a bedroom. It was almost tropically steamy inside. Diffused white, green, and blue light filled the interior. It rippled across the room, making everything look as if it were underwater.

The furnishings themselves were solid and heavy. There was a lace-covered bureau, a standing Tiffany lamp, a bed table covered with clean, lacquered, ceramic pottery, and a huge canopied bed.

Grim slithered through the little hole. He stood on the other side of the door. He slowly took off his hat and pulled down his glasses. It would have been like being inside a diamond had it not been for the smell. The stench of disease and defecation permeated the room.

Grim started toward the bed. At first the thick, satiny, bone-colored sheets seemed to be flat, but as he got closer, he could see a frail, sweaty form lying there.

Grim walked around the bed and stood between it and the night table, almost reverently—his hat in his hand.

He looked down into the face of a once beautiful woman. She was still fragile and pure, like a porcelain doll. Her cheeks were sunken, but her classically lovely bone structure still shaped her face. Her hair was limp but still glowed with auburn embers. The freckles across her nose seemed about to fall off.

Her eyes were tightly closed. Her breathing was uneven and soggy. Sweat covered her like a layer of skin. Her mouth was moving, but only small, unintelligible sounds came out. She must be having a nightmare, Grim thought.

"Pneumonia," his god said.

Grim looked over his shoulder to see a thick washcloth lying in a ceramic bowl. He wet it with water from the ceramic pitcher and carefully laid it on the wan woman's brow.

Her eyes snapped open, panic blinding them. Grim was sure she would have screamed and fought, but she didn't have the strength. Her frighteningly thin form could only jerk weakly in place.

Grim tried to back up out of her sight, but her green eyes captured him. He froze as her head slowly turned toward him. By the time that obviously painful motion was complete, her gaze was steady and serene.

Instead of shock and fear, her expression held only thanks. Her jaw worked, her mouth finally opened, and she spoke three almost inaudible words.

"Are you Death?"

Grim couldn't answer. Instead he approached the bed again.

"Please say you're Death," she begged him.

He soothed her forehead with the water.

She moved her head back again, so that she was staring up at the ceiling. "No good anymore," she said. "Just as well. I'm no good to him anymore anyway. Can't sell me like this. Not even to the ones who like them skinny." She tried to laugh but failed. She couldn't even cough. It sounded as if she was choking. Finally she relaxed.

"Please be Death. I've prayed to God to send you

here. I've prayed every night and every day. I've made this a temple for you. I've worshiped you. Please do not forsake me."

Even that effort was too much. Grim could feel her temperature rising, even through the cloth. Her fever raged. He watched her descend into delirium.

"Beauty lasts forever," she gasped out, starting to thrash feebly. "Beauty lasts forever. It can't be destroyed. It can only turn on itself." He saw her eyes cloud over. She could no longer see him. He saw her fingers try to grip the sheets from beneath. "Eaten away from the inside. Betrayed by beauty. Beauty rages and destroys. They love you, and they take a piece . . ."

Grim gripped her shoulders, hoping to keep her still. It was like pressing on a dying bird. Her body continued to tremble. "He loved me. Even after, he still loved me. He said I was special. He said I could still make him happy. Happy, I wanted to make him happy. It was never better then. Every kiss was the last kiss. Every touch, every caress . . . every *fuck*."

The word was harsh and horrid in this ethereal room. She spat it out, almost sitting up. It changed her. She became like a drowning victim, trying to claw her way back to air and life.

"He loved me!" she tried to shriek, the words tearing through her stretched, clogged vocal cords. "He gave me to them! Every nine months! Every nine months, another. Every year! Every year!"

Grim was afraid she'd tear herself apart in his hands. Her face turned dark red and the veins on her neck grew fat and pulsing. But finally she fell back so suddenly that he was left holding his hands in midair. He could see that she had no awareness of where or who she was.

He heard distant crying.

He did not know whether it was the voice of a child . . . or a god.

"My children," he heard her say. Then her fingers gripped his shirt with a strength he couldn't believe she still possessed. "My children!"

The fingers loosened and the hand dropped. Grim carefully lifted it away from him, seeing the jade circle on his belt buckle—the symbol of life.

More's the pity: she wasn't dead yet.

All Grim could do was stand by the side of the bed, his fists tightly clenched. Her last words echoed in his mind. "My children . . ."

"Look," said his god, the words hoarse.

Grim turned his head to the left. The curtains behind the bed's baseboard were more than decoration. He reached out, grabbing a fistful. He pulled it aside.

There was another door there. This one was not glass. This one was padded steel.

Grim left the woman's side. He moved purposefully beneath the curtains, his fingers wrapped around the doorknob. He twisted it and swept the partition open.

A wall of crying hit him.

It was like throwing open a dam. The wails were like water washing across him, covering him, drowning him. The cries were as loud as screams. They were high-pitched and incessant. Grim realized he had stumbled upon a soundproofed room. It was as if the cries had been collecting inside, threatening to burst the enclosure.

Grim was frozen in panic and shock. There was nothing in the small room except five cribs.

They were the best cribs money could buy. They were beautifully made and expertly appointed. The colors were both blue and pink. The walls, ceiling, and floor were heavily padded. The smell of waste was even worse in here.

"Move," said his god.

Grim did not.

"Look," said his god.

Grim refused.

"Now," said his god.

The dictator moved his feet. Grim looked down.

Children were in the cribs. Naked babies lying in their own filth. Grim could tell from their expressions that they were insane. Only four screamed. They wouldn't stop. They couldn't. The fifth one was dead—shriveled and curled on its side in the fifth crib.

No one heard Grim's scream. It was swallowed up by the sound of the bureau exploding through the front wall of the greenhouse. The heavy piece of furniture hit the roof but didn't break.

Grim came out of the destroyed wall, flying. He landed near the bureau and paused only to grab it again. With a roar, he swung it above his head and hurled it into the door leading downstairs.

The bureau smashed into kindling, and the door bent inward. But the door was made to swing from the inside toward the outside. Grim panted like a bull. He threw himself against the obstruction with a grunting cry, then snapped the long steel pins out of the hinges holding the door.

He threw it open from the wrong side. It flew across the roof, hitting the low restraining wall.

Grim didn't bother with the stairs. He vaulted over the banister and dropped to the third-floor landing. The alarm horns were blaring. Already doors were opening and young women were running for their lives.

"Street!" Grim bellowed, hurling girls aside. He

raced through every sumptuous apartment, knocking over anyone who got in his way. "Street!"

A bulldozer of a man came out into the hall, cinch-
ing a short robe around him. "What the . . ." was all
he got to say. Grim leaped into the air and planted
his foot in the man's throat.

The man made a gurking sound and hit the wall as
if yanked by a steel cable. His eyes were wide open
in surprise as Grim grabbed his arm and threw him
through the third-floor banister.

The man hit the opposite wall, bounced, fell to the
stairs, and slammed all the way down to the second
floor, bones snapping.

Grim leaped after him, also hitting the opposite
wall but landing on his feet and running down the
remaining steps.

"Street!"

On the second floor there were more women running and screeching in fear. Grim stood in the middle of their pimp's dreadful crib, grabbing them by
the throats as they went by.

"Street!" he screamed, slamming them up against
the wall. "Street, Street, Street, *Street!*"

"Shouldn't be a problem," Street Wise was saying
calmly.

A smile played around the lips of his companion,
the only person he respected and took orders from.

They sat in her Riverdale house, less than ten
miles from his crib. The home was tastefully decorated in somber hues of dark wood and copper. They
had just finished a delightful breakfast, after a long,
hard night of activity.

Street finished the last of the croissant and straw-
berry preserves, then carefully wiped his lips. He
took a final swallow of café au lait. He wiped his lips
again. They gleamed, soft and pampered.

"I really don't foresee any difficulty," he elabo-
rated, his syllables careful and softly accented. From
which country his accent came, she was never able
to pinpoint, although she knew the man himself
came from Costa Rica. He smiled, eager to satisfy his
associate.

He had great admiration for this person. He felt
this was the only person on the planet who truly
appreciated him. This person was the sole justifica-
tion of his life. This was the patron of his art.

"I am not so sure," said Muriel Holford. She was a
middle-aged woman with a kind face and a placid
disposition. She exuded calm. Sometimes she was so
calm, it was scary.

"And neither should you be," she continued.
"Hope for the best but plan for the worst. I'm told
the police want to question you about a shooting
incident on One Hundred and Twenty-seventh."

"Circumstantial," said Street. "There's no eyewit-
ness placing me on the scene. There are other eye-
witnesses who can place me elsewhere." He
shrugged. "Besides, the weapon is gone." He made
little smoke-puff motions with his hands. "As if it
never existed."

"Even so, dear, I will not be happy if you are
distracted. I need you more than ever now."

"No distraction," he promised. "If need be, I can
go underground. For weeks at a time. Months. I've
done it before."

Muriel smiled. "I know, dear. I depend on you,
you know that."

Street nodded. "And I, you."

Muriel started to clear the blue-and-white bone
china plates. "We're doing quite well," she said.
"The time is right. I think we can move ahead." Her
words were as calm as always, but Street could feel

her added excitement. He couldn't help feeling a new thrill himself.

"Yes?" he said, with just an edge.

"You have done very well," Muriel said, coming back from the kitchen, wiping her hands on her apron. "Very well. The force of your actions is tangible. I think, with your help, the energy is sufficient to start. But you must tell me, with all honesty. Is there anything which could disrupt the flow of events?"

Street smiled. He sat back, putting an arm over the chair. "On the contrary," he replied. "The only problem is a positive."

Muriel frowned. She did not like the word "problem."

"One of the trim," Street quickly continued, forcing himself to remain assured. It was amazing how this innocuous woman intimidated him. "She may have been the 'inside' for this police action at the shack."

Muriel looked away, busying herself with clearing the rest of the cutlery. The scene looked like any other in millions of dining rooms across the nation. "Oh?" she said placidly. "What makes you think so?"

"She was acting strange. There was an edge of contemptuousness in everything she did."

Muriel laughed quietly. "What language. Can't you just say 'uppity' like the rest of the city?"

He smiled back, warmly. "No," he said. "I can't."

"In other words, dear, she was acting as if she knew something you didn't. She had a secret."

"Exactly," said Street. "And she was spending money. *My* money."

Muriel looked up in mock shock. "Another man!" She went back to her clearing. "Are you losing your internationally famous touch, dear?"

"No," he said. "She was losing hers."

"I hope you talked to her, dear." Although she

kept her head down, Street could see her begin to smile in anticipation.

"I did." They both had images of the "discussion." *Screams. Slaps. Terror. Sobbing.*

"Was it enough?" she asked.

"No," he answered. "It wasn't."

Muriel looked up in pseudosurprise. "Whatever did you do?"

Street's smile was at its widest. "I sent her to my room."

For a moment, it seemed as if the woman was going to squeal with glee. Instead, her smile matched Street's until the palatable joy that had infused the room subsided.

Finally Muriel Holford finished clearing the table. "Well, that's nice, dear. That's very nice."

Betty had to stop crying. She no longer had any breath for it. She couldn't scream—for all the good it would do her.

Her mouth ached. Her fingers were numb, her fingernails torn and bloody. It felt as if her hands were stitched into electrical outlets. It felt as if all her bones had been split open. Mucus covered her upper lip. Saliva covered her jaw.

She tried to pull the gag off again. It was no use. Her hands were free, but the leather strap between her teeth was affixed around her head by a small lock that had its own metal tongue and clip. There was nothing to untie, no buckle to unfix. She needed the key, which was nowhere near her.

The strap kept the Ping-Pong ball on her tongue and upper palate—away from her teeth. She could make sounds, and could just barely manage words, but she couldn't get enough volume for a shout. Street was taking no chances. He didn't want anyone to take her out of his room.

It was a five-foot ball of thick steel mesh. It sat in the sewers beneath Broadway and Nagle Avenue, at the mouth of Harlem River Bay. It was held there by a chain. The only exit was a three-by-three hinged mesh door. It was sealed shut with a larger lock. The only way out was by another key. That key was close by.

It was tied around the neck of a rat. One of the fifty rats inside the cage with her.

Betty had placed her feet on either side of the cage and pushed herself up into the very top of the crosshatched steel ball. The rats could no longer sniff or run across her feet. But she couldn't reach them, either. Instead she looked down at all fifty of their scurrying forms with their brown fur, black eyes, and quivering dark pink noses.

Every one of the fifty had a key tied around its neck.

Betty had been in Street's room for almost an hour, but she still couldn't bring herself to touch the rats. She could imagine Street capturing every one of them, securing them down, and tying the keys around their necks. She could imagine him smiling all the while, enjoying his precise handiwork, reveling in the plan. What she couldn't imagine was trying to pull the keys off their gnawing, disease-ridden faces herself.

Fine, her brain screeched. Let him punish her. She deserved it. She had gotten out of line. She admitted it. She didn't tell him about Grim, but she knew she had gotten too sure of herself because of the beast. She had toyed with the idea of escaping to him. She would have let Grim protect her from Street.

But it was just a fantasy. She tried to tell Street that, but he wouldn't listen.

So now she was here. And here she would stay, she

thought, until she learned her lesson. Soon she would gather the courage to try getting the keys—trying each one in the lock until one worked. Soon. As soon as she got her wind and wits back. If she thought of Grim long and hard enough, she would find the courage. She knew she would.

It had just turned seven o'clock.

Betty heard something in the sewer tunnel.

At one time, when Manhattan was in its prime, the sewers were cleaned out every night at 4:00 A.M. But as the city grew older, the attention to detail and devotion to duty grew lax. Now the night shift waited until the day shift arrived before both opened the rusted, creaking valves that sent a torrent of water into the underground pipes.

From inside the sewer, the sound of the water was like a tidal wave and earthquake combined. The walls and ground shook. The ceiling rumbled. The rats squealed. Betty couldn't hear whatever sounds she made.

Her eyes widened as the solid tube of liquid shot at her. It slammed into the steel ball, hurling it off the ground. The chain held. She was thrown into the very corner of the metal circle.

Her head broke the surface. The water was still rushing through, lifting the cage, but it filled up the sewer tunnel only halfway. Betty blinked, trying to spit out the offal-filled water from behind her gag.

Suddenly she saw the rats, trying frantically to stay on the water's surface, all around her head.

They were climbing on her. They were trying to gain purchase on her arms, torso, shoulders, neck, and skull. They bit and clawed.

Betty almost went insane. She couldn't stay there, but she couldn't dive either. The rats were everywhere. There was nowhere for her to go.

Then she heard it. The second roar of water. Another valve had been opened.

Something clicked in her brain. *If the first rush of water filled the tunnel only halfway, the second would . . .*

"Find the key," Street had said. "Find the right key and get out before the second wave covers you. . . ."

The girl went mercifully out of her mind.

PART TWO

What the mother sings to the cradle
goes all the way down to the coffin.
—Henry Ward Beecher

7

Captain Bender knew he was in trouble when he saw the patrolmen crying.

He recognized both men. Mallory had been on the force for seven years. His partner, Kulinsky, had been on the beat twice that long. Both men had seen terrible things before. But here they were—Mallory leaning on the roof's short embankment wall, sobbing, and Kulinsky just standing beside the greenhouse's doorway, fat tears running down his face, soaking his moustache.

Lieutenant Chang was just inside the unusual glass structure, talking with his medical examiner. Bender could see them through the big hole in the front wall. He reached them just as the doctor was finishing up.

". . . Given just enough sustenance to keep them alive, but for the most part their basic needs were ignored. From what I can see, their urine and stool samples are full of blood."

Bender stopped short when he saw the figure on the bed. The covers had been thrown back. The sheets beneath her were thick with blood and waste stains. The woman herself looked like a concentration camp victim. She couldn't have been more than sixty pounds . . . if that. Her skin was as thin as parchment and it hung on her like melted rubber.

The most horrid thing was even though her face was sunken and her eyes were closed, she was smiling.

Bender could hear the screeching of babies in pain from the adjoining room. He stopped in his tracks and turned his back on the scene. He didn't need to see this. He couldn't let this astonishing cruelty distract him. Within moments, Lieutenant Chang was at his side.

"Jesus, Vic," said Bender. "What is going on? It's like . . . people are using the latest atrocity as inspiration. They see it in the paper or on TV, then try to outdo it! It's like people are testing us. Every time I leave the office, it's like a fight to see if I can remain unshakable."

"I doubt it's personal, Frank," said the lieutenant.

Bender turned his head and stared at him, his expression hard. "What is it, then, Vic? What is this if not personal?" Chang didn't bother answering.

Bender forced himself to calm down. "Okay, fill me in," he said.

"Welcome to the fabulous, previously unknown Street Wise crib," said the lieutenant. "This"—he pointed his thumb over his shoulder—"was his 'penthouse.' The woman is . . . was Jane Weston, once one of his prime prostitutes—the QE2 of his fleet."

"AIDS?" Bender asked.

Chang nodded.

"The children?"

"We won't know for sure until all the blood tests

are done, but we're guessing they're hers. We're also guessing AIDS for them." Here even Chang became sad. "They *can't* stop crying, Frank. The oldest one is almost four."

Bender walked away—closer to the destroyed door leading downstairs. "Jesus, Vic," he repeated, shaking his head. "Jesus." He stopped and turned. "What did he have them up here for? Punishment? A warning?"

"The few we were able to find downstairs . . . and revive . . . said they never knew they were up here. They were not allowed on the roof. Strict orders. Seems Street didn't want anyone in the neighborhood to know his herd was being stabled here."

"Then why?"

Chang shrugged helplessly. "You may have been right the first time, Frank. Punishment. Jane Weston got AIDS. Maybe any client Street didn't like got Weston. But why he made her have the babies is beyond me."

Captain Bender looked down for a few moments, then leaned close to Chang. "It's not beyond me. Street is scum. He wants to be evil. Completely evil. But he doesn't have the brains for it. So when something horrible like this drops in his lap—when this Weston girl asks for an abortion—he just says 'no.' He wants complete control. He wants his minions to suffer. He wants to be god."

"Or the devil," said Chang.

Captain Bender considered that for a second, then marched away from the greenhouse. He went past Kulinsky into the brownstone. Lieutenant Chang was right behind him. They had only to look down to see the devastation. The once perfect walls had holes in them. There were bloodstains. The banisters and stairs were broken.

"High-class hookers were lying all over the place,

Frank. Some were in shock. Some had concussions. One or two even had fractures. The manager of the apartments—a muscle-bound lunkhead named Steve Messert—is in the hospital in critical condition. Someone used him as a basketball on the floors, walls, and stairs."

The policemen walked down to the second floor where more Ninety-third Precinct officers were going over the place with fine-tooth combs.

Bender looked back at Chang. "No hoop, huh?"

"No hoop. He just dribbled the guy until he wouldn't bounce anymore. Those who could remember—and talk—described their assailant as some kind of monster. Some only remembered ashen teeth. One even described him as a 'barbecued skeleton.' That's when I called you, Frank."

"Good to know my inter-precinct memos are getting read."

"That's not it," said Chang. "The central computer is automatically cross-referencing whenever a description overlaps with the boy you're looking for."

"Anybody else get called?"

"Sure. The chief and the commissioner, but neither wanted to come near this place. After the press problem at the K Club, they didn't want to do any more explaining. The word from on high is, and I quote, 'Treat it like an ordinary call.' "

Bender snorted, remembering the scene on the roof. "Anyone recall what my boy wanted here? Did he say anything?"

Chang checked his notes. "Seems he was looking for Street Wise."

Bender nodded. "That's what I was afraid of. Any chance I can talk to Jane Weston?"

"She's in a coma, Frank. The M.E. says there's

probably brain damage. Even if she comes out of it, she'll be in no condition to give state evidence."

Bender really didn't care about that, but he didn't say so to Chang. He wanted to know more about his personal quarry. He already knew the monster was dangerous. Now he needed to know whether it was dangerous just to Street, or to everyone in the tri-state area.

His thoughts were interrupted by a call from downstairs. "Uh, Lieutenant? There's some reporters at the door."

"What?" exploded Chang. "How did they get here?" He looked accusingly at Bender. The captain was devoid of expression.

"Couldn't keep this a secret for long anyway, Vic," Bender said with philosophical sarcasm. "Too much 'human interest.' Which reporters?" he called down to the patrolmen covering the front door. "Which station?"

"Channel Six," came the answer.

Bender nodded, his suspicions confirmed. "Yeah, they probably bird-dogged me, Vic. Sorry."

"Then *you* deal with them," the lieutenant said angrily. "Sir."

"It might be a good idea if you . . ." the captain started, then let the sentence trail off. He realized that if he tried to duck the reporters, they'd know they were onto something. Besides, Chang had enough to deal with, as two of his men were already blubbering. "Dismissed, Lieutenant," he said instead. "Keep me informed, Vic."

All anger left the lieutenant's face. "Thanks, Frank. Good luck."

"You too, Vic," Bender answered, knowing what Chang had to face on the roof. "You too." The captain walked heavily down to the first floor.

They were all waiting for him outside. Big-time

Sam Niven had retreated to stand next to the Channel Six *U. R. There News* van, parked across the street. But standing beside the Ice Pick was newswriter Warren Malone. Bender was surprised they didn't have someone with her cue cards with them.

"Captain, Captain," she cried, moving in quickly as he descended the brownstone's steps. She pointed her mike and Jonathan aimed his video camera. "So sorry to hear about your ex-wife's remarriage."

"You shouldn't be sorry," Bender said without pausing, delighted that she tried this diversion. "You should congratulate us. She no longer has to live with a man who is forced to desert her at all hours of the day and night. Instead of bringing home the bacon, I'd come home with stories that would make her lose her appetite. I'm very happy for her. And you should be too."

Bender wasn't a captain for nothing. He had gotten Ashley Smith off onto one of her favorite tangents. "But you, Captain Bender," she said with a heartbreaking expression of sympathy. "What about you?"

He gave her his widest smile. "No more alimony," he replied.

Malone nudged Ashley, showing her his notes. She made a face, but turned back to Bender with renewed conviction. "Reliable sources tell us this is a scene of unspeakable horror, Captain. How does this tie in with your work at Central Division? Does it have anything to do with what happened at the K Club last night?"

They must have seen a crying policeman, Bender realized. They also must be incredibly desperate for ratings. Every other local station would probably wait for the police press division and newswire releases. And any other local news team would have sent a reporter, not their on-air anchorperson.

"It's too early to say, Ashley," Bender answered.

"What *exactly* happened in there, Captain?"

Bender considered the question, then thought it best to leave the wording up to the public relations department. "No comment." He tried to move farther down the steps, but Ashley and crew only moved forward to cut him off.

"What *exactly* is the goal of your unit at Central Division?"

Bender saw no harm in answering that, and plenty of harm in not answering. They'd wonder what he had to hide and be all over his superiors downtown. That wouldn't make his bosses comfortable. They had enough trouble with the idea of a "barbecued skeleton" as it was.

"We're a motive-oriented major crime unit responsible for the investigation of seemingly motive-less crimes of a violent nature," he told them in fluent cop-speak.

"How *exactly* does that tie in to what went on here?" Ashley demanded, pushing the mike at him more insistently.

"All right, all right," said Bender, not wanting to leave Lieutenant Chang holding the bag. "We have an unknown alleged perpetrator who may have been responsible for violent actions both here and at the K Club last night. The M.O. in both cases is similar."

"'Search and destroy,'" Ashley read from Malone's pad. "Both of these establishments are owned by a pimp known only as Street Wise. Is that not so?"

How did they get that information? Bender wondered. His suspicion that they had a p.i.—pig informant—inside the department was confirmed. "That has not been completely established at this time, Ashley."

"Now, come on, Captain," said the perfectly groomed woman with derision. "Is this the start of a" —she checked Malone's pad of paper—"vice war in the city?"

Bender could see he was in a no-win situation. He couldn't dissuade them from that theory without hinting that this destruction was somehow connected with the deaths of five serial murderers and a half dozen pushers in the past few weeks. It was time to cut his losses.

"No comment," he said, pushing his way through.

"Hey!" said Ashley, quickly checking her nails to make sure none were broken.

The captain had succeeded in demoralizing the troops. They slowly made their way back to the van and their news director. Only Jonathan stayed in place, videotaping Bender's retreat to his car.

Bender was unlocking the driver's-side door when a strong feminine hand fell on his arm. He noticed the fingernails were short and unpainted. He looked up into cold, hard blue eyes, set in an unblemished, pale face surrounded by almost pure yellow hair.

The first word that entered Bender's mind was "angel."

"It's not a vice war," Melanie Merrick told him. "It's important that you know it's not the work of another pimp or angry customer. It's not the start of a vice war. It's something better . . . and something worse."

The Arnold family had come to the end of the line. They had seen every doctor and effectively depleted their life savings, their parents' life savings, and their friends' kindness. They had seen every minister and priest, and their fingers and knees were rubbed raw from praying. Their eyes were dry and bloodshot from crying. Their throats were tight and thick from arguments and recriminations.

So when the hospital counselor called to say he was sending a social worker over, Everett Arnold said nothing. He didn't even thank him. He just hung up the phone and returned to his chair in front of the television.

"Evelyn," he called, not caring whether she heard or not. "The hospital is sending a social worker over." He stared at the game show without seeing it.

It happened that his wife did hear him. She turned her head but said nothing. Just a few days before, she would have yelled back, lashing out at him, but she no longer cared. What was the point of arguing over another intrusion? After all, what was one more oversympathetic, platitude-mouthing, useless person in the house?

Instead, she turned back to her daughter . . . clutching her limp hand in both of hers, staring at her pain-racked face.

When the doorbell rang, Everett went to get it without a word. He opened it without looking, then went back to his seat in front of the television like a zombie.

The social worker came in. She stood in the entrance to the plain but well-kept living room and sized up the situation. Without changing her brisk posture or attitude, she went over to the television and switched it off.

Everett Arnold looked up without complaint. The social worker looked into his empty eyes.

"I'm Muriel Holford," she said. "From now on, think of me as your television."

It wasn't long before she came quietly into the daughter's bedroom. Evelyn reared up, her mouth opening to launch a blistering attack. Muriel silenced her with a quick, efficient signal, saying, "You don't want to disturb the child."

Evelyn watched in stunned silence as the social worker walked along the other side of the bed and looked down on the suffering young girl. "What a beautiful child," she whispered, and her left hand moved.

Evelyn only got out the word "no," and even that wasn't at full volume. Then both she and her husband saw the miracle happen. When Muriel touched their daughter's brow, the pain on the girl's face subsided. Her sleep suddenly became untroubled.

When Muriel looked back at the Arnolds, their mouths were open in astonishment.

"Who *are* you?" Evelyn asked.

"Your friend," said the social worker. "Your only real friend."

"They said we'd never have a baby," Evelyn said, sniffling. "Not one of our own. So when Pamela came along, we thought it was a miracle."

"Ev was in her forties when she became . . . with child," said her husband, "so you can imagine . . ."

"Of course," said Muriel. "The joy. The concerns. The fears."

They were having tea. The first tea they had had since their daughter was diagnosed. They sat around the living room, eating cookies and sipping orange pekoe. Muriel had made it herself. The sun seeped in from behind the curtained and shaded bay window.

"Yes," said Evelyn. "But everything went all right, thank God. Everything went . . . perfectly." She became preoccupied, distracted. "I was so certain then that it was a sign . . . she was truly a miracle."

"She *was* a sign," Muriel said sharply, regaining Evelyn's attention. "A sign that for every joy . . . there is sadness."

Everett nodded his head. "Now that happiness is like . . . a punishment."

"Ev!" his wife said with shock.

Muriel smiled inwardly. Ev and Ev. How cute. "You felt you were being punished for your happiness?" she said aloud. Before they could answer, the social worker continued. "Oh, I've seen it again and again."

She put down her teacup and stood so they had to look up at her. "Having invested all their hopes and dreams into the sum total of their life and love together, the poor parents of an only child are visited by tragedy. A reminder that they must not love too much . . . or they will pay for it."

Now she had them agitated.

"H-how could we have known?" Evelyn finally stuttered. "We thought Pamela *was* love."

Muriel nodded. "A symbol of your love together . . ."

"I worked hard all my life. . . ." Everett said.

"We bought this house. . . ." said his wife.

"I practically built it. . . ."

"We gave her everything. . . ."

"She was so young, so full of life . . ."

"So vital, so smart," Muriel urged.

"Yes," said Evelyn Arnold. "Yes!"

"And then came the cancer," the social worker said sadly, lowering her head.

"Yes," Everett echoed with finality.

"What could we do?" Evelyn pleaded. "We tried everything! Ev took early retirement. . . ."

"They cut my pension," he said bitterly. "Twenty-five percent—"

"It didn't matter! We gave everything we had to our child."

"The insurance would only pay seventy-five percent," Everett continued. "Then fifty—"

"It made no difference!" said his wife. "We'd do anything . . . everything!"

"The specialists," Muriel interjected. "The therapists. The counselors. The miracle cures . . ."

"Yes," said Everett. "Nothing worked. We . . . we couldn't stand seeing her in that hospital anymore. No one cared. We brought her home . . . we had to bring her home—"

"What did we do wrong?" Evelyn sobbed. "Why did this happen to us?"

"Did you pray?" Muriel asked gravely.

That brought the Arnolds up short. Evelyn stopped crying and blinked the tears away. "Of course."

"First every Sunday," Everett said to himself. "Then every day. We gave all our money to the doctors . . . then the church. We prayed for a miracle."

Muriel Holford looked at them very steadily and seriously. "To whom?" she asked.

They stared at her. They stared at each other. Finally Evelyn leaned forward. "I beg your pardon?"

The social worker was unfazed. "To whom did you pray?" she asked again, as if it were the simplest question in the world.

"Why," said Everett. "To God, of course."

Now Muriel Holford looked honestly perplexed. "Why?"

"What?" said the man.

"I don't understand," she told them. "Why would you pray to God? He's the one who gave your child the cancer."

The room was deathly silent.

"Yes, but—" Evelyn started.

All Muriel cared about was the "yes." "What did you want from Him?"

She let them take their time. She didn't supply the

answer for them. It was vitally important that they think it was their logic.

"For . . . forgiveness?" Evelyn finally said.

"For what?" Muriel asked with seemingly honest interest and concern. "What did you do wrong?"

The Arnolds could only stare at each other.

"For . . . forsake Him?" Everett asked.

"So He smites your innocent daughter with cancer?"

By now the Arnolds were dreadfully confused. They looked everywhere but couldn't escape the logic. Their daughter was in her room dying because they loved her too much.

Muriel picked up her teacup and saucer. "I'm afraid that is the way religion works," she said regretfully. "Unfortunately, the Bible is full of fine print."

"What can we do?" Evelyn wailed, wringing her hands.

Muriel Holford, well known as one of New York's finest, most considerate, most respected, most successful social workers, took a sip of her tea.

"Have you ever," she said reasonably, "considered praying to Lucifer?"

8

They recognized each other. The last time Bender had seen Melanie, she was sitting primly in a hospital bed, quietly giving her statement to a police stenographer. She had explained the details of the massacre in a gentle monotone—as if discussing a menu.

She had maintained that Jeremy Bancroft attacked her without provocation, and that her life was saved by conscientious derelicts who came between her and the mass murderer's knife. Once the killer had been scared away, she called the police before collapsing.

She had looked different then. Meek, submissive, confused. Now her hair was pulled back in a tightly woven tail that rested on her shoulder like some sort of sleeping pet. Her face was devoid of makeup. A pair of classic Ray Bans hung around her neck by a dark brown cord.

The sunglasses lay on her chest, which was cov-

ered by a burly black turtleneck. She wore dark wool
slacks and flat black leather boots. Her hands were
clasped on her lap as she sat beside Bender in the
sedan. Her expression was hard.

She remembered him as a doorstop. That was all
he had done in the hospital—stand beside the door,
watching her talk. When she was through, he left
first. She knew he was the superior officer. She could
tell by his attitude and the way everyone silently
deferred to him.

"Why is a captain doing his own legwork?" she
wondered aloud.

Bender tried to study her posture and expression,
but he couldn't afford to take his eyes off the road for
long. There were too many potholes and crazy driv-
ers.

"Come on," he said casually. "We both know this is
more than your common, ordinary, run-of-the-mill
investigation." He wanted the words to be light, but
they seemed to thud to the floor.

"Okay," he grumbled. "You told your little story.
I'll tell you mine. I've racked up all the favors I'm
going to get. I've played all my cards. No man is an
island? Don't tell that to Central Division captains.
You ever see those buoys at the beach? Ever wonder
what they're for? They're markers. Just markers. So
are we. So am I. We mark depth and time." He
grinned at the image. "Bobbing in the NYPD sea."

He took a left at Ninety-sixth Street, past the police line blockades, and into Central Park. Melanie
watched his profile as the brick and glass gave way to
trees and multicolored, dying autumn leaves.

"So that means when there's an investigation that
no one else wants to touch with a ten-foot pole, it's
given to one of us. We get the politically hot jobs. So
if it blows up in our faces, we're pensioned off like we
never existed. 'Captain Bender? Oh, he's gone now.

That idiot screwed up good, didn't he?' They can smile and wave and get their promotions without fear while we're out fishing or sucking on a gun barrel somewhere."

He had wanted to be straight with her, but even he was surprised by the vehemence of his reaction. Maybe it was because he knew that of all the people in the city, only she would completely believe his theory. That gave them a kinship. He looked over to check her reaction. She was looking back steadily, without expression.

Bender returned his attention to the road, winding through the nearly empty park. "You saw him, didn't you?" he asked.

Melanie turned to look out the passenger window. She took in the flowers and hills and rock formations, imagining she was back in the suburbs.

"For a while I thought he was consciousness itself," she said absently. "I thought he had to be aware and a witness to everything while we escaped through sleep."

Bender shook his head. "We don't escape through sleep."

"But we know it's not real. We know it when we wake up."

"*If* we wake up," said Bender.

"*That's* death," said Melanie. "Neither of us are dead. Not yet. Not even him. He isn't consciousness. He's action itself. He sleeps. But when he's awake, he sees what we all see." She looked back at the cop. "The only difference is that he can't turn away. He has to do something about it. He cannot witness injustice and do nothing."

"Who is he?"

Melanie started, as if the seat gave her an electric shock. She opened her mouth, but nothing came out.

She turned back to the window. "I don't know," she finally said. "I was hoping you would."

"Where can I find him?"

She looked out the front windshield. "I was hoping you'd know that too."

Bender frowned, frustrated. "Okay, then, Mrs. Merrick. How did you find *me*? I left strict instructions to tell no one where I was going."

Melanie looked down. "I didn't find you," she said. "I found them. The children."

Bender's head snapped in her direction. Her voice had gotten so soft he could hardly hear her. And he wanted to see if she was lying. But according to her expression, she was not testing or probing him. She knew what had been in that penthouse glass room.

Melanie's eyes were filled by the greenery around them. "The last time I saw him," she said, "he was in the middle of a beautiful field. The sky was the purest blue, clouds the purest white, the grass a hill of emerald green. The trees were deep brown, and their autumn leaves every color imaginable. He looked like he couldn't believe it. A monster like him didn't deserve such a paradise."

Bender was getting impatient. This junk didn't wash. If she had not been speaking so clearly, he would guess she was drunk or stoned. "Where were you?" he asked, trying to snap her back to reality.

"Above him," she answered simply. "I'm always floating above him. Looking down on him as he dreams." She finally looked back at Bender, not caring whether he believed her or not. "I have these dreams. That's where I see him."

"Mrs. Merrick . . ." he groaned.

"Let me finish," she said. "Then you can drop me off and forget about it if you want. I'm telling you what I know, and that's all I can do."

Bender gripped the steering wheel tighter, scowling.

Melanie said the rest, her voice a calm monotone.

"He was astonished. He thought he had actually reached heaven. That's when I realized that his mind had to show him this beauty or else he couldn't stand it. But even then, the truth was breaking through.

"In the distance, he heard crying. It was a single voice at first, and very far away. But soon it gained volume and dimension. There were two crying voices, then three, then four, and then five. By then the crying was like the wind . . . no, like the atmosphere, everywhere and always.

"He looked all around, trying to locate it, trying to stop it. Then he felt the wetness on his hands. He felt it everywhere his body touched the ground. When he raised his hands, they were covered in tears."

"I thought it would be blood," Bender interjected sardonically.

"Let me just say it," Melanie said with tired irritation. "You think I don't know how stupid this sounds? This is what I *dream,* Captain Bender. You don't think I'd rather live without this? Yes, I saw him that last time. And he looked exactly the way he did in the dreams. The same dreams I've had *every single night since my husband died.* Every night since my husband *was murdered*! All right? Happy now?"

Bender shook his head, chastised. "Sorry, Mrs. Merrick. It's just kind of hard to accept, you know?"

"Captain," said Melanie patiently, "you have a man who looks like death warmed over, walking around, twisting the heads off pushers and pimps. Tell me how hard this is to accept, okay?"

"Sorry," said Bender. "Sorry, sorry. Go on."

"I'll make it short and acceptable. He went nuts. And not 'fun' nuts like Daffy Duck or something. You know how emotions are magnified in dreams? Imagine rage, horror, frustration, and agony combined, filling your brain, blocking everything else out. He tore the placid image apart, trying to find the source of those cries. Soon I could see nothing else but his screaming face."

The two were silent while Bender drove down Park Avenue toward the Pan Am Building.

"Okay," the cop finally said. "How did you find the place?"

"I had this dream on the train," Melanie said flatly. "His screams had an echo. I followed them. That's the only way I can describe it. There's my stop. Pull over at the next corner, please."

Hardly thinking, Bender did as she asked. They were amid the finest corporate buildings in the city. "Wait a minute," he said as she started to get out. "What did you come here for?"

"To visit some friends," she answered. "There was a time the dreams stopped, Captain. Right after Jeremy Bancroft died. I think our monster was wounded."

Bender nodded. Evidence justified that theory. Melanie stepped out to the curb.

"But the dreams came back, Captain," she said, leaning over, looking through the open passenger door. "He's on the move. He's seen something else. Something he has to do something about."

"Stay out of it, Mrs. Merrick," Bender told her. "Go home. Leave him to us. We'll stop the dreams."

"That's what I'm afraid of," she said before she slammed the car door.

Bender watched her walk toward the front of a black glass building. It was a strong stride, with the natural feminine rhythm cut to a minimum. He saw her stop by a gold sign just outside the revolving door. He strained his eyes to read it.

"Dice-Corp: The DiCenzo Corporation."

He saw her shoulders straighten. Finally she went inside. He thought about going after her or getting out and calling to her.

Instead, he pulled the car into traffic and drove back to Central. His office was as he left it. After spending the many weird minutes in a car with the fresh-faced blonde, he couldn't help noticing the worn metal desk, the chipped wooden chair, and the window so smog-encrusted the city looked sepia-toned.

Bender sat down, smiling in spite of himself. He could imagine her flying through dreams.

He looked at the spot on his desk where the photo of his ex-wife used to be. He looked around carefully, trying to memorize everything. If this case continued the way it had been going, it wouldn't be long before he was a tired, retired old man somewhere, trying to decide between taking a security guard job and blowing his head off.

Captain Bender picked up the police directory, then grabbed the Touch-Tone phone and pushed ten numbers. "Westport Police? This is Captain Frank Bender, Central Division, New York City Police Department. I'd like to talk to the detective who handled the Geoffrey Robert Merrick murder. . . ."

The Channel Six *U. R. There News* team watched the videotape with a combination of pride and irritation.

"Look, look," said Nancy Loman, the producer, her finger jabbing at the image. "Look at them push. They're not supposed to do that!"

"Nance," said Manny Steiner, the news editor. "They were trying to get babies into the ambulance without impaling them on cameras or lights. We're not supposed to do that, either."

Nancy folded her arms. "It's a question of First Amendment rights," she said, then sniffed. "They were trying to keep us from informing the public of their discovery."

"Nance, they were trying to get four sick children to the hospital."

"They were trying to keep us from filming," she insisted.

"How would you know?" Warren Malone complained. "You weren't even there."

Manny could feel the chill covering the producer like the next ice age. That was another bone of contention lying on the table in front of them. Ever since Sam Niven, the news director, had gone into field work, Nancy was feeling increasingly paranoid and unloved.

"Thanks, Warren," Manny said under his breath.

So now, instead of giving voice to her fears, Nancy was taking Sam Niven's side in everything with the passion of an overprotective mother. "You can see it," she said stridently, waving at the monitor. "You can see it clearly."

"What exactly *are* we seeing?" asked Tom Templeton, the coanchor of Channel Six's 5:00 and 10:00 P.M. newscasts. Sam had been spending so much time with Ashley that he had thought it best to include Tom in their meeting.

"AIDS babies," said Sam, watching the video intently, already editing it in his head. "One of our stringers got the word at the hospital. And I *like* the shoving, Nancy. It gives the film urgency and a reality it wouldn't have otherwise."

"AIDS?" Ashley echoed, acting as if someone had said "money." "They actually kept the children with AIDS in the house with them? That's amazing."

"That's barbaric," said Nancy, sitting.

"It's incredibly rich with story possibilities," Warren said.

"But how can we get the full horror across?" Ashley wondered.

"I'm sorry?" said Tom Templeton. "What do you mean? You just read the copy and show the videotape. The words and images speak for themselves."

"Not anymore," Smith countered. "Tom, our viewers see this every day."

"This?" Tom said incredulously.

"Or something like it," Ashley replied.

Manny interrupted cautiously. "She may be right, Tom. Our stories have gotten pretty rough lately."

"Like for the last five years," said Warren. "One disaster and atrocity after another."

"It all looks the same," Ashley complained.

Tom started to tense. "This is beginning to sound the same as the time you introduced bantering, Sam?"

But the news director wasn't listening.

"Don't be afraid to try new things, Tom," his coanchor urged.

"I'm not afraid of trying new things, Ashley. I'm trying not to trivialize the news any further."

"That is exactly what we're trying to do as well," Ashley said in triumph. "It's all beginning to sound the same."

"And look the same," said Warren.

"That's because we're making the news look and sound the same as cop shows!" Tom exclaimed.

Manny disagreed. "No, the average viewer can distinguish between fantasy and reality, Tom."

"That's not what I'm saying!"

"We need to shake them up," said Ashley. "Get them to take notice. This is an important story. They have to *feel* these children's pain. They have to understand."

Tom Templeton folded his arms and sat back. He had seen this before. The staff was always looking for new ways to get attention, ratings, and advertising dollars. When they went into this kind of a feeding frenzy, he thought, it was best not to bleed.

"What do you have in mind?" he asked calmly.

Ashley looked at Warren Malone. Warren looked at Sam Niven, but the news director was still looking at the videotape. The writer looked at the anchorman.

"Dramatizations," Warren said.

Tom considered it. The national networks were using them, although they gained fame in syndication. He should have known it was only a matter of time before they reached Channel Six.

"I'm not an actor," he warned.

"Not you," Warren assured him. "The human interest stories. You know, Ashley's specialty." The anchorwoman was positively beaming with anticipation.

Tom looked at Manny Steiner. "We can really boldface the pathos," the editor said, almost apologetically. "It could really have impact."

"Hey," said Sam Niven. They all looked at their fearless leader. He was watching the section of the videotape where Captain Bender was beating his hasty retreat.

Sam pointed at the screen. "Who's that?"

They all looked at the distant form of a young blond woman talking to the cop at his car.

"She's too far away," Warren complained.

"I can't make out her features," said Nancy Loman.

Just then the image magnified. "God bless Jonathan," Sam marveled. "I can always depend on him to know what's important." The screen was now filled with the back of Bender's head and the blond woman's face.

"That's better," said Warren, admiring her handsome features.

"She looks familiar," said Ashley, who usually never forgot the competition.

"Another reporter?" Sam asked.

"I don't know . . ." said Ashley.

The news director looked at the news editor.

"I don't recognize her," said Manny. "She's not a stringer as far as I know." He looked closer. "Too young to be anything but an on-air correspondent from a cablevision station. Maybe one of those Connecticut outfits."

Sam studied her serious, intent face. "There's something . . . special about her," he said. "I feel it. She's important, somehow."

"To what?" Tom wanted to know.

"To . . . this thing," Sam replied. "This . . . whatever it is. Whatever is going on in this city right now. What happened here and at the K Club are connected. We know that. Bender said so. But we don't know how. This girl . . . whoever she is . . . may be the key." He turned to his producer, with the silent speaking image of Melanie Merrick over his shoulder.

"Nancy, I want you to find out who this girl is. I want to know everything there is to know about her."

Nancy responded with a mixture of relief, thanks, and panic. It was nice to be wanted again, but she had to cover her ass in case of failure. "I'll do my absolute best, Sam. And better. But . . . uh . . . do you need it for tonight? My contacts may not be able to work that fast."

"Only tens of millions of people in town, Nance,"

said Warren. "Shouldn't be a problem." He got a look that could cut sheet metal.

"I want that information," Sam intoned. "And if I can't get it from you . . . I'll get it from them." His abrupt arm motion seemed to include everyone outside the conference room walls. He turned back to the video monitor and pointed at the blonde.

"One way or another, that face will be on the Channel Six *U. R. There News* tonight."

9

Muriel Holford came home early, as she often did. Her busiest time was lunch and immediately after—when distraught men, women, and children flooded her office with calls.

She had built her business slowly, but doctors, clerics, and those in the law industry marveled at her energy and dedication. Her consulting fees were reasonable and she guaranteed results. In fact, most of those who recommended her couldn't remember a single incident where a customer or client expressed dissatisfaction.

Muriel Holford: Social Worker—She Delivers.

Street Wise came out of the kitchen, carrying a tray. On it was her silver tea service, two bone china cups, and a plate covered with homemade cookies.

"Oh, you dear," Muriel exclaimed, putting down her leather attaché case and taking off her coat. "I daresay they're wasting your true talents downtown. You are a gentleman's gentleman."

Street put the tray on the living room coffee table, then bowed slightly from the waist as she approached. He wore a tailor-made suit, as usual. He would have looked more at home at an exclusive club . . . except for the pallor of his skin.

Muriel sat on the edge of her chair, collected some Ridgeway Majesty Blend and a pastry, then sat back with a comfortable sigh. She kicked her sensible shoes off, put her feet up on the ottoman, and took a bite from the thick cookie.

"Oh," she cried. "These are heavenly! What are they?"

"Chocolate orange chip," he said, sitting down nearby and taking his own teacup. "It's my favorite ice cream flavor, so I figured, why not?"

"Heavenly," Muriel repeated, tasting the light chocolate mingling with the hint of orange. "If you'll excuse the expression."

They looked at each other, feeling the same excitement they had felt the first time they laid eyes on each other, the day that one of Street's stable had panicked and called the number a sympathetic cop had given her months before.

The prostitute had poured her heart out to Mrs. Holford, telling her every tale of Street's cruelty she could remember. The social worker promised to come right over.

The pimp had beaten her to it. When Muriel finally arrived in the tiny, run-down entryway of the girl's building, she heard muffled screams from upstairs—even through the security door. Muriel had to use a credit card to slip the lock.

She found Street Wise in the girl's cramped studio apartment, beating her with a studded belt. He had ripped open the back of the girl's shirt, and her skin was livid with welts and bleeding bruises.

The two had looked at each other from across the

room. Muriel saw an elegant, tightly muscled young man with handsome features and tight black hair. Street saw a kind-looking woman of medium height and build wearing well-cut but conservative clothes. But there was something about her . . . something else . . . something he recognized. . . .

"Stop this instant!" Muriel had cried, her hand up in the universally recognized position for halt.

The prostitute's head had turned quickly in the direction of the front door. Muriel saw that a pair of panty hose had been tied between the girl's teeth.

"No, no, no," said Muriel, marching in. "That won't do at all."

Street backed off, confused, his hand going in his pocket. "Hey, who is this?" he asked no one in particular. He looked at the hooker, who was kneeling on the floor, panting in pain. "Your mother?"

"In a way," said Muriel, who took the girl's arm and helped her to her feet. She pointed at the hooker's face. "Did you do this?"

Street had backed to the center of the far wall, his hand still in his pocket. He quietly and carefully said: "This is none of your business, miss. This woman is my friend."

Muriel smiled. She already knew Street was remarkable. The prostitute had told her so. And now, instead of swearing and faking bravado, the man had calmly and civilly asked her to leave.

"I'm afraid it is, young man," Muriel replied, just as civilly. "This young lady asked me to come over and help."

"She has no right . . ." Street said, stepping forward.

"You should be ashamed," Muriel interrupted, fussing over the sobbing, frightened girl. "Here, dear, let me help." The hooker couldn't undo the tight panty-hose knot at the back of her head. Street knew that something special was happening here. Any other social worker would have been screaming at him. Instead, this woman's bright eyes focused directly on the struggling girl.

"Look at this," Muriel continued, unraveling the gag. "Hardly effective. I could hear you all the way down the street. Are you all right, dear?" She patted the hooker on the shoulder. "Stand up straight, dear. If you made any more noise, the neighbors would have surely called the police simply for the nuisance value. Put your head back, dear. Open your mouth. I have something that will help. Wider."

And, as Street watched, Muriel Holford took a small, red rubber ball out of her purse and popped it into the girl's mouth. Then she grabbed the girl's wrists.

"There," she said to him, twisting. "*Now* you can tie the panty hose."

Street reacted immediately, then got another pair to tie the girl's wrists behind her. Muriel helped as the girl yelped in disbelief.

"Now her volume is cut down at least fifty percent," the social worker informed him, closing the apartment door. "I usually use it as a doggy toy, to distract any overzealous watchdog, but it has its other uses."

She watched as Street disciplined his charge. "Not only does it pry the jaw open," continued Muriel, "but it pops back into the throat occasionally to cut off the air. Keeps them quiet, and weak."

Street continued to berate and abuse the girl, then warned her what would happen if she ever disobeyed again. He threw her on the bed.

"Oh, I *am* disappointed," Muriel said. "I've heard *such* good things about you. You call that a punishment?"

She led Street into the kitchen, had him turn over

the kitchen table, lash the girl spread-eagled to the four table legs, and placed her in front of the open refrigerator. Muriel then fixed the automatic ice maker so it wouldn't stop. Finally she pulled the ice tray out.

Every few minutes ten ice wedges rained down the open freezer compartment onto the wriggling, moaning girl.

"Best I could do on short notice," Muriel explained. "It's not agony or ecstasy, but it'll have to do." She took the man's arm and led him to the front door. He glanced back at the prostitute.

"She'll get free," Muriel assured him. "Eventually. Meanwhile, you and I should have a nice long talk."

"It was love at second sight," Street would later say. She had found a good right arm, and he had found a sanctuary. The attraction between them was powerful and palatable. They were mother and son . . . and more.

Now he sat in her orderly, comfortable home on the quiet, residential street. He had gone underground: no one would even think of looking for him here.

"You're quite a chef," she told him, finishing off the cookie. "Your many talents amaze me."

"Least I could do," he said humbly. "How was your day?"

To all the world it would have looked like any other late afternoon in any other house in the nation. Loved ones greet each other, do kind things for each other, inquire as to their well-being. Only here the man was an expensively dressed, smooth-skinned young sadist. The woman was a plain, placid, middle-aged monster.

"Ah!" she said, smiling widely. "I daresay there's more evidence that the time is right."

"Your meeting with the Arnolds went well, I take it?"

"Very nicely," she confirmed. "An almost textbook example. They feigned shock, but I could see their minds working. It's like selling an encyclopedia. It's already sold once they let you in the door. All that remains is eliminating their doubts."

"Ah, but an encyclopedia isn't free."

"Neither is this," Muriel said evenly.

"Of course. But you know what I mean. Like drugs. The first taste is free."

The woman laughed. "You should have seen their faces when I touched their daughter."

Street was pleased the liquid tranquilizer worked so well. Muriel kept it in a gelatin capsule that she broke just before she placed her palm on the suffering girl's forehead. "What happened?"

She told him.

"We couldn't," the Arnolds had said.

"Why not?" she had asked.

"Well, isn't Lucifer evil?"

"A common misunderstanding," Muriel had told them. "Satan isn't evil. Satan is a fallen angel. Evil is an entirely different thing."

Street laughed quietly. "An interesting distinction. No, Satan isn't evil, with a capital *E*. But he *is* evil, isn't he?"

"Not at all," Muriel chided. "Are you evil?"

Before he could nod, she interrupted him.

"Not completely," she said. "After all, you baked these cookies. Who are any of us to say what evil is? Who are any of us to judge the Devil? Let's just say he is interested in evil. I think it's safe to say he collects it. I'm counting on that."

Muriel had explained to the Arnolds what the Devil was. A fallen angel, someone with the power to aggravate God and counteract His work.

That excited and shamed the Arnolds. They asked with trepidation if praying to him would lead to repercussions from God. Muriel told them the Devil would protect them.

How could they be sure?

Muriel pointed at their daughter's bedroom. God had not prevented the social worker from bringing solace to her, had He? If Satan could cure their daughter, would they believe?

"Yes," they said.

"Then ask him," Muriel had said. "Pray to him."

Street Wise was leaning back in the chair, looking at Muriel through veiled lids. "Think they will?"

Muriel finished her tea. "Wrong question. Do I think they are, at this very moment? Yes, I do. They will do anything to save their daughter." She studied his smug, disbelieving face. "But don't think they don't know what's coming. Don't think I don't know that in the back of their minds they're remembering that Satan's payment is their souls. I'm counting on that too."

Street started to clean up their high tea. He chuckled at the thought of Muriel's complicating the Arnolds' already devastated lives.

"What is it?" she asked him.

He stood directly in front of her chair, looking down at her dowdy form. "I have to admit I admire you," he confessed. "I couldn't do what you do."

"Nor I, you," she said, smiling. "Two sides of the same coin, my dear. Two parts of the same forest. You're hell's son, but I am the hell mother."

Street nodded his head. "I can understand it. I can understand how they would buy it. It's something they need to hear. I do the same thing to the trim. But I've got to know. Do *you* buy it? Do you believe the junk you're telling these people?"

Muriel was sitting so far back in her chair that her

face was completely in shadow. Street could hear her calm words, but he could see only small sparks of late-afternoon light coming from the whites of her eyes and teeth.

"My darling," she said, her voice a sexy, husky whisper, "you don't understand. It *works.*"

He grimaced, moving his head. "Yeah, I know. It works on my bitches too. A golden line of bull works anywhere."

She smiled. He couldn't see her expression of supercilious pity. "No. You still don't understand. It actually works. Not just on them. To them, for them. You don't think I would have claimed so many if it didn't, do you? It works. It really works!"

Then she leaned forward, picked up the TV remote control, and pushed his leg. "Now get out of the way. Oprah's on."

"Melanie, my dear! What a pleasure to see you!"

Valentino DiCenzo came around his huge desk and walked across the big office, his arms out.

Melanie Merrick stood near the farthest red leather chair. The president of Dice-Corp could feel the chill in the air, so by the time he reached her, his arms were lower. She allowed him to take both her hands.

"What a pleasant surprise," he said. He knew it was trouble when she didn't even say "I hope I'm not bothering you." Instead she smiled without humor and with very little warmth. But her gaze was even and strong.

His own gaze dropped first. He surveyed her plain, severe outfit. He dropped her hands and headed for the cappuccino bar, which took up most of the wall near the entrance.

"You look tired, my dear. Can I get you anything?"

He started making himself an espresso. He figured he'd need it.

"No, thank you, Val," she said to his back. "I'm fine. I came during business hours for a reason."

"Please," he interrupted, looking over his shoulder. "Sit down. Make yourself comfortable. I'll be right with you."

Melanie sighed, went to the chair nearest his desk, and sat. She let him play around with the espresso machine while she looked out the nearly wall-size picture window to her left. Manhattan clawed the sky.

DiCenzo had granted her an open-door policy since the death of her husband—one of his most promising (and youngest) vice-presidents. He and his wife considered Melanie family and had told her so. Louise was anxious to see Melanie whenever she was in town, and often invited her to shopping sprees and parties—careful not to try making any matches yet. They all had a warm place in their hearts and minds for Geoffrey.

Only today was the day when family pressures came home to roost. Val could feel how heavy the atmosphere in the office had become.

Melanie waited until after the machine spit out the thick, steaming black liquid before speaking again. "You know why I'm here, don't you?"

She turned in the chair in time to see Val's back hunch and his head droop slightly. He looked into his coffee. "I don't know why I drink this stuff," he finally said, heading for his chair. "Louise says I might as well put a straw in the La Brea Tar Pits." He sat heavily and looked the blonde straight in the eye. "Yes, I can imagine why you're here."

"Well?"

"I'd rather you tell me, just in case. I don't want to make a fool of myself unless I absolutely have to."

"You have to," said Melanie. She wasn't trying to make him squirm. That was just the way it was. She liked him as a friend, but he was a businessman first. If he thought she was going to choke at the last minute, he had another think coming.

"It's been months since my husband was murdered," she said evenly. "Did he die for nothing?"

"Melanie . . ." he said with a mixture of helplessness and sympathy, his hands wide. She disarmed him by remaining silent. He was left to watch his word dangle, then drop. Finally she let him off the hook.

"What is the status of the Northern Plan?"

"Melanie, you have to understand . . ."

She raised her hand. "Don't, Val. Don't. Give me the respect you would have given Geoffrey."

DiCenzo wrestled with his emotions, ashamed of himself. He was treating her as if she were a reporter or something. He had been prepared to trot out the camouflage and bull so the status would remain quo. He was treating her like one of his wife's friends, not one of his.

"I'm sorry," he said honestly. "I apologize. It's hard for me to remember that women are people. The old Italian machismo, I'm afraid. Our hormones get in the way and we try to treat you like children. And stupid children at that. I hope you will forgive me."

"I don't want you to be sorry. I want you to tell me the truth."

"Of course. Melanie, you know the Northern Plan was risky and unpopular. It was only by your husband's energy and force of will that it was passed. And it was only your husband's skill and passion that I trusted to make it work. Now, with him gone . . ." DiCenzo didn't see the need to continue.

Melanie pressed him. "Is it canceled? Has it been officially rescinded?"

"No."

"It's just lying dormant."

DiCenzo nodded.

"So. Your holdings in Central and South America remain in place and active. You're still accepting drug money."

With anyone else DiCenzo would have fought vehemently against that conclusion. But they both knew that more than half the money made there was in some way connected to the cartels.

"Probably," he said truthfully.

Melanie's voice was even and clear. "Geoffrey died for nothing."

"Melanie!"

"You don't think I'm going to let you off easy, do you, Val?" she said, leaning forward. "And I'm not going to get hysterical and dissolve in tears, either. I'm just going to sit here and tell you the truth. Geoffrey died because he was crazy enough to suggest you try to work around the drug pushers, and you're letting his killers get away with it."

DiCenzo was stunned to his seat, gripping the arms tightly. "Melanie," he managed to get out. "You've . . . I've never . . . Good Lord!"

"What a surprise, huh?" she goaded. "The man I loved gets brutally murdered, half my life gets blown away, and I don't just stay at home, frightened out of my wits, and cry my head off. What a shocker, right?" She leaned back, crossing her legs. "Well, I got news for you, Val. Geoffrey is still alive." She pointed at her head. "He's right up here."

"Jesus, Melanie," DiCenzo finally said. "I knew . . . I mean, Geoff's murder . . . and then that Cryst character trying to kill you, but . . . I had no idea it affected you so much."

She leaned forward again, pointing at him. "Wait a second. Maybe all this death has affected me. I won't deny it. You try going through something like that and see how you like it. But if you're suggesting for a minute that all I've said is the result of leftover shock . . ."

"No, no, not at all," said Val, waving his hands. "It's just that I'm not used to you like this. You caught me by surprise."

"Dump your preconceptions, Val. I've had to."

"All right, Melanie, all right." DiCenzo straightened, preparing himself. "You're right. Nobody wanted to take up the Northern Plan, and I've let it slide. But not for the reasons you may think. First, I didn't want anyone else to get killed. And second, I didn't want some incompetent asshole taking over and blowing it."

Melanie considered what he said. She leaned back, satisfied. She was willing to believe he didn't have anyone else of Geoffrey's caliber. "How about Keith Sullivan?" she said from the depths of the chair.

"What about him?" DiCenzo retorted.

Melanie's face came out of the shadows. "He spent a few weeks trying to convince me that he wanted to follow in Geoffrey's footsteps. Maybe now's the time for him to prove it."

"Sullivan?" DiCenzo echoed. He always thought the two hated each other. At least Sullivan, once the youngest VP, had hated Merrick. Merrick had hated no one as far as DiCenzo knew. He certainly hadn't liked Sullivan, but Keith gave him plenty of reasons.

DiCenzo thought harder. He had to admit that recently he had detected a change in Sullivan. Ever since Merrick's death, he had been calmer, less antagonistic, less competitive with his own associates. He had slowly begun to take on the attributes DiCenzo had so envied in Merrick. But DiCenzo had attributed that to Merrick's absence. Sullivan no longer had to prove himself . . . until now.

DiCenzo pushed down the intercom button. "Ms. Corser? Get me Keith Sullivan, will you? Ask him to come into my office." He leaned back in his chair, swiveled to face Melanie, and smiled.

She did not smile back. She leaned away from him and closed her eyes.

The phone rang once, then stopped. Seconds later it rang again, and stopped. Seconds after that it rang ten times before it was picked up.

"Broad River Market. Can I help you?"

"This is Masterson. May I speak to José Rivera?"

"This is he," said Juan Ruiz.

Ruiz stood behind the counter of the small convenience store he had bought (so he wouldn't go nuts from boredom), surrounded by chipped tile, faded nailed-on paneling, cigarettes, lottery tickets, newspapers, magazines, paperbacks, candy, doughnuts, corn-cheese-potato-and-pasta chips, ice cream, juices, soda, coffee, and booze. He wore a T-shirt and jeans.

"Boy," said a customer holding a six-pack. "Craziest phone-answering method I've ever seen."

"I want to make sure they're serious," Ruiz told him, with a wink.

"I've been given the Northern Plan," said Keith Sullivan. He had been given the code name "Masterson" for Sky Masterson, the leading man in the musical *Guys and Dolls.* Ruiz had seen it as a boy and liked it. He never forgot the number "Luck Be a Lady Tonight."

"Good," said Juan. From the background noise, he could tell Sullivan was calling from a pay phone. Ruiz rang up the six-pack price.

"Not good. It was on the request of Merrick's widow."

Juan smiled. Everything about America entertained him. He enjoyed the way all his customers and the neighboring stores accepted his obviously fake name without question. He was Hispanic, so why shouldn't his name be José Rivera? José for José Jimenez, and Rivera for Chita Rivera.

"Even better," he said. Another customer asked for a pack of Camel Lights.

"Don't you get it?" Sullivan's voice seethed on the already crackling line. "If I screw up, they'll know something's up."

"No, they won't," Juan said, practically in a sing-song.

"I'll be slitting my own throat. If I screw up, they'll *fire* me."

"Then don't screw up," Ruiz said pleasantly, giving a customer his cigarettes and matches. He took the money and slid it into the cash register. "Do the most complete, researched, thorough job you can." He waited until the customers had left the store.

"What?" said Sullivan.

"Do your work," Ruiz said. "Sweat, slave, struggle. Stall."

"Jesus," Sullivan complained. "It's not that easy."

"You decide," Ruiz told him as another customer came in. "Either they slit your throat or I do."

"Holy . . . be cool, will you?"

"My idea is looking easier all the time, isn't it?"

"Okay, okay . . . just relax, all right?"

"You too, my friend," Ruiz advised, watching the new customer check out the newspaper rack. "Think it over, and don't worry. We'll do whatever is necessary to make sure everything works out just right. Remember?"

Juan Ruiz, the assassin known as "The Student,"

hung up the phone. The customer put the *Daily News* on the counter, checking his change.

"Pretty tough on him, huh?" the customer commented.

"Ah, who wants them calling, anyway?" Ruiz replied. "I'd rather concentrate on my customers. Thirty-five cents, please."

10

The Arnolds seemed delighted to see her. The
difference in their attitude was immediately ap-
parent. Everett all but threw open the door, his
face restructured with hope. His inner light grew
even brighter when he saw who was standing there.
Muriel Holford was ushered in like visiting royalty.

"Evelyn," he called. "Look who's here."

Evelyn Arnold came out of her daughter's bedroom like a television hostess about to bestow gifts
on a lucky contestant. Her arms were wide, welcom-
ing the social worker to her humble abode. By the
time she reached Muriel, she was practically bab-
bling with excitement.

"She slept without pain for the first time in
months. Her eyes cleared, I could see it. She recognized me. She took one look at me and smiled. For
weeks we've had to stay in the room with her, each
holding on to one of her hands, squeezing and praying, while she would scream and cry. But now she's

getting better. I can tell. She's not sweating. We've had to feed her intravenously, but today she was strong enough to have soup. I can't tell you . . . I can't tell you how much . . ."

Evelyn was rubbing Muriel's hand with excitement and nervousness. Muriel was certain she would start kissing her ring in another few seconds. Everett was standing beside them, beaming, one hand on each of their shoulders.

"All in one day," he said with happiness and disbelief. "All in one day!"

"Yes," said Muriel, pulling her hand free and leading them into the living room. "You see? What did I tell you?"

"It's a miracle!" Evelyn whispered, as if afraid the wrong force of nature would overhear.

Muriel laughed. "Please. There is no more reason to be afraid. You'll see. Pamela will just keep getting better and better."

"Thanks to . . ." Evelyn tried, her back hunching. "Thanks to . . ."

"No, no, no, no," Muriel said soothingly, helping Evelyn into her easy chair. "Please sit down, Mrs. Arnold." She looked toward Everett. "Mr. Arnold?"

He reacted like a rabbit caught in a spotlight. "Uh . . . what? Can I . . . um . . . get you anything, Mrs. Holford? Something to eat? Some tea?"

"No, thank you. I'm quite all right. It's you who should take advantage of this. You can finally relax, after all this time. Please sit down, Mr. Arnold."

Everett mumbled agreement and went quickly to his chair. He sat beside his wife. They both looked up with fright and anticipation.

Muriel looked down on them with a wide smile, trying not to laugh. "No need to thank Lucifer," she told them. "You hold the fate of your daughter in your own hands, just as you always have."

Everett blinked. "What . . . what do you mean?"

Muriel put her arms wide in the small living room —a living room built very much like her own. "All you had to do was ask. The power was there, waiting."

The Arnolds looked confused, and slightly distrustful.

"That's it, then?" said Evelyn.

"Of course."

"And Pam'll get better?" asked Everett.

"Of course not."

The Arnolds looked at each other as if they were the last couple on the *Titanic*.

"But you said . . ." Evelyn started.

"You can't expect Lucifer to assume things," Muriel said smoothly. "You asked him to make your daughter better. He did. But you can't expect him to cure her, completely cure her, without asking."

Muriel was using the Arnolds like yo-yos. She loved watching their faces fall, then firm up. It was like dropping babies and catching them just before they hit the floor.

"So, all we have to do is keep praying to him?" Everett asked hopefully.

Muriel considered the question carefully. "Curing cancer," she mused. "A tall order. It's not the sort of thing he can do for free."

If the Arnolds were anxious before, now they were paralyzed. Muriel watched as they looked into each other's eyes. She saw their lives and their love for each other go by. She saw their desperation and terror at the thought of the unknown. And she saw their daughter—the one symbol of everything they were, separate and apart. To lose her was to lose all purpose to their existence. She saw the bleak emptiness that would mark their remaining time if their child was to die.

They looked back at her with tragic conviction. "All right," said Evelyn. "We understand. We're ready."

Muriel made a point of pursing her eyebrows. "For what?"

"For what you have to do."

"I'm sorry," said Muriel. "You've lost me. What exactly did you expect me to do?"

"To . . ." Evelyn licked her lips and leaned forward. "Well . . . don't you . . . Don't we have to give up our souls?"

Muriel let the reactions sweep over her as if it were the very first time this had ever happened. First, she feigned surprise. Her mouth and eyes widened. Then realization. She leaned back, looking at the ceiling. Then delight. She laughed as if she really meant it. It was a friendly laugh, as if they had told a good clean joke.

"You thought . . . your souls? Oh, no, no," she said, waving her hands and keeping her expression kindly. "Of course not. You've been watching too much television. It doesn't work that way. It may have once, but not anymore. No, now all you have to do is keep praying to him. Keep worshiping him."

"That's all?" Everett said incredulously.

"Why, yes . . . essentially." Muriel wiped her eyes and went to the guest chair, diagonally across from the television. She started chuckling again. "You thought . . . I had come . . . to collect your . . . Oh, that's funny. That's funny." She looked back at them. "And very sweet," she assured them. "No. I just came over to see if everything was all right. If there was any problem, I hoped I could advise you. Ev, I think I could really use that cup of tea now."

Everett looked at his wife. "Of course, of course," she said quickly. "I'll get it right away."

By the time she returned, the two were leaning
back, their feet up, watching the news. They had it
on Channel Six. Muriel wasn't surprised. It made
sense that, during their time of torment, they would
have relaxed by watching other people's pain. It was
a fairly basic human trait.

Evelyn let them take their cups from the tray,
then returned to her own seat, warming her hands
with the steaming liquid. With all their money gone,
they couldn't afford to have the furnace on too often.

They watched a report about the pervasive, destructive influence of pornography, without a flicker
of reaction.

"Of course," said Muriel absently, "your worship
will have to be complete."

"Oh, yes," said Evelyn. "We wouldn't want anything to go wrong."

They continued to talk without looking at each
other. They remained riveted to the striking television images. Ashley Smith was walking through the
U. R. There News team's re-creation of a prostitute's
crib.

"You know," Muriel continued. "Reject the Lord's
work and teachings. Eliminate any hint of his presence. . . ."

Channel Six had created a stunning special effects
video version of the greenhouse interior, with "ART-
IST'S CONCEPTION" in block letters across the bottom of the screen. Completely wrong, but stunning.
The last days of Jane Weston were lovingly re-cre-
ated in ninety seconds.

"Is that the payment?" Everett asked. "That's it?"

Finally Muriel looked back at the Arnolds. "No,"
she said patiently. "That's just part of the proper
worshiping. You can't fake it. It has to be honest."

"Yes, yes," said Evelyn. "We understand." They

were so relieved not to have to give up their souls that they were ready for almost anything else.

Muriel looked back at the television. "Jane Weston" had just died.

"There are plenty of souls. Lucifer doesn't need those. He needs understanding. He needs to know how . . . strong . . . human beings are. He needs to know what you're willing to do to make your dreams come true."

"We were ready to give up our souls!" Evelyn exclaimed.

Muriel smiled upon the righteous woman. "Now, Ev," she said gently. "That's easy. Really. But how willing would you have been to give up your daughter's soul?" Mrs. Arnold's reaction of fear and revulsion was all Muriel needed. "You see? Giving up your own soul is simple. But don't worry, Satan doesn't want Pamela's soul either. He wants to save her."

Evelyn, who looked about ready to have a coronary, relaxed. Muriel looked back at the television where Ashley Smith was talking intently into the camera without blinking. Something about a tangled web of perversion, greed, lust, and violence.

"No," said Muriel blandly. "The payment is with knowledge. Satan wants to know the parameters of the human mind. He needs to know his minions."

"How?" Evelyn asked.

"Tell me," said Muriel, looking at the Arnolds. "What's the worst thing you could do to another person? What's the most evil thing you can think of?"

The only sound in the room was made by the television. "The big questions remain," Ashley Smith intoned. "Who caused the death and destruction at the K Club in Harlem and the luxurious town house in Washington Heights? Was the violence connected, and how? What is Central Division doing about it?

And what place does the mysterious blond beauty have in the investigation? You saw her for the first time last night on our award-winning newscast, and still, twenty-four hours later, her place in this perplexing, frightening mystery is no clearer. If you have any information, call the Channel Six hotline twenty-four hours a day. . . ."

Muriel glanced back at the TV, the image of the beautiful woman filling her vision. For the first time in her visit, her thinking lost its firm control. There was something about the face that intrigued her . . . that reminded her of something, or someone. . . .

"What do you mean?" asked Everett. "Like killing someone?"

Muriel returned her attention to the matter at hand. "Maybe killing," she encouraged. "But how? And who? It can't be just killing a stranger. That's evil, but stupid. It has no . . . weight. No value."

"Rape?" Evelyn said in a tiny voice, as if the word escaped her mouth.

"Again, who?" said Muriel. "A friend of your daughter? Another cancer patient? Again, evil, certainly, but with no resonance. Rape would be truly evil only to someone who couldn't be raped, for some reason.

"Think of evil as a pool," Muriel suggested. "And each evil act as a pebble. What we need is one that will make the most ripples. A simple killing or rape would have a very limited effect on the rest of the world."

"Sabotage?" Everett thought aloud, watching the reports of international friction on the newscast. "Terrorism?"

Muriel shook her head curtly. "Far-reaching effects, perhaps, but it's scattershot. We want particular, personal things." She saw it was time to shock them out of their self-inflicted stupidity. "For instance," she continued mildly, "say if the doctor who was treating your daughter held back a cure because he had been raping her every day and didn't want her strong enough to accuse him."

The Arnolds' complacency shattered.

"There!" cried Muriel. "Feel that horror? Feel that dread? *That's* the sort of thing we're looking for."

"But . . . but . . ." Evelyn sputtered. "That's . . . terrible. We couldn't possibly . . ."

Muriel's face darkened and her voice became low and threatening. "That's what Lucifer needs. Do you want your daughter to get better, or don't you?"

Everett was about to stand and order the social worker out of his house when the image of his peacefully sleeping daughter entered his mind. He felt his wife's hand on his arm. He slumped back in his chair.

"Come now," said Muriel, back to her considerate self. "Think. You knew it wouldn't be easy. The last few months haven't been easy, have they? But now, finally, it's working. You can't stop now. You've finally found the answer. Don't let the worst happen because you refuse to take responsibility for your thoughts. Let your mind go. What's the worst thing you could do?"

Muriel watched as all the bad things in the Arnolds' life came back to haunt them. She watched as all the things they kept locked up in the back of their heads came creeping out, filling their minds' eye. She watched them relive all their hatred and envy. She watched them recall all their own stupidity and avarice. She watched as they redirected it. They rejected their own complicity in their lives' disasters—and blamed them on someone else. They remembered what they had hoped would happen to their contemporaries, peers, and competitors.

She saw that Everett had something. She saw the

man actually blush with shame. It was more than his own self-loathing directed outward. He had dredged up something so shameful it was in an entirely different category.

"What?" Muriel asked.

Everett Arnold's eyes were brimming with tears. "We won't have to do it, will we? Tell me we won't have to do it ourselves."

"Of course not," Muriel said with complete conviction.

"No more after this, right?" Everett begged. "All he wants is the worst thing . . . the most evil thing we can think of, right? I don't want to have to actually do it. I *couldn't* do it!"

"I said you wouldn't, didn't I?" Muriel said impatiently. "What do you want me to do? Swear on a *Bible*?"

"All right," said Everett, getting his strength up. "All right. If it will save our daughter—"

"Ev, wait!" his wife cried. "What if . . . *he* does it? The Beast . . . How could we live with that!"

"You're not exactly in a bargaining position . . ." Muriel began.

Pamela Arnold cried out in her sleep.

Her father and mother froze in place, their fingers clawing their chairs. The shriek had been sudden and painful, as if she had been stabbed. It had been a short screech that completely died out almost as soon as they heard it. It had no echo, as if it had never occurred.

Everett leaned forward, putting his face in his hands. "Forgive me, forgive me, please," he was saying. "It happened when we ran out of money. When they promised to help and nothing happened. I hated them then so much. I'm sorry . . . I'm sorry . . ."

Evelyn embraced her husband, soothing him. "It

can't be that bad," she whispered. "Please. Remember, they forsook us. They lied to us. It *can't* be that bad . . ."

When the Arnolds looked back at the social worker, Muriel Holford's eyes were even brighter, her gaze firmer, her posture stronger. Her expression was totally assured.

"Tell me," she demanded. "Right now."

I Sister Agnes Dunning left the school grounds on East Seventy-fifth Street at 4:15 in the afternoon. She had seen the children onto the buses at 2:15, then stayed after to help tutor the slower learners in math. She said good-bye to the Mother Superior and the principal, then made her way down the long block toward First Avenue—where she could catch the bus.

It was a partly cloudy day—the perfect fall day, she had commented to one of her fellow teachers. She expected it to be sunny in spring, hot in summer, cloudy in fall, and snowy in winter. The cool gray days were her favorite days in these months of regeneration and hibernation. It was her favorite season, because it reminded everyone that death was a part of God's plan. It was as natural as life.

This block was like a channel into civilization, she thought. Because of the large recording studio across from the school, there were very few shops, apartment houses, windows, or doors facing the street on either side. It was an oasis of severity in a city of exploding activity, lights, sounds, and colors. Except for the graffiti, of course.

Most of that had been scraped off or painted over, but there was still some hint of it left, representative of the destructive forces around them. Heaven help them, they tried to keep their students safe from the temptations of drugs and ignorance, and were largely successful. But every now and then, a misguided child with a spray can stumbled upon their sanctuary.

Sister Agnes Dunning lowered her gaze and shook her head—with a little smile. She walked past a blue van. She didn't notice a well-dressed man coming from a recessed doorway on her right. Not until he was almost alongside her, digging in his jacket pocket, did she notice him.

She gasped, stopped, and stepped back when she saw him pull the small gun out.

Sister Agnes laughed at her own foolishness. The gun was bright orange. It was practically clear plastic. The smiling young man was holding a water pistol.

She looked up into his mirth-filled eyes. "My, you gave me a fright," she said. He said nothing, just kept smiling. Sister Agnes put one hand on her waist and waggled a forefinger at him. "Now, you're not going to douse me with that thing, are you?" He still didn't answer. "You do, young man, and you won't be in my prayers tonight."

With that, she turned away and continued her walk to the corner. She didn't see the man squeeze the trigger, but she felt the cool liquid splashing on the side of her face.

She was about to chide him for his mischievousness, when she discovered that her knees had gotten weak. She couldn't quite turn around; it was as if she had suddenly lost all sense of balance.

She was stunned to discover that the side of her face was stiff. She wanted to cry out, but her mouth was numb and frozen in position. She thought in panic: *Am I having a stroke?* No. The books said she would hear a buzzing, ringing, or music, and she would smell something noxious.

Instead she could vaguely hear the traffic, and she smelled her own panic. Sister Agnes felt her arms waving by her side. She felt herself falling. She saw the gray sky. She thought she would feel pain when she hit the sidewalk. She was frightened she'd cut her head on the curb. But she only felt restraining hands. She felt herself floating, then flying.

Then the sky turned dark, and she felt nothing.

Just before she awoke, Sister Agnes realized that it had not turned night. The sky had not turned dark. It was as if a metal sheet had been pulled across the heavens. No. She had been thrown into the van. The dark sky was the vehicle's ceiling.

Abduction, she thought. But this was not El Salvador. This wasn't even Harlem.

She opened her eyes and looked upon living hell.

She was lying on her back on a mattress. The mattress covered the floor of the van. She was looking at a curtain that covered the back of the front driver and passenger seats. It closed the rear, seatless section from any pedestrian's view.

She looked at her body. Her feet were strapped together at the ankles and knees. The packing tape squeezed her support hose. Her arms were lying straight, along the sides of her body. Her hands were covered in packing tape from the tips of her fingers to her forearms.

That was not the worst. The worst was that her

plain blue skirt had been pulled up to her hips. The tape had been wrapped around the very tops of her thighs so her outstretched hands could be affixed to them.

Sister Agnes tried to sit up and cover herself, but she felt hands restraining her. She looked up. Above her was the man who had shot her with the water pistol.

No. Not water. It had been something else.

He was still smiling at her the same way he had before. The smile was infuriatingly patient and comforting. He held her down with one of his arms behind her, fingers wrapped around her right shoulder. He stroked her forehead with the other, pushing her matted brown hair out between her eyes and her glasses.

She tried to ask what he wanted but discovered that the packing tape covered her lips as well. It sealed them together so she could only mumble and hum.

"So plain," he was saying, as if telling her a bedtime story. "At first I wanted to find the youngest, prettiest one possible, but then I thought, why? First, a pretty nun may have joined the order because she could sink no lower. A pretty one might have become a nun to escape her beauty. Then it would have been too late.

"Second, why rest on my preconceptions? Why depend so thoroughly on my own good taste? A pretty nun would make a pretty picture. And this is not a pretty picture. This isn't a joke. It isn't a game. Not really. This is it. This is the ultimate test of your fealty. So for that, I said to myself, why not get someone real?

"Besides," he said, looking into her eyes, "a youngish, ugly nun is sure to be a virgin."

Sister Agnes tried to scream and struggle. He

shushed her and continued to stroke her forehead.
He hadn't even taken off the half-habit head covering. She lay stiff and tried to pull free.

"Oh, stop," said Street Wise, still smiling. "Your
hands are together. I did them that way on purpose.
As a favor to you. Why don't you try praying?"

The van slowly made its way through growing
rush-hour traffic. It went south to Twenty-third
Street and cut across west to Tenth Avenue. It
turned left and headed to where the city broke up
into Greenwich Village, SoHo, and the lower West
Side.

Here the side streets were empty of tourists, com-
muters, or residents. Here there were long stretches
of warehouse property and meat-packing facilities.
Here the roads were still made of cobblestone, and
they broke off into interesting patterns. A van could
get swallowed up in here.

When the curtain between the storage space and
the driver's seat was pulled back, Sister Agnes was
shocked to see it was a thin woman driving.

"We're here," the driver said.

Audrey Buckman closed the curtain without
expression, opened the driver's-side door, and
dropped out to the cobblestones. She could see West
Street, the docks, and the Hudson River to her left—
between the squat, dark buildings. To her right were
about a half dozen blocks before civilization started
up again. If it was dusk in the Village, then it was
already night here.

She got out the keys and unlocked the garage's
sheet-metal door. She pulled it open, got back into
the van, and drove into the building. She quickly
stopped the vehicle, turned off the engine, hopped
out again, closed the sheet-metal door, and switched
on the lights.

Three hanging bulbs illuminated the long, high interior. It was lined with solid steel support beams covered in dust. There might have been a long opaque window set high on the far wall, but it was so crud-encrusted, it was impossible to tell.

The remnants of a workbench lined the far wall. The floor was littered with cans, bottles, wrappers, large oil drums, broken furniture, and a gutted piano.

Audrey Buckman walked back to the front of the van. She looked to the left, at the corner of the gloomy, cavernous work space. A man stood spread-eagled against a bedspring.

The covering and guts of the bed had been ripped away so only the steel skeleton was exposed. The man's body made an X across it. He was about six feet tall, balding, and paunchy. He was still wearing most of his clothes. He had on dark scuffed shoes, black pants, a shiny black short-sleeved shirt, and a clerical collar.

He stood, his arms, legs, and eyes wide, staring back at Audrey. She wore a short-sleeved man's T-shirt, gloves, jeans, and high-heeled brown suede boots. She was five six, on the thin side, with wiry, muscular arms. He could say nothing to her because packing tape was wrapped around his head, covering everything from just below his nose to his chin.

Audrey slapped the van's side door twice. She waited to hear the lock go up, then pulled the sliding door back. Street Wise still sat with the nun.

"I don't believe you two have met," said the pimp. "Sister, this is Audrey. Audrey, this is the sister."

Audrey almost waved "hi" before walking away. She headed toward the bedspring while Street slid out of the van. As Audrey got closer to the priest, she could see his wrists and ankles glimmer. The naked yellow bulbs were reflecting light off the wire wrapped around his limbs and the frame's metal coils.

Street grabbed Sister Agnes by the ankles and started to pull her out. "Audrey is a very nice person," he told her. "Recovering alky. Fifteen months sober." He called after the other woman. "Isn't that right, Aud?"

Audrey waved without turning around.

"Go easy on her in your prayers, Sister," Street continued. "She's had a tough life. Husband beat her. Sometimes really bad. Put her in the hospital a dozen times. Had his rap down solid. 'Trying to keep her straight,' he said. 'Tried everything, but all she understood was violence.' Blamed all the destruction on her. Pleaded self-defense. They bought it."

Street got the woman on her feet. She had to hunch down slightly as the tape at her thighs pulled at her arms. She lowered her head in shame.

"Aud tried everything," Street continued, closing the van door. "Nobody would listen. Until a fine social worker came along. Fine social worker."

Street came back to the nun. "Funny," he said. "After that, Aud's old man started to come down with really nasty diseases. Bleeding welts, running boils, little animals crawling out his orifices—even psoriasis so bad he looked like a Sicilian pizza."

Street laughed, put his arms around Agnes's shoulders and under her knees, then hefted her in his arms. "So be kind, for her sake. Me? You can send me to hell for all I care."

Audrey pulled a Full Auto Minuteman knife from her pants pocket, flicked it open, and carefully cut the tape across the priest's lips. She pulled an edge free and slowly tore it from his skin. She didn't care whether it ripped his hair out or not.

The priest didn't complain that much. Sister Agnes gasped when Street brought her close. She saw a single strand of silver wire had been affixed around the man's head, in between his lips and teeth. It dug into the sides of his mouth.

Even so, he tried to speak.

"We . . . don't . . . pray . . . for . . . damnation," he said painfully, carefully. "We . . . pray . . . for . . . salvation." Drool coursed over his lower lip and dribbled across his shirtfront. Sister Agnes began to cry.

Street put her down, on her feet, so she'd have to remain standing. "Good for you," he told the priest, slapping him on the chest. "What's your name, Father?"

He blinked, gasped, and swallowed. "Vogel," he was finally able to say.

"Well, hello, Father Vogel. Say hello to Sister Agnes. Her mouth is a trifle occupied at the moment; please don't take it personally. I wanted to fill it with something appropriate, but couldn't risk her choking to death. No, we have something entirely different in store for you."

"Why?" gasped the priest, rocking his body on the springs.

Street shrugged. "Don't ask me. I am only a humble servant. I do what I'm told. I'm only following orders."

Audrey grimaced and motioned Street ahead. "Come on," she complained.

Street pouted at her. "I don't think you've got the proper spirit of the thing. Wait till I tell Mommy on you."

"It's already a production number," Audrey said dourly. "We don't need comic relief."

"Oh, very good," Street replied with sarcasm. "Being sober does wonders for your wit, Buckman."

Audrey grimaced again and walked away. She leaned on the worktable and folded her arms. She looked away from the pimp—not with disgust, but with disinterest.

He followed her gaze, glancing to his right in time to see the carefully struggling nun lose her balance and start to topple over. No one did anything to cushion her fall. They watched, motionless, as she fell heavily on the cement floor sideways. Sister Agnes lay in a cloud of slowly settling dust.

"Anxious, are you?" Street said affably. "All right. We'll get started." All signs of amusement left his face. From now on, it was all business. He looked at Audrey, motioning toward Vogel with his head. The pimp went over to Agnes and started to pry and pull off her gag.

Audrey walked over to the upright bedspring set, leaned over, and reached for the priest's waist. As he shook in the wire restraints, she pulled down his zipper.

Street had removed the gag and was freeing the nun's wrists from her thighs. Gasping, the first thing Agnes did was push down her skirt.

"No need for modesty here," Street said softly. "Not now." He curled his fingers inside her leg taping and yanked it off violently. Agnes squealed as the glue tore her stockings.

"Stop . . . it!" Vogel choked out. "Stop . . . it!"

Street Wise stood, looking at him with mock amazement. "Stop this? All right. But all you get is one wish. That was it. From here on, you've got no say in the matter." He looked down at the cringing nun. "All right, Sister." He cocked his head toward the priest. "Get going."

Agnes looked up, her eyes blinded with tears. "What do you want with me?"

"Hey, it's one thing to be pious, it's another to be stupid. What do you think I want? Vogel is standing up there, all ready and waiting for you. Do what comes naturally, lady."

The nun collapsed, sobbing.

"Strength!" Vogel managed to cry. "Strength, Sister."

Each word was a terrible effort. The wire dug deeper into the sides of his mouth, drawing blood.

Street sneered at him. "Save it, Padre," he told him. He looked back down when he heard the nun mumbling. Listening more closely, he could make out her prayers.

"A little late, Sis," he grumbled, tapping her on the skull. "Come on, get going, we don't have all night."

Sister Agnes raised her head and started to wail. Street Wise slapped her sharply across the face.

The blow was strong. He used his entire palm and caught her full in the face. The sharp crack went through the cavernous interior like a thunderclap.

For a few seconds, there was total silence.

"I don't know," said the nun, rubbing her cheek, "what you want."

Street Wise knelt down beside her. He spoke to her quietly, but his voice was hard. "I want you to display your love of God, sister. I want the ultimate show of respect, by using the equipment the Lord gave you for one purpose and one purpose only."

Audrey Buckman rolled her eyes, but the nun could only stare at the man in growing awareness and horror.

"No," she whispered.

"No!" the priest shouted.

Street looked at him with patient disdain, looked back at her in expectation, then nodded. "Yes," he said, then grabbed her by the hair and dragged her over to the boxspring. He threw her down at the priest's feet.

Father Vogel moaned. "Don't," he told the sister. "No sin."

She covered herself with her arms as best she could with her bound hands, even though she was still clothed. She was already going into shock. "Yes," she agreed. "I cannot commit sin."

"No," the priest repeated. "No . . . sin . . . in God's eyes."

Street strode over to the upright boxspring. He stood beside the holy man and woman. "Yeah," he said, putting his elbow near the priest's head and leaning. "Tell me about it, Padre. Tell me about God, will you?" He kicked at the nun. "Come on, Sister, up at it."

"No!" Vogel yelled. His eyes sought the pimp's face. "Kill us."

"No way. You've got to do the wild thing."

"The . . . Lord . . . won't . . . blame . . . us. No. We . . . won't."

Street grabbed him by the ear and shook the man's head, digging the wire into Vogel's flesh. "This isn't an exercise, Father," he growled. "What do you think? God is testing you?"

Slowly, carefully, with his eyes looking forward, Vogel got the words out. "This . . . is not . . . our Lord's . . . work."

"God!" Street exclaimed. He let go and walked away in disgust. "Always an answer. Always a way to crawl out." He spun back on the two. "Tell me, somebody! What kind of God would let me do this to you? Why is He letting me get away with this?" He practically ran back to the bedspring. "What kind of God, Father? What kind? Why doesn't he smite me down? Why doesn't a lightning bolt rip through the ceiling and tear me in half? Explain this to me, Father. Tell me the truth!"

The only sound in the building was Sister Agnes's sobs.

Street Wise shook his own head and walked away.

"They won't be committing sacrilege if we force them," Audrey told him. "I guess God recognizes extenuating circumstances."

Street waved his arm as if dismissing them. "That's not what this is all about. All right, then. You get him ready." Suddenly the pimp marched over and grabbed the nun by the hair again. He dragged her toward the van while Audrey knelt in front of the priest.

Street retaped the nun's tear-covered mouth. He pushed her on her back. He grabbed each of her legs, bending them back and taping her shins tightly to her thighs.

Audrey reached into the priest's zipper and opened her mouth.

The bedspring was lying flat on the ground. Father Vogel was still attached to it, spread-eagled. Sister Agnes's hands were bound behind her. More tape affixed her arms to her torso. Both shins were taped to her thighs so she had to sit in a kneeling position. Pieces of her panty hose lay around the naked box-spring.

Her legs were taped and tied to the metal coils and slats—on either side of Vogel's hips. The man and woman were bound together; the priest lying on his back, the nun seated.

Both were motionless, as if they were dead.

Street Wise and Audrey Buckman surveyed their handiwork. Audrey watched without expression. What she had already seen, felt, and done in her life left little room for shock, faith, belief, or trust. She continued her existence with all the fervor of a zombie.

The pimp, on the other hand, looked upon the scene with a certain pride and zealousness. "So," he said strongly, his words filling the room. "Your God isn't so great, is He?"

He wasn't expecting an answer. He waited until the words had bounced off the walls and ceiling, and their echo completely died out.

"Yes."

The word might have come from above. Nothing but Father Vogel's lips had moved.

Street Wise's eyebrows sank into a V, and his upper lip curled. He was fed up with their blind conviction. "How can you say that?" he demanded. "How can you . . . lay there . . . and say that?"

Vogel turned his head, ignoring the wire cutting into his face. He looked directly into the pimp's eyes. "Because," he said, blood pouring from his mouth. "He would forgive even *you*."

The pimp finally exploded in anger. "Congratulations!" he yelled, moving in agitated circles, waving his arms. "Congratulations! Now I want to kill every single fucking one of you. I want to kill—no—torture every stinking priest until I find one who cries and whines and begs and shits in his pants!"

He stopped dead in his tracks, beside Audrey. He held out his hand. "Give me your knife." The woman frowned, dug in her pocket, and slapped it in his hand as if she were a nurse and he was a surgeon.

Street marched over to the boxspring, flicking the blade open. "Fine! You're so blind. Stay that way." He grabbed each of their skulls and cut a thin, deep, straight line across the tops of their foreheads. Vogel shuddered, shouting in surprise and pain. Agnes screamed, shook, and cried.

The pimp stepped back as the blood began to slide down their faces in a sheet, like a dropping curtain.

Street gave the knife back to Audrey. "Man!" she

said, then carefully and slowly wiped the blade on his shirtsleeve. He just stared back at her and smiled.

"I'll never wash this shirt again," he told her.

She nodded her head at the boxspring without looking. "What about them?"

"They'll die," said Street. "Loss of blood, starvation, whatever. And you know what? Just before they die and find out eternity is a deep, dark, maggot-infested nothing, you know what'll happen?"

Audrey didn't answer. Street waited almost a half minute while they stood face to face and said nothing. Finally he turned and went to the van.

She went to the garage door, unlocked it, and pulled it up. She stuck her head outside, looked both ways, then gave him an all clear. He started the engine and drove out. She stepped onto the sidewalk, closed the door, locked it from the outside, and hopped into the passenger seat.

It wasn't until they were well on their way uptown that she finally answered.

"What?" she said.

"They'll forgive me," Street said with simple derision. "Assholes."

12

All Detective Wade's associates at the Connecticut police station were duly impressed.

"Ooo," they said in the parking lot, locker room, and cafeteria. "Big man in Manhattan. Big Apple boy toy."

In spite of the ribbing, Wade couldn't help being a trifle impressed with himself as he drove the blue sedan into New York.

Not only had he been called to assist the NYPD in their inquiries, but by no less than Captain Bender of Central Division, whose reputation reached throughout the East Coast. Most fellow officers assumed he was the model for almost every big-city cop on television. He was blunt, determined, tenacious, intelligent, and built like a battleship.

Wade pulled off at the Ninety-eighth Street exit and joined the twenty-four-hour crawl across town. He steered the car east, toward Central Park.

Bender had instructed him to get onto Central

Park West and turn left on Seventy-second Street into the park, but he found the entry blocked by wooden police line markers. He took the left anyway and pulled as close to the barricades as possible. He was blocking traffic, and the cars behind him let him know how they felt about that in no uncertain terms —with both a male chorus and a horn section.

Wade spotted a bored cop standing to the far left. The Connecticut cop rolled down his window, waved, and showed his badge. The policeman nodded and started to pull a barricade aside.

"Who are you seeing?" the policeman yelled. Wade told him. The officer nodded again. "Head down about a half mile, go under the bridge, and get ready to take the sharpest right you've ever seen in your life. The opening in the fence is narrow, so watch your side-view mirrors. Watch the curb bump too. Good luck finding a parking space."

Wade stared at him incredulously. "Have a nice day," he drawled.

"In your dreams," he heard the cop mutter before he rolled the window back up.

The officer hadn't been exaggerating. Wade drove into the shade of overhanging trees. The road went down as if it were an entrance to the underworld. Stone walls loomed on either side. He saw the bridge ahead and slowed as he went under it.

The right was indeed sharp—practically a forty-five degree angle to the street he was on. And it was immediately after the bridge. Wade cursed as he took the turn too wide. He quickly checked the rear-view mirror. Seeing no one, he awkwardly backed up and tried again.

The wheels whined and the steering column shook as he forced the vehicle into the narrow gap in the chain-link fence that surrounded Central Division on three sides. The building itself was forbidding and depressing. It was made of rock, squat and long, with brown circular windows that had to have dated from the nineteenth century.

Wade was particularly aware of his parking responsibilities. He didn't want to block any vehicle that might be needed in an emergency. But there just didn't seem to be anywhere to go in the cramped lot. He couldn't park on the street—the roadway was too narrow. Finally he pulled his car as close to the building's back door as was safe.

Finding the entrance was another trick. The only thing inside the back door was a plain, severe stairway, leading down. Wade tried the door at the bottom. It was locked. He thought about knocking, but went back upstairs. He circled the building twice before returning to the locked door.

He knocked. It was immediately buzzed open. He stepped into what looked like an accounting office. He was surrounded by simple green metal partitions with pebbled glass running across their tops, behind which he could make out rows of desks and casually bustling activity.

There was another doorway in front of him. He stepped across and knocked. He waited almost a minute before it was opened.

"Detective Wade, Westport, Connecticut, Police, to see Captain Bender," he told the young man in tie and shirt-sleeves.

"Yes, sir," said the man. "We've been expecting you." He led the way through the mass of desks. Wade saw all sorts of men in ties and shirt-sleeves—on the phones, at the water cooler, at their typewriters, and manning the bulky computers that lay on a table along one wall.

Along another wall, he saw a glass partition. Behind it were women on radios and women watching security camera monitors. Sexism still lived at Central. The other two walls were taken up by small, square cubicles that served as offices.

"You had a good time watching me?" Wade asked the man leading him.

"Yes," said the man without turning around. "As a matter of fact, we did."

Wade imagined they had the same kind of fun with all newcomers who tried to park and find their way inside.

"This is Captain Bender's office." The young man motioned toward a plain door with a pebble-glass window.

"Thanks," said Wade, knocking.

"Come."

The room barely contained the captain. Bender lived up to his description. He had a boulder of a head, covered with Irish moss, set on a thick neck. His whole body seemed to express a single message: *Nonsense: I don't take it and I don't dish it out.*

Wade felt an immediate kinship with the man. They were both too old and too lonely to notice anymore. They both avoided office politics like the plague and had therefore been frozen in place. They were two difficult demons sent to work in purgatory.

But Bender intimidated the heck out of Wade.

"Wade?" Bender said, getting up halfway out of his chair and putting out his hand.

The detective nodded and put his own meaty hand into the captain's. They shook, neither giving an ounce. Bender sat again as Wade took the one available seat and looked around.

The captain was certainly not anal retentive. He and dust had a long-term contract and he seemed happy to give the stuff many surfaces upon which to rest. He had many citations and awards, but they were all buried under piles of papers resting on file cabinets.

"Had to use a crowbar and dynamite on your chief to get you out here," Bender said, checking some memos on his green desk blotter.

"Yeah," said Wade. He wasn't surprised.

Bender looked him in the eye. "What were your orders, Detective?" he asked, handing him a paper. It was to Wade from the governor of Connecticut, hoping that Wade would extend every courtesy and urging him to cooperate to the best of his ability. It ended with a suggestion that he foresaw great things for the detective. I.Y.D.S.T.U (if you don't screw this up).

"You work fast," said Wade.

"Faxes." Bender shrugged. "What *aren't* you supposed to tell me, Detective?"

Wade ran his hand over his face. "Not much," he finally said. "Just that my department didn't want to solve the Merrick murder, and they have no intention of doing so."

Bender watched Wade carefully. He wanted to make sure the detective was being straight with him, and not just grinding some personal ax.

"How about you, Detective?" the captain asked evenly. "You want to solve the Merrick murder?"

"I like my job," Wade replied, just as evenly. "But yeah, I'd like to close the case . . . if I can."

Bender harrumphed and leaned back in his chair. "I gathered as much from your chief."

Wade went pale. "He said that?"

"Not in so many words. He made a big deal about how they were slaving on it, then couldn't name any particular investigator. When I finally dragged your name out of him, he made sure I knew you were no longer on the case and couldn't be the slightest help to me."

Wade visibly relaxed. Bender decided not to follow up on that . . . for the moment.

"So. What do you say, Wade? You going to be no help to me?"

The Connecticut cop smiled. "Hey. You didn't hear anything from me. What do you want to know?"

Bender didn't stand on ceremony. "What happened to Geoffrey Robert Merrick?"

"I think . . . we think that he was killed by a professional on the orders of some Central or South American drug cartel."

Bender interrupted. "Staff or free-lance?"

"I'm guessing staff."

"Why?"

"Merrick had just created a plan for his company, the Dice-Corp, to get around cartel contributions. If the bad guys wanted the message—not to screw with them—clear, they'd use one of their own messengers. To show off their power and influence."

Bender nodded. "Go on."

"Sophisticated bomb in Merrick's car. Very powerful. Installed while he was in Manhattan and the vehicle was in the train station parking lot. We can only assume the explosive was set to go off after the key was placed into the ignition. No matter what he did, turn it or remove it, the bomb would go off."

"What was the body's condition?"

Wade was surprised by the interruption. Especially since Bender's words were suddenly cool and his attitude remote. He wasn't even looking at Wade. Instead his right ear was pointed at the detective's mouth.

"You had to see the explosion's aftermath, Captain," Wade said slowly. "There was hardly enough left of the car to tow away. The interior was burnt to ashes. We assumed that . . . the body was cremated."

"You found a shoe," Bender said.

"Yes. It had been thrown clear. But chewed up. Broken. Burnt."

Bender pursed his lips together, nodding curtly. "Nobody saw anything?"

"Too late at night. Merrick's car was parked too far away from the main lot area. But I found a few people who said they saw a fairly tall, fairly good-looking, athletic Hispanic wearing sunglasses who watched Merrick boarding the train that morning."

"A little too hot and heavy for the town to handle, eh?"

Wade shrugged. "All I know is that I was taken off the case. Pardon me; I was informed that other investigations should take priority."

"Diplomatically put," Bender remarked. "Think your hit man flew the coop?"

"I'd be astonished if we found him within a hundred-mile radius of Westport by now," said Wade. "Probably flew in, took a limo, did the dirty, took the limo back, and flew out. He could be in any major North or South American city by now, maintaining his masters' schedules. This guy is probably a career killer—punches a time clock, works nine to five, another day, another death, another ten thousand dollars."

Bender considered what Wade said carefully. "I'll access some files," he decided. "The FBI routinely check on the comings and goings of cartel suspects within our borders. The CIA will probably have a book full of Central American hitters' descriptions and lifestyles. Maybe we can match up some sort of composite."

Wade nodded. "Impressive."

Bender shrugged. "No problem. Remember, our boys in D.C. want these bastards as much as we do . . . paranoid political conspiracy theories aside."

The captain stood, putting both hands flat on his desktop.

Wade stood as well. "What if the theories are true?" he asked.

Bender gave him a patient smile. "Even if the President is in bed with the drug-smuggling scumbags, there are always some good cops salivating at the thought of bringing them all down. Want some coffee?"

The two moved out into the sea of desks and made their way to the water cooler. Beside it was a small table with a two-urn coffee maker. Both men took it straight, in small Styrofoam cups. Wade noticed that Bender was looking through the glass wall, and followed his gaze. They watched a few video screens that were fast-forwarding through local newscasts.

"Come on," said Bender. They went into the room. It was quieter in there, and darker.

"Hi, Marge," the captain said to the policewoman making transcripts of the programs. "All set?"

"Just hit the play button, Captain," she replied, pointing to a small remote-control unit lying on top of one of the video machines.

Bender did as he was told, and two nineteen-inch monitors were filled with the face of a beautiful, blue-eyed blonde. "Know her?" the captain asked Wade.

"Melanie," the detective said in surprise, then regained his composure. "That's Melanie Merrick, Geoffrey's widow."

"I know. What's your relationship with her?"

Wade repressed the "What do you mean" he felt popping up his throat. "Paternal," he ultimately said. "She was given a raw deal. I . . ." Wade knew it was unwise to tell Bender about his off-duty actions, but decided that the captain would treat him worse if he wasn't totally honest. "I told her the

situation. I . . . basically said that if she wanted jus-
tice, she'd have to get it herself. I promised to help in
any way possible."

Wade got what he pretty much thought he was
going to get. Bender just looked at him, allowing the
detective to read the reprimand in his face. It was
ten seconds before the captain spoke.

"You *do* like your job," he said. "Maybe too much."
He freeze-framed the television picture. Melanie
was caught mid-word. "An insane news team has
adopted her," Bender continued. "They stole her
image, stuck it on the stove, and turned up the
burner. They still don't know who she is or where
she fits in on this thing, but they're asking the entire
city to find out." He clicked off the machines, returned the remote, and marched back to his office
without another word.

Wade followed humbly behind. It wasn't until they
were both inside with the door closed that Bender
turned on him. "Man, if you're going to put a civilian
on the battlefield, you damn well better make sure
you're in front of her, not behind her. What were
you thinking? That once she was killed, maybe you'd
be there to get a picture of the murderer? That
maybe you could find a clue on *her* burned body?"
He sat down in disgust. "That is, if you even found a
body this time. Maybe just her shoe. Then at least
you'd have a set."

Wade took it, knowing everything Bender said to
be true. He had told Melanie the truth, but only
because he didn't want to do absolutely nothing. He
had not been willing to risk his pension, however.
"Guilty," he finally responded, and not with pride.

Bender's expression was still tinged with disgust,
but also understanding. "Don't worry, Detective. I
didn't call you here to ream you out. Well, not just to
ream you out, at any rate."

Now that the Connecticut detective's guilty conscience had been exposed, he was no longer nervous or ashamed. "You called me here to find out about Geoffrey Merrick's body," he said.

Bender looked up in surprise.

"It was the only unusual question," Wade explained. "Also the only one when you weren't looking at me straight."

A tiny passing cloud of respect shaded the captain's face, then disappeared. "You told me your story, Detective. I guess I owe you one. Earlier this year, we found four teenagers in a deserted railyard. Two had the front of their skulls caved in. One had his neck snapped. One had his wrist broken. His balls were so high between his legs he might have swallowed them.

"Some days later it looked like a tornado had gone down Avenue A. About a dozen alleged drug pushers were shot and beaten to death. Their skulls were pushed in, their necks broken, their *spines* snapped. A little while after that we found what was left of Jeremy Bancroft. His remains fit in a beaker."

"Sounds like somebody's doing your job for you," Wade commented.

Bender's expression went blank. He might as well have been a statue. His words were quiet, flat, and direct. "Our job is not to slaughter people."

Wade licked his dry lips. He cleared his throat.

"Earlier this week somebody broke up the K Club in Harlem," Bender continued. "Later that same night somebody broke up a hooker's palace in Washington Heights. Somebody fast, strong, and brutal. Same M.O. Same broken, snapped bones."

"What do you think?" Wade wondered. "This hit man?"

"Not the hit man," said Bender.

Realization smacked the detective—with a wet fish. "You're kidding."

"Maybe," said Bender, getting up from his chair and studying the walls of his office. "All I know for sure is that in almost every case our boy left witnesses behind. And in almost every case the general consensus was that he looked like a broiled skeleton."

Wade felt as if he had been nailed to the chair. "Did your boy have only one shoe?" he asked weakly.

Bender didn't get the feeble joke. "That I don't know. What I do know is that the case has been dropped in my lap. The commissioner doesn't like it. The P. R. people tell him our boy makes the cops look like idiots. Ineffectual idiots. His common sense tells him that innocent bystanders are hurt in any war, whether it's between us and them, or our boy and them. And I tell him it could be just a matter of time before our boy goes completely bonkers and starts slaughtering anyone within reach."

Wade's mouth was dry. "Sooner or later you'll catch up to him. . . ."

Bender was studying his citations for bravery. "I'm not going to be too happy when he starts seeing us as his enemies either."

Wade stared at the floor. "It couldn't be. . . . You had to see the car, Captain. There's no way that anyone could have survived that!"

Bender finally turned back to his visitor. "No corpse, Detective. That's all I wanted to know."

Wade's mind was reeling. "Melanie," he suddenly blurted. "Do you think she knows?"

"I think she may have guessed," Bender said gravely, coming back to his desk. "I'm certain she doesn't want to believe it either. Last time I saw her it looked like she was refusing to let herself believe it. But I can tell you one thing for sure. She knows our boy. And when we catch up to him, she's going to be right there . . . in the middle."

Keith Sullivan's breath had caught in his throat when he saw her. He had walked into DiCenzo's office completely unsuspecting, then she turned her head toward him. She was sitting in the red leather chair, her yellow hair curtaining her face. When she turned, her blue eyes piniored him like lighthouse beacons.

Her skin was so smooth and creamy. Her features were so serene and full. His heart beat faster. All his nerves tingled. He felt his flesh reddening. Then they gave him the Northern Plan and panic set in. Unable to think, he phoned his contact. He bitterly regretted the call afterward.

He had walked out into the hall, trying to decide what to do. He figured a long lunch would help. Incredibly, the hall was clear of other executives. Incredibly, the elevator responded within seconds of his pressing the down button. Incredibly, there was only one other person in the elevator when the doors opened.

Sullivan knew it had to be fate. It was a sign from greater powers—greater than even the cartel. Melanie Merrick looked at him without expression as he stepped into the elevator.

Nothing was said as he pressed the lobby button, the doors closed, and they started downward. As befitted Dice-Corp, the elevator was well appointed with sumptuous wood paneling, carpeted floors, and old-fashioned light fixtures.

Finally Melanie looked at him. He had not taken his eyes off her.

"Thank you," he said.

"For what?" Her reply was stubbornly oblique.

"For trusting me."

They didn't speak for another few floors. Incredibly, the car didn't stop and no one else got on. Another sign that this meeting—that everything concerning the two of them—was preordained.

"Nothing has changed, Mrs. Merrick," Sullivan said, the emotion welling inside reminding him of his schoolboy infatuation with his first English teacher. "My respect and admiration for you only grows. You trust me to continue your husband's work. I appreciate that. And I want you to know: you *can* trust me."

Melanie looked at the perfectly dressed young executive with the lovesick child's face. She glanced over the elevator door, seeing the lights between "2" and "L." She waited until the "L" lit up, then abruptly hit the "Door Close" button.

The car lurched, knocking Sullivan into the wall. Melanie's feet remained anchored to the floor.

"You admire me, you respect me." She was nearly mocking him. "Time for talk is past, Keith. Trust you? Why? I've already had Geoffrey. I'm not going to settle for less. Think you're as good as him? Prove it. Then we'll talk." She looked him up and down, her gaze settling on his stunned face. "Maybe."

She released the "Door Close" button and walked out.

Keith watched her go as the people who had been waiting for the elevator filed around him with irritated, impatient looks. He watched her march toward the front doors, her firm, round body covered in thick, bulky black, her tightly braided ponytail swinging.

And he realized he wanted her now more than ever before.

More than anything.

13

Street Wise stood in the wide doorway between the front hall and the living room until Muriel Holford noticed him. She looked over from her seat in front of the television.

He stood, head down, with a huge grin on his face. He wore a dark rust-colored suit made of almost Day-Glo fiber. His tie was black, with small red triangles on it.

His pure white shirt was splattered with red.

It looked like a design that had been purposely placed on the garment. Framed and hung in a gallery, it would have ranked with the best of modern art. The crimson was splashed below the tie and spread behind either side of the suit jacket.

"Heeere's Johnny!" Street said.

Muriel laughed in appreciation. "My darling!" she said, getting up and throwing her arms wide. They embraced. She held his shoulders at arm's length and surveyed him again. "What an entrance!" she gushed.

Street looked down, rubbing his shirt between thumb and forefinger. "Dried, I'm afraid," he said. "Can't share this with you."

"You already have," Muriel assured him. "More than you could ever know. Hungry? You must be hungry, dear, after such an arduous day. Let me heat up the veal."

Street waited until she had prepared the meal and he was sitting down to eat before he spoke again. "It would be veal," he commented. He sat on one side of the large butcher-block table in the corner of the expansive, airy kitchen. The social worker came across the white-and-black tile floor from the industrial stove.

"Of course," Muriel replied, putting the white stoneware plate down in front of him. "They pen them in, chop off half their legs, and stuff them with nutrients. It's the only way to slaughter. *Bon appetit.*"

Street grinned at her again. "Thanks." He took his first forkful. "Superb. Delicious."

"Thank you, dear," she said, putting her chin on the back of her folded hands. "How did it go?"

He told her. Her eyes got brighter with each detail.

"I knew it," she said when he finally concluded. "I could feel the power growing inside me." She poured him some more red wine.

"Uh-huh," he commented, taking another bite of the veal and buttered vegetables. "You sure you're not pregnant or something?"

Muriel laughed, and went to the refrigerator to start preparing his dessert and coffee. "In a way," she murmured.

Street looked over his shoulder at her. "How does that work, exactly?"

"How does what work, dear?"

"The power stuff. You feeling the power of what I'm doing and everything."

She smiled at him from the icebox. "You don't believe it, do you?"

He shrugged, looking at his plate. "Hey, all I know is I don't feel what you're doing. I don't get, like, a psychic message every time you freak out or something."

"You don't try, dear," she said, returning her attention to the fridge shelves. "If you worked at this as long and hard as I have, it would work for you as well. Just because you can't feel it doesn't mean it doesn't happen."

"I didn't say that," Street complained, leaning forward in the U-backed wooden chair. "I just want to know what it's like, that's all."

Muriel stopped in the middle of the kitchen, looking at him as if he were a precocious child. "Well, isn't that sweet?"

"What?"

She went about her preparations, waving a finger at him. "Don't think I don't know what's going on here, dear. The energy is rising. You can feel it too. And you can't help feeling just a little bit afraid, right?"

"What are you talking about?" he responded angrily.

"See? You're getting defensive. Come on, admit it. Aren't you just the teensy, tiniest bit concerned about what you're feeling?"

"No!"

"Come now, darling. When you watched them dying, weren't you just a trifle afraid? Didn't you feel just a flash of fear? Didn't you think you might possibly be dealing with powers greater than you?"

She stood with her back to him, pouring the coffee beans into the little electric grinder. He opened his mouth to deny it, then snapped his jaw shut. He thought back to just a few hours before.

"There is no God," he finally said, returning to his meal.

"I didn't say that," Muriel told him pleasantly. "I said 'powers.' You felt it, didn't you?"

Street finally, reluctantly agreed. "I felt *something*. . . ."

"Of course," said Muriel. "You felt the energy. That is all you're trained to feel. But I feel more. I can collect the power inside me. I can direct it. I can control it."

"Yeah," Street drawled. "Sure. So okay, make the percolator float across the room to me."

Muriel shook her head with sad amusement. "It doesn't work that way, dear. You can't use the energy to make things float. That's a magic trick. You use the energy to control the energy."

"Huh?" Street exaggerated the word with impatience.

"Think of it as a laser," she suggested. "A dissipated laser does nothing. A concentrated laser can cut through anything."

"So what are you going to do?" he said with sarcasm. "Cut through a vault? Rob a bank?"

Street saw the muscles in her neck get tight. He saw her shoulders bunch. But then her anger passed and she was her calm, patient self again. "Don't be stupid, dear."

"I'm not being stupid," he flared.

"You're just upset that you haven't found any sort of direction or redemption yet."

"Admit it!" he yelled. "We're just killing guys for

the hell of it. Man, I do it because I like the rush. That's it. The rush of power, babe. There's nothing else."

She turned to glare at him. "You're wrong. You're more wrong than you've ever been in your life. There's a greater power in all this. And we can tap into it. We can *be* it."

He was on his feet. "Prove it, bitch. Prove it!"

They tried to outstare each other for a few moments, their backs bent. But then Muriel relaxed. She stood up straight, and smiled.

"Oh, no. You don't get off that easy. I'm not going to let you ruin it before everything is ready." She turned back to the counter and continued mixing his dessert.

He turned back as well, sitting at the butcher-block table in disgust. "Yeah, right," he grumbled, picking up his fork. "Always have a way around it. Always have a way to slip out." He called over his shoulder. "You sound like *them.*"

Muriel dropped her spoon with a clatter. "All right," she said evenly. "Darling. Dear. Haven't you ever wondered why no one has ever seen God or the Devil? With all the good and evil in this world, why can people only *hear* them? 'The Lord spoke unto me,' they say. Or 'The Devil told me to do it.' "

He turned in his chair and looked at her. He accepted the truth of what she was saying.

"It's because they are out of our physical reach. They exist on entirely different physical planes. Once you realize that truth, you can proceed."

"Proceed? To what?"

"What do you think? Why do you think I've had you do all these things? The AIDS woman. Her babies. Your room . . . that cage you have in the sewer. This, what you did tonight. Everything we've done before. It's all collecting, adding up. It's building up to something. We're so close. I can feel it."

"What?" Street exclaimed. "Feel what? So close to what?"

"The bridge," she said. "No one will use the power of good to make a bridge for God to return to this world. They're too afraid of Him. Religion has seen to that. It has made them all feel unworthy. They are afraid of what He might do to them.

"But that cannot stop us. This world should belong to Satan. It already does. All that's left is to build him a bridge upon which to cross over from his world to ours."

Street Wise stared at her. Finally he broke their gaze and shifted back to his plate.

"Other worlds," he scoffed. "Bridges. Just more bullshit."

Muriel raised and shook her head, her hands pointed to the ceiling. "Look," she said. "Don't you understand how much power, how much energy there is? Can't you see what a miracle we are? Haven't you ever wanted to fulfill your destiny as a human being? I mean completely fulfill it—do everything you can to be everything you can?"

He kept eating.

"Idiot!" she cried. "My husband tried. He did everything in his power to understand existence. He filled this house with arcane books and knowledge. He studied mythoi. He respected the supernatural and was willing to believe anything. He made only one mistake. He chose to follow the path of good."

Street picked up his plate and put it in the sink. He went back to the table and waited for the coffee to brew.

"There's a problem with good," she stressed regardless. "You can't do anything with it. It's its own reward. Unlike evil, it cannot be taken to an extreme. If it is, it *becomes* evil."

Muriel went over to sit beside the pimp. "Do you want to know or don't you?"

He looked at her with veiled eyes. "I'm listening."

That was all she needed to hear. "He died. He died with nothing to show for it. It wasn't a horrible death. It wasn't revenge from above or below. He was an old man who smoked too much, drank too much, and ate too much. He died of a coronary and that's it. He left behind his house, his books, and his one wish for me."

"I can just guess," said Street, holding up a hand. "An army commercial. 'Be all that you can be.'"

"Yes," said Muriel. "Yes. But don't you see? That's what they're counting on. That we'll think it's all stupid and useless and not try. That we'll remain blind to the power and energy that we can harness. We can."

It was like throwing water balloons at a brick wall. Muriel finally leaned back and yelled, pointing at the doorway. "You want me to prove it? Go see Buckman's husband in that hospital! Go see Pamela Arnold!"

The first hint of honest doubt showed on Street's countenance.

"There!" she said with satisfaction. "No floating percolators. That's not the power."

"Okay," he said. "So answer me. Why are you having me do these things? Yeah, I know it's leading up to something. And yes, I felt it tonight and damn it, I was scared. You happy now?"

Muriel laughed with joy and went to take him in her arms. He angrily pushed them aside, but she only laughed again and continued her embrace. This time he allowed it. Suddenly he was holding on tight.

"Oh, my dear," she whispered. "My love. It's all right. You'll see."

"Why?" he choked out.

"Darling," she cooed. "I can feel the power inside me. You have created that power with your actions. We are so close to having enough strength to actually alter reality."

She felt him start, as if getting a tiny electric shock. "Yes," she continued. "Yes, to be all that we can be, we only have two choices. Good or evil. Good will get us nothing. It will put a ceiling on this existence. But evil will give us unlimited power."

"What power?" Street scoffed.

"Not what," Muriel immediately replied. "*Whose*. We will have power over others, but what's more, we will have power over *their* power. We can, and will, take their power to feed ours."

Street Wise looked lost.

"Think!" she demanded. "Why am I having you do all these things? Why not, as you hope, just kill the victims? Because the torture magnifies their emotions. And emotions embody human power. It enhances a person's strength and desire. It fills a human being. And that's what we take. That's what we need to make this work. Burning, bright, human beacons for the gods to follow." The woman laughed silently, her shoulders shaking. "A landing field marked by human torches."

Street leaned back, looking at her from arm's length. She could see he still didn't completely believe her but was willing to try anything she asked. "What do you want me to do?"

She smiled and he could feel her strength. He could practically feel the power. "We're so close," she said. "So incredibly close. We just need one thing more. One final act of concentrated evil to push us over the top."

She released him and went back to the counter. He sat at the table, stunned into silence, looking down at his bloodstained shirt. She finished mixing the whipped cream and poured it over the combination of fresh fruit and different-flavored cake crumbs. She poured the coffee and served the dessert. Finally she sat back down beside him.

"It's time," she announced brightly. "It's time for a *service.*"

She ran laughing across the field to him. She wore a light, flowing summer dress. She held the straw hat with the light blue ribbon around the crown. The sky was blue, the clouds were white and fluffy, the air smelled sweet, and the breeze felt refreshing. The long green grass waved. The thick brown trees were filled with rustling green leaves. The birds chirped happily. Even the sun seemed to be smiling.

Grim stood, waiting for her—his arms at his sides, his teeth clenched.

As she grew closer, he could see her features. Her brown hair bouncing against her thin neck. Her close-set eyes twinkling with merriment. Her flat nose pulled even wider by her joyful smile.

Her name was Betty and she was running to embrace him.

Her arms were stretched out to enfold him. They met, her body hitting his.

She exploded against him, as if her skin were made of brittle paper.

She erupted, washing over him, her body tearing apart.

He saw her eyes tear out of their sockets, her jaw come apart, her teeth start to spill, her hair caving in to her unraveling brain.

It all hit him full in the face.

He was blinded by the blood and brain fluid so he

couldn't see the rest. But he could feel it. He could feel her bones turning to powder. He could feel her internal organs hitting him like sacks of rubber. He could feel the rest of her fluids soaking him.

Grim stood in the field, shivering. He waited until the girl was just a puddle of human parts at his feet.

Even before he wiped the goo from his eyes, he heard the crying.

Grim looked across the field. He saw a small form kicking and waving its arms some yards ahead. It was nestled in the tall, thick, soft grass. He decided he had little choice but to go to it.

He walked toward it. Not slowly, not quickly, but at his natural pace.

It was a crying, naked baby. Something was coming out of every orifice. Tears, saliva, mucus, urine, and excrement. Blood was oozing out of its ears.

Grim turned around. There was another crying baby in the tree. He looked the other way. There was a crying baby in a flower bed. He looked up. There was a crying baby in the clouds.

Grim looked off into the distance. He saw plants growing. In each of their stalks and trunks, misshapen, crying children started to form. The field was filled with screaming children, their faces contorted. He couldn't move, lest he step on one. They hemmed him in, this sea of undulating screeching flesh.

Grim stood perfectly still, letting the cries tear his eardrums. He remained motionless, without expression, as the tortured infants covered the ground for as far as the eye could see. . . .

He finally woke up.
He heard one word.
"Street," said his god.
Grim had gone crazy. He had left the pimp's crib

with no information. He had searched the streets for
hours, days. He had gone to One Hundred and
Twenty-seventh Street. He had gone to the Lenox
Terminal. He had gone to Forty-second Street. He
had gone to Park Avenue South. He had gone to
West Tenth Street.

He had gone everywhere anyone dressed like
Betty was. He had prowled every alley and every
roadway. He asked all the women, and the men.

"Street?"

"Hey, buddy, you're standing on it."

"I don't know and I don't care."

"I'm not one of his bitches."

"He ain't here tonight."

"He's gone underground."

"The heat's on. He's gone into hiding."

"Not here, baby. No Street here."

Grim had looked until he was weak with exhaus-
tion and hunger. He ate some garbage and kept going. He even looked in the sewers. He wandered the
subway tunnels, remembering that was where his
other evil had ultimately gone. The evil named Jeremy. Grim had killed him, but Street remained out
of his reach.

He had walked and walked until he couldn't keep
himself from stumbling into walls. He walked until
his knees gave out. He fell to his face on the sidewalk. He got up again and kept going.

He crawled back into the High Bridge Park area.
He dragged himself to the one place he felt safe. He
collapsed in the cellar of the condemned apartment
house where he had met her.

There was hardly anything left of the men he had
killed there. The rats and wild dogs had fed on them
for days. The stench was horrible, even for him.

Grim imagined he could hear her calling from
above. He pulled himself up the steps and lay on the

first-floor landing. It took him hours to get to the rear apartment. He kept losing consciousness, falling into the black, dreamless pit where all he could hear was his god screaming.

Grim's fingers and knees were bleeding when he finally got to the mattress. He just managed to hold the digits before his eyes, smiling at the sheen of scarlet. It meant he was still alive. He was not yet completely lost.

He crawled onto the bed. He laid his arm over on what had been her side of the padding, imagining the feel of her form and the smell of her skin. He imagined hearing her words lulling him to sleep.

He thanked her for her company and thought of his angel.

The sleep and dream demons had come for him at last.

They had done their best, but he had suffered their onslaught without fear or oppression. He knew he was safe with them. They weren't telling him anything he didn't already know.

Betty was dead. The children suffered.

Suddenly Grim sat up.

It was night. He was not alone in the room.

The eyes that glowed there were not the eyes of rats or dogs, which would have been low to the floor. These eyes floated in the air at least five feet off the ground. Grim couldn't see the walls or floors. They were covered in shadow, cast by the figures that filled the room.

He looked around him. There were broken shoes and dirty feet completely surrounding the edge of the mattress. Grim looked up. Thin bodies wrapped in ripped clothes stood there. Their dark, smudged, discolored faces looked down on him. Their blood-shot eyes watched him.

They stood, in the room, out in the hall, and on the stairs: silent, unmoving.

Grim thought they might be his army of dead, coming to claim him. But he eliminated that thought almost immediately. He could distinguish between hallucination and reality, between sleep and awareness. He could now watch both from a distance.

Grim narrowed his eyes and remembered. He recognized them. Not from their features, but by their bearing and attitude. He could practically read their aura. He sat and waited, unafraid.

"King Grim."

He turned to the one who had spoken. The man had ventured onto the mattress, on one knee. His hair was like chipped nails driven into the edges of his skull. His face was wide, with large, fluid-filled eyes and a red, rutted nose. His lips were cracked and discolored, with black strips along them. His pockmarked skin was livid. Gray stubble covered his chin.

Grim smiled his awful smile. "Nathan?" he said, putting his hand out.

He meant to pat his friend on the shoulder, but was too weak. The derelict caught the hand instead and kissed it with reverence.

Nathan held his deity's hand against his rough cheek. Large tears rolled out of his eyes. "Yes, my lord," he whispered. "Yes."

Nathan had saved Grim's life. He had found him, crumpled and unconscious, by the railroad tracks in the Bronx. He and some other derelicts had carried him into the Lightning Street Railyard nearby and kept him safe, warm, and fed during his recuperation.

Nathan had thought the man was a message from God. More than that: a messenger. Nathan had lost his way waiting for the resurrection. He had drunk himself into a stupor from which there was no return. But there was redemption. This horribly burned, disfigured, wounded man had to be it.

The only sign Nathan had been given was the remnants of the shirt the wounded man had worn. On it Nathan read three letters, and named his deity.

G.R.M. Grim.

Their king had saved them when the killers came for them. Grim had defeated the Firebeaters; Nathan had followed his king when he left to find his angel. He had helped his king protect the angel from the horrors stalking her.

And he had followed the small dots of blood King Grim left after vanquishing Cryst, the King of Killers. They led him here.

Nathan had passed the word that their king was still among them, and waited for his return. Now he held his king's hand. Grim looked in wonder at the fetid bandage that kept Nathan's right palm together. He remembered: Jeremy Bancroft had stabbed through it, trying to get at Melanie Merrick.

His tears joined his friend's in welcome and gratitude.

The derelict turned to his brethren in exultation. "He lives!" he cried in his cracked, ruined voice. "He lives!"

The others shouted and babbled, some in confusion or insanity, but some in celebration. Grim was their king. He had to be. It was the only explanation for his existence and powers.

Grim could imagine them shuffling through the city. He saw them marching down this street like the living dead—answering a call, a rumor, a hope that a purpose to their existence could be found. He could see Nathan raving to them about redemption and salvation with a conviction no normal man could possess.

He could imagine the word traveling throughout the homeless population. Only the mentally disturbed ones would respond. The poverty-stricken, luckless, sane ones would ignore the call. Their lives were bereft of such absurd hope.

Grim watched their sad, feeble celebration and accepted it. Like it or not, want it or not, he was their leader. For the moment, at least.

He smiled and nodded at Nathan, who cried and laughed.

So be it, thought Grim. *We all have our gods to worship.*

PART THREE

If I cannot bend the gods,
I will let hell loose.

—Virgil (70–19 B.C.)

14

"Channel Six *U. R. There News* line. Can I help you?"

"Uh, hello. Um, I know who that blond woman is. The one you're showing on the Five O'clock News? Can I get any money for this?"

"You got any proof?"

"What?"

"Proof. You know, proof."

"But I know who it is!"

"Pardon me, miz, but so did everyone else. We've already received hundreds of calls. How do we know you won't just give us the name of your sister, daughter, girlfriend, or hairdresser? Half the time, all these tips led to people who didn't look anything like the woman we featured. The only thing they had in common was being blond. And most of the time they were bleached blondes."

"Uh. How do you know the girl you featured isn't a bleached blonde?"

"Look at the eyebrows, Miz. The facial fuzz. Do *you* have any proof?"

"Well, yeah, I guess so. But are you going to pay me, or what?"

"Please hold."

"Hey, don't go putting me on hold!"

"Do you want me to find out whether they're willing to pay you, or what? I only answer the phones around here."

"Oh. Okay, then."

"Please hold."

"Hello?"

"Hello."

"Who's this?"

"Who's *this*?"

"Sam Niven, news director. You say you have proof of the woman's identity?"

"Yeah, I guess so."

"What do you mean, 'I guess so'?"

"Are you gonna pay me?"

"If your information turns out to be accurate, we would be willing to reimburse you for your time and effort."

"How much?"

"That depends on the accuracy of your information."

"Five hundred bucks?"

"It's useless to discuss amounts until we know whether your information is correct."

"Yeah. I guess that makes sense. . . ."

"Please, if you don't mind, we're trying to prepare a newscast here—"

"Okay, okay. But you're willing to pay me, right?"

"We're willing to reimburse you for your time and effort, yes."

"That means, pay me money, right?"

"I've already wasted too much time—"

"Okay, okay! I'm a nurse, all right? I was on duty when they brought her in, okay?"

"Brought who in?"

"Look it up. Not in New York papers. In Connecticut. That businessman guy; the one who was blown up in his car in the train parking lot. You know?"

"Geoffrey Merrick?"

"That's him. His wife. It's his wife. She was attacked by that Bancroft guy."

"Cryst . . . the King of Killers?"

"That's what you called him. Jesus, what a stupid name."

"We have no information that she was attacked by Jeremy Bancroft!"

"They kept it secret. They figured she had already been through enough."

"How do you know all this?"

"I told you. I'm a nurse. I was on duty when they brought her in. I heard them talking about it. I heard everything. Now listen, I got some car and garage payments, okay?"

"We'll have to check this out—"

"Christ, mister, there's gotta be a picture of this blond bitch someplace! Check her wedding announcement or something. She's pretty young. They couldn't've been married that long. Now I want five hundred dollars—"

"If this checks out, we'll pay you. Hold on and give your name to the receptionist."

"Don't you go putting me on hold again—"

But it was too late.

The receptionist held the phone and looked up at the news director. "You want to pay her?"

"Sure," said Niven. "This sounds like the real thing. As soon as I give you the okay, send her a hundred bucks."

"A hundred?"

"Yes, a hundred! What is she going to do? Sue us? If the hospital finds out she blabbed, they'll get rid of her—union or no union. A hundred . . . and she's lucky to get that!"

It was midnight at the Riverdale mini-mall. With space so much in demand and the zoning laws so restrictive, real estate developers were not able to build the massive shopping centers you could see in New Jersey and Connecticut. Instead of steel, cement, and glass creatures stretching over hundreds of acres, complete with amusement parks and food courts, they were only able to fashion city blocks into pale plagiarisms of suburban glory.

The Triangle mini-mall, at the intersection of Irvin and Waldo Avenues, was a perfect example. It was not simply a one-sided drive-in. The stores were in a narrow, two-story rectangle, facing both in and out. Each of the shops had two entrances, one facing the various streets, and one facing in on a small rectangular courtyard.

It was a masterpiece of urban planning. In the one relatively small space, the designers and engineers had crammed triple the usual amount of stores. Instead of one big store taking up the block, they now had three: one on the Irvin and Waldo Avenue sides, one on the Broadway side (which made up the base of the street triangle), and one on the second floor.

In the center of the courtyard was a small park area, highlighted by a six-foot circular fountain with colored lights. Into this mini-amphitheater came furtive, nervous people.

Street Wise watched them from his vantage point at the back door. The only unused space in the structure was this narrow hallway, hemmed in by store walls. It allowed the store managers to reach both sides of their shops when they opened in the morning.

The mall had no security. It was considered a waste of money. Each store had iron gates that were locked down on either side of the shops—over the windows. And each store had its own alarm, if a window was broken. So there was no night watchman coming in and out every hour. There were no security patrols prowling the parking lot. These people could come and go without witnesses.

The anxious, guilt-ridden people watched Street Wise back. He could tell by their expressions they didn't trust him. Why should they? He was the one person among them who looked special. He was the one who dressed the best. Some others wore suits, but none wore an Italian tailor-made suit. He was also the best-looking and the most assured. He was also the most exotic, by comparison, the rest being pasty-faced and dumpy.

Muriel Holford was standing at the pimp's side. As her minions found places to sit around the dry fountain, she whispered in Street's ear.

"There's Herb Resnick. He's the manager of this place. He'd never admit his son is gay, and when the kid got AIDS, it put him over the edge. That's the Conroys. Their eight-year-old daughter was kidnapped by child pornographers, who then came back for their five-year-old son. Over there is Florence Menozzi. After almost forty years of marriage, her husband got Alzheimer's. I love it; there's the Beaumonts. He was found guilty of insider trading and tax evasion. They couldn't stand the thought of losing their stuff. Next to them is Willis Farmington. Walks well, doesn't he? He used to be paraplegic. Audrey you know. Hello, Audrey! Wave, my dear, wave. That's it . . ."

Muriel started to make her way over to the center

area, stopping to chat pleasantly with each sitting group. Street remained where he was, watching. He could see that the people were tense until she approached, then made a great show of being friendly. It was like a cocktail party where the guests hated one another but would do anything not to show it. They were united against Muriel by one emotion, but it was the most powerful: fear.

They were all salt of the earth, Street thought derisively. It was just as Muriel said. They were all normal people who had been visited by tragedy. They were all people who had need of a sympathetic ear. They were all her social work clients. They were not the only ones she had given an option to. But they were the ones who took it.

He saw the Arnolds sitting there, trying not to attract any attention. Street laughed to himself. Ev and Ev probably thought they were the only "normal" ones here and everybody else was a rabid, foaming Satanist.

Street wondered if Resnick's son knew what his father had done to "cure" him. He wondered if Resnick, Jr., was now disease-free and dating girls. He wondered if the Conroys ever told their children how they got them back. He wondered what happened to the kidnappers, if anything. He wondered if Florence ever told her now lucid husband about her semiregular rituals.

And he wondered who gave Muriel which ideas. Who suggested the AIDS hooker? Who suggested keeping the AIDS babies? Whose idea was the sewer ball? He could certainly guess whose idea it was to meet here. That was obviously the work of Muriel herself. No abandoned church for this lady, no, sir. It made far more sense to have her ceremonies in this, "the Modern Cathedral."

Muriel had finished "working the room," and was

making her way to the center of the padded bench-like seats. "Come on, everyone," she said, urging them forward. "I don't want to shout. You don't want me to shout, do you? So, come on. Everybody gather round. Come right up front. I won't bite." She laughed. "Neither will any of you. You're all just good neighbors. They're nice folks, just like your-selves. Come on!"

The group reluctantly shifted down and closer to-gether. They tried not to look at one another, but some couldn't avoid glancing around furtively.

"That's better," Muriel said pleasantly, then clasped her hands in front of her, looking around with a smile. "It's *so* good to see you all tonight. I'm so glad you all could come, because this is a momen-tous occasion. This is a night you should remember for the rest of your lives."

She let that sink in, enjoying their expressions of paranoia, fearful anticipation, and discomfort. Street could see that a few had become philosophic about the whole thing. Willis, especially, was looking studi-ous—as if this were merely an interesting hobby. They all had to rationalize it. Some were just better at it, that was all.

Muriel looked over her minions, enjoying their conflict. Her power was in their torment. She rev-eled in their anguish, letting it feed her. She wouldn't have enjoyed it half as much if they had been ready and willing to join her. Now they were truly trapped: they would never be innocent again.

"Thanks to your efforts on my behalf," she finally continued, "your loved ones are safe and well, and your lives are better than they've ever been. But it is only from the collective energy of your thoughts and desires that these benefits are maintained. As long as you continue to worship, pray, and most impor-tantly, think, all will remain as it is."

Street could see and hear the collective sigh of
relief ripple through the crowd. He smiled and
shook his head, knowing what was behind those in-
nocent-sounding words: worship, pray, and think.
These people read the papers and watched the
news. They had to know about Jane Weston and her
children by now. No one had discovered Betty or
Vogel or Agnes yet, but these people had to suspect.
They *had* to.

The pimp looked at their faces. He could imagine
them looking at their saved loved ones and forgetting their doubts or suspicions or concerns. "God's in
his heaven, all's right with the world!" But somewhere, in the back of their minds, they had to wonder . . . *Which atrocity was I part of? Whose idea
was that?*

"But," Muriel went on, "what would you say if I
told you we are preciously near the time when I will
not require even that!"

The hope on their faces was aching and heartbreaking, but then it was gone—replaced by suspicion.

"It's true," the social worker said. "That's why I
called you here tonight. Lucifer is nearly satisfied.
We have built him a foundation upon which he can
rest. All we need is one more brick. Just one. Sepa-
rately you have each come up with an idea worthy of
him. Together I hope we can think of a concept that
will be the fitting peak of our accomplishment."

She looked and smiled at each of them. But only
Willis Farmington was willing to speak. "What do we
have to do?"

"Just what you did before, but here and now—in
company. You have to inspire each other. You have
to share your ideas and build upon them. We have to
come up with a final concept with which to convey
our thanks and hope for the future."

"You mean," said Willis, "like sacrificing a baby or something?"

No one's look of distaste could surpass Muriel's own. "That is exactly what I *don't* mean," she said.

"What's wrong with that?" Willis wondered, suddenly defensive.

Muriel wrinkled her nose. "*Anybody* can do that. Everybody does! When they start, they think killing an innocent child will get Lucifer's attention. It might have once, but not anymore. It's boring. Any idiot can do it. How hard is it to take and slaughter a defenseless child? What brains does that take? Know what you get when you kill a baby? A dead baby."

Street chuckled.

"It shows your desire, but no intelligence—no flair," Muriel insisted. "Everybody's killing children today because it's easy. And you know where their sweet little baby souls go? Straight to heaven. Why should Lucifer be interested in that? You won't get his attention with that junk. Come on, people, think!"

"Then how about starting a teen division of our . . . club," said Harlan Beaumont. "I'm sure we could get lots of young people, and all their energy as well."

"No, no, no!" Muriel groaned. "Why do you think there are no teenagers here already? I talk to plenty in my work. There'd be no problem convincing them . . . and that *is* the problem! These idiots will accept anything, go along with anything if it gives them an excuse to do whatever stupid thing they want to do.

"But they don't *believe*. They don't believe in anything, not even themselves. They have plenty of energy, sure, but it's flopping all over the place. It's completely dissipated." She made a fist. "He needs *concentrated* energy. Thick, heavy, powerful."

Street chuckled again. It looked like a satanic tele-thon.

"Don't you understand?" Muriel pleaded. "Remember what you came up with before! We need something special. Not things anyone could do. Think of it as an orange. We've got to squeeze *all* the juice out of it. . . ."

The pimp watched them closely. He saw their brains working. He saw their eyes moving. He realized that the one thing they wanted to avoid was responsibility.

Muriel saw it too. "Come on, my dears," she urged. "You know what I always say. 'You must take responsibility for your thoughts.' Come on, tell me. Tell me now."

They started talking, reluctantly. They each came up with horrors close to their own experiences, but none had what Muriel was looking for, what she called "verve."

They kept at it until Street could see one man in the back sit up straight. He looked as if he had taken a glance into his soul and seen a big hairy spider. The pimp put two fingers in his mouth and whistled sharply.

Everyone froze and looked at him except the man in the back. Street looked at Muriel and pointed at him. The social worker looked up and recognized the expression.

"Mr. Barker?" she said sweetly.

"I . . . I . . ." the bearded, bespectacled man stammered. "I . . . saw a news special on television the other night. It was . . . all about the country's most famous serial killers, you know? And, like, in every case, there seemed to be one girl who got away, you know? There was a girl who identified Ted Bundy, and one who described David Berkowitz, right?"

Muriel Holford's smile got broader as the overweight, balding man reluctantly continued to speak. She already knew where this was going. And she loved it.

"So I was thinking," he said, his words becoming dry and hollow, "wouldn't it be terrible if . . . if somebody purposefully stalked and killed these survivors? I mean, it was bad enough they were attacked, maybe raped, and almost killed before, but for someone else?"

Muriel just stared at him, her eyes bright. She kept looking at him, saying nothing. She smiled and smiled and smiled.

"I mean," he finally said. "If somebody else went after them. If a second killer made a point of murdering the people who got through the first time . . . It would be like one of those slasher movie sequels."

Muriel showed her teeth. She stretched her arms out. "Thank you," she said. "Thank you all so much. I cannot tell you what a thrill this is. Do you know what this means? This will do it. I feel it. This idea will actually do it. In just a few hours . . . at the very most, a few short days . . . we will have collected enough energy to power a complete transformation." She looked at them all. "You won't even have to pray anymore!"

They looked as if that was too much to hope for.

"Yes, it's absolutely true," she maintained. "We will be his children, his chosen ones. We will be his beloved and under his protection. We will be able to have anything we ever wanted, whatever we wished for." She saw their expressions. "You don't believe me? Well, you didn't believe I could cure your loved ones either. But you know that's true, don't you? You know that now."

Muriel started up the padded steps that doubled as

their seats. "Be ready," she said. "If you value your lives and your loved ones' lives, go nowhere for the next two days. Stay, wait until you hear from me. In forty-eight hours, we will come back here one last time. And then, my friends, all will be well. You will be able to go, safe and happy, into new lives."

Street watched their faces as the social worker approached him. Their fear and doubt slowly changed as they thought about their loved ones' recovery. Some might have thought it was a dream or a hallucination, but then they realized it made no difference. If it was a dream, it was a wonderful one that never ended. Muriel Holford had given them something every human desired. A supernatural system that worked. A deity that returned their calls.

The social worker stopped next to Street. She continued looking at the door while he remained watching her club minions.

"You want I should off a survivor?" he inquired mildly.

"Not off," she answered. "Take. Keep. And bring here."

"Got anybody in particular in mind?"

Muriel Holford smiled with total power. "I know just the girl. . . ."

15

It was only about twenty miles from the Broad
River Market to the back hills of Westport. Driving the Chrysler he had bought, Juan Ruiz prepared his mind-set.

The people who lived here were hedonistic scum.
Ruiz had been catering to them for the past few
weeks, so he knew whereof he spoke. The parents,
who had made the money and settled here, were
moving to Florida—leaving behind their consum-
mately spoiled children. The once traditional,
unique suburb was rapidly being taken over by
snobs, studs, and sluts.

Ruiz enjoyed the occasional vistas of green, feeling
the bile load his throat when the natural New En-
gland beauty was interrupted by squat brown corporate buildings, trashy modern mansions, and
rambling structures that looked like Victorian
houses with thyroid problems.

These fools had no idea the way real people lived,

Ruiz decided. They deserved to have their eyes opened, painfully.

So the assassin known as The Student was ready to hate everything about Melanie Merrick when he pulled into her neighborhood. He thought it looked like the kind of block you'd see on any American TV sitcom. Perfectly manicured lawns, smooth paved streets, handsome elm trees trimmed into shape, and stuccoed, shingled, two-story houses—complete with silver mailboxes set near the road.

Not much cover, he judged. Hardly important. He was here for basic reconnaissance only. The woman had already set the Northern Plan onto Sullivan. If she had had an "accident" after her husband's murder, it might have looked suspicious, but to kill her now that she had put a bug up DiCenzo's bum would only rally the troops.

At the moment, all Ruiz wanted to do was get to know his subject. He always studied each of his targets in detail. Just because she wasn't an assignment—yet—didn't mean he shouldn't start surveillance. Besides, he was going stir crazy. He wasn't used to being told to stay put.

As he put the special telescoping sunglasses on, he couldn't help thinking about why he was here. Her damn husband hadn't seemed to stay dead. Ruiz could have sworn he had seen the charred corpse of Geoffrey Merrick get up and run into the flames of the burning car.

But he knew that wasn't possible. He told his superiors nothing about it. Yet, still, they detected his new attitude. They picked up on his sudden nervousness and doubt. They had put him out to pasture to tend to the cows already in place; it was his job to control the situation here.

And he took his responsibilities seriously. Undead victim or no, Ruiz was going to make sure there

would be no trouble with Dice-Corp. He studied and
memorized the layout of the Merrick home. He saw
Geoffrey's widow was not unduly paranoid. Some
window curtains were wide enough to let him peer
through.

He saw some activity in the upstairs bedroom. He
could clearly see a phone sitting on a bed table. He
could even hear it ringing in the distance. He reminded himself to plant a listening device on the
outside wall as soon as possible. He sat straighter
behind the steering wheel as the woman came into
view.

Melanie Merrick was wearing blue jeans and a
white shirt. Although both were fairly loose, the
firmness of her form was unmistakable. Her shining
yellow hair was in a loose ponytail. Her movements
had the assurance and strength of a fit and able female.

Juan Ruiz watched her pick up the phone. He was
trying desperately to hate her. Instead new emotions disturbed him. Desire. Both to possess and im-
press her.

And even worse, pity. He suddenly felt sorry that
her husband had been killed. For a split second, he
forgot who killed him. Juan Ruiz felt a chill he hadn't
experienced since the night Geoffrey Merrick died.
It scared the hell out of him.

"Hello?"
"Melanie?"
"Yes?"
"This is Detective Wade."
Melanie's manner became brisk and professional.
"Hello, Detective. How are you?"
Wade's manner was anything but conciliatory. He
was breathless, both angry and amazed. "Listen, I'm

sorry, are you near a TV set? Have you seen the news today?"

"No. Why?"

"Damn. Turn it on. Channel Six."

"Detective . . ."

"Just do it!"

"Hold on." Melanie scrambled over the bed, still holding the phone receiver, and grabbed the re-mote-control unit. She rolled back to the phone, stood, and pointed the black box at the cyclops eye. "I got it," she said while the set warmed up. "What's going on?"

Her words faded as the image emerged. Melanie Merrick looked into a mirror.

Her face filled the screen, her head and mouth moving in slow motion.

"Oh my God . . ." she moaned.

". . . repeat, has been identified as Melanie Mer-rick, the widow of Geoffrey Robert Merrick, who was brutally murdered just a few weeks ago. . . ."

"Melanie?" Wade called into the phone.

"Shut up," she said.

". . . has become our angel of mercy, the symbol of this city's violence. Has her terrible experience led her to become a champion of the victim, or are these heinous new crimes somehow connected to the brutal slaying of her husband, who was a vice-president of the prestigious DiCenzo Corporation, otherwise known as Dice-Corp? Mrs. Merrick, though not a Manhattan resident, has been seen reg-ularly on our streets, often in the company of Cap-tain Frank Bender of Central Division. The only official word from the NYPD is a tersely stated 'No comment,' but sources close to their investigation tell us that Mrs. Merrick is indeed helping them with their inquiries. . . ."

Finally Melanie's face was replaced with Ashley

Smith's earnest features. "Meanwhile the violence continues in our fair city. Earlier today city mainte- nance workers found the remains of what appear to be three male Caucasians in an Upper West Side tenement that was scheduled for demolition. Ac- cording to medical examiners, it will be some time before positive identification can be made since the bodies were apparently eaten by both rats and wild dogs. . . ."

Melanie hit the remote control's mute button a few seconds too late. She had the graphic description of the newly found corpses rattling around her brain while she yelled at the detective.

"Why didn't they just announce my address and phone number? What do those maniacs think they're doing? What is it—they decided I haven't suffered enough? How did they find out?"

"I don't know," said Wade. "Captain Bender is chewing everyone's head off trying to find out."

"It won't help anything now."

"Have the press reached you?"

"No!"

"Good. That means our cover is still fairly water- tight. They've already called headquarters trying to get your number, which means they've called every- where else too. You wouldn't believe it. They've said they're relatives of yours, they're insurance investi- gators, even long-lost friends of your husband."

"I believe it," Melanie replied, her voice begin- ning to crack. "The question is, what are you going to do about it? I can't have these people camped out on the lawn, following me around, picking through Geoffrey's charred bones!" She choked, fighting for breath.

"Melanie, please," Wade said quickly. "Take it easy. We can get you out of there. We can put you in a safe house."

Melanie snapped back to composure. "What do you mean, 'we'? Since when does the Connecticut Police have safe houses? What are you going to do, rent a room at the Westport Inn? A corner suite overlooking the indoor pool?"

"Melanie, I'm not at the Connecticut station. I'm in New York, at Central Division. I'm assisting Captain Bender. He's got his hands full, but he's empowered me to speak on his behalf. Say the word and we'll get you out of there for as long as this thing takes."

Many thoughts raced through her mind as she held the phone. She wanted to strangle personally whoever had thrown her to the wolves. For a moment she wondered whether Bender did it himself just to get her to talk, but she decided against it. She remembered his face and manner. He wasn't that devious.

"Melanie, are you there?" Wade called. "Are you okay? Listen, no strings attached. We're probably as angry as you are about this. Just say the word and I'll drive out there personally. Just say the word."

Sudden fear pushed out any other thoughts from her head. She could imagine Ashley Smith leading her troops across the border and through the front door. She could see the Ice Pick shoving the microphone in her face.

"How did you feel when you heard your husband was brutally murdered?"

"How did you feel when you saw his charred, bent, broken body?"

"What was he like in bed?"

Melanie gripped the phone tighter, looking down at it and speaking directly into the receiver. "Okay," she said. "The word."

*   *   *

Juan Ruiz's curiosity got the better of him. Besides, he couldn't stay in the car any longer. The ceiling and doors seemed to be moving in. The dashboard seemed to press against his knees.

He moved carefully around the side of Merrick's house. It was still early enough that most of the block was either at work or shopping. Even so, he walked over as if checking the address for accuracy. Anyone watching would assume he was lost and trying to find his way.

He palmed the tiny suction cup bug in his right hand. All he had to do was place it against the base of any window and he could pick up sound vibrations from inside. It would do until he could replace it with a more sophisticated listening unit that would allow him to hear even her breathing.

Ruiz got around the side of the house and out of sight. The shrubs were well trimmed, but he could still use them as cover in the fenceless yard. He had just pressed the bug in place when he heard a car drive up. He risked a glance through the window.

The living room was clear. He could see straight into the front hall from this vantage point. And unless Melanie put her nose against the glass and looked to her far left, she wouldn't see him.

He heard the doorbell.

Melanie heard the doorbell. She checked her bedside clock while she pulled on the black zip-up jacket. Sixty-five minutes from Manhattan. Wade must've burned rubber and had the sirens going through midtown. Thank heaven he kept his Connecticut approach silent. She didn't want to alert any Channel Six stringers.

She checked her pockets. Money and credit cards. If she wanted books to read or hair dye to disguise herself, she could always ask her guards at the safe house to get it for her.

The doorbell rang again.

"Coming!" she cried and headed downstairs.

Ruiz heard someone else coming around the side of the house. He crouched behind the bush and flattened himself against the side wall. From his vantage point, Ruiz could see a tall, wiry-muscled, dark-haired woman wearing gloves. She held in her hands a thickly folded handkerchief and a small black leather sack.

Ruiz was surprised and impressed. This was either a kidnapper or a thief.

Wouldn't that be a kick: Ruiz becoming bosom buddies with Merrick's widow by saving her from a violent criminal?

He heard the doorbell ring again. There must be at least two of them. He heard Melanie yell, "Coming!"

Melanie raced down the steps as she finished putting on her jacket. "Just a minute," she called. She grabbed the front door handle, pushed down the latch, and swung the door open without looking. "Come on in, Detective," she said, heading for the kitchen. "I just have to unplug the major appliances and I'll be right with you."

She went through the bright, airy room, disconnecting the stove, microwave, blender, can opener, portable television, and radio. She had decided to let Wade off the hook. It wasn't his fault that Channel Six had dug up her identity. And, in this situation, it was better to have the cops—local, state, *and* New York City—on her side.

She came back through the dining and living

rooms. She went right past the living room window. She hurried back to the front hall.

"All set!" she said brightly, hopping into place right in front of the door.

Street Wise smiled and shot her full in the face with his water pistol.

Ruiz watched them drag the woman to the van parked all the way up the driveway. He had moved to the corner of the house, where the front and side walls met. The blond woman looked exhausted or slightly drunk. The handsome man in the suit held her around the waist. The dark-haired woman stood on her other side, gripping the blonde's arm.

Ruiz knew an abduction when he saw it. He had plenty of experience in them, both in witnessing and in carrying them out.

He was tempted to race to the rescue. Although both kidnappers looked capable, he had no doubt he could handle them. He liked the look of the guy—it might be edifying to take him on. But before he could do so, he had to answer the question "why?"

Why were they kidnapping Melanie Merrick? Were Ruiz's people supporting him in the field without either his knowledge or his permission? Very unlikely, even though he had shown hints of self-doubt. He had done too much work for them, too well, for them to double-cross him. They knew what he was capable of, at his best.

Then again, these were drug lords he was working for. Who knew what they would do once they started sampling their own product? It made them nuts enough to try the absurd and the impossible.

The Student told himself to stay out of it. If these weren't cartel operatives, he couldn't risk getting involved. If they were, it was important not to let the cartel know he was aware of their duplicity. When the boss gets stupid, it's every killer for himself.

The two kidnappers got into the van after putting the blond woman in the back. All the doors were closed. The engine was started. The vehicle rolled down the drive and drove away.

Juan Ruiz came out from cover, tossing and catching the suction bug in his hand. He wouldn't be needing it. It was time to head back to his store and relieve Sally behind the counter. The recent high school grad had a hard time making change, even with the cash register's help.

He needed to think this turn of events through completely. How would this abduction affect the Dice-Corp investigations? Was there any way the situation could be traced back to the cartel? More importantly, was he being set up as the fall guy?

Ruiz had unlocked the door of his parked car and was just about to get in when yet another vehicle drove up. The sedan pulled into the Merrick driveway and a thick, wide man in a raincoat and hat ran out. He was at the door, knocking, before the engine had even died.

Ruiz didn't wait to see any more. He got in his own car, turned on the engine, and drove away.

When she didn't answer, Detective Wade broke in. He stood in the front hall, hunched over, his fingers curled into fists.

"Melanie?"

The name echoed through the empty house.

16

Angel of Mercy, Angel of Death;
Send me to my final rest.
Angel of Heaven, Angel of Hell;
Show me to the place you dwell.
For in that place I shall lie;
Lest I wake before I die. . . .

Melanie could feel her throat tightening, even in sleep. It was the one physical movement she was aware of, as her mind was seized by the emotion of tragedy.

She felt like crying because this was her first nightmare since Geoffrey's death. The others had been his. But this one was completely her own. She was not observing this one. She was inside it.

The first tragedy was that it wasn't special. It wasn't a unique nightmare. In fact, it was one of the most prevalent. She recognized it as soon as she was hurled into it.

She was flying and falling. When she woke, she'd supply the emotional context for her takeoff and height, but the actual nightmare started in midflight. She recognized the environment. Below her was the battleground. She supposed it was the one for her life or soul. The one her dream monster fought on.

She couldn't perceive any particular skirmish, but

the gray sky was filled with dark white mist. The ground was pockmarked with craters and rubble. The sites were marked by coarse black lines that might have been barbed wire, or they might have been scars.

Melanie shot across the sky and through the clouds. At first she thought she was flying, but then she felt the tendrils of gravity pinching at her. The joy of freedom was immediately replaced by sadness and fear. She had not been flying; she had been thrown.

She began to lose altitude. Even though she tried with all her mental and physical might to stay airborne, she started to fall. It was unavoidable and inevitable. Hitting the ground held no terror for her. She knew this was a dream. It was the sense of futility and failure that tore at her.

She began to spin. The ground below twisted in her vision, as if the earth itself had become a whirlpool. She felt the diaphanous robe she was wearing begin to bunch and twist, binding her. She felt the wide sleeves snapping in the increasing air pressure, slapping her cheeks and mouth.

She fell; she dived. She lost all sense of direction or balance. The brown dirt became her sky as she flailed and kicked, her blond hair covering her face like a hood. She saw and felt dust wrapping around her, enveloping her. It seemed impossible for her not to smash into the hard rock below.

But instead of crashing into the ground, breaking into taffy pieces held together only by rent skin, she sank into the soil as if it were liquid. But rather than slowing and then floating, she kept dropping, cutting through as though she were a spike that weighed millions of tons.

She cut through dirt, mud, and rock. She cut through slag and oil. She dived farther and farther until she neared the white hot core at the center of the earth.

The light blinded Grim. He had to put his hand on the alley wall so he wouldn't lose his balance.

It wasn't like a headache. Grim didn't get headaches anymore, not in the human sense. He could scarcely differentiate that pain from the pain of his existence, which he always felt. Never not feeling it, he wasn't aware it was not natural.

He knew where the light was coming from. He knew it was not a flash, spot, or headlight pinioning him at the corner of the alley mouth. He knew it was coming from inside his head. It was his angel, trying to show him the way.

He blinked tightly, willing the blinding flash to go. It finally receded, then winked off altogether. Grim did not take his hand from the alley wall. He continued to lean, breathing deeply. He had to. For the first time in his undeath he felt nausea.

He had never felt it before, even when looking upon the crying children. He had no sense of disgust, only rage and pain. He did not know why he suddenly felt sick and confused. It couldn't come from his angel. She was his sun, his warmth. She would not, could not, bring him this.

He asked if his god was punishing him for some reason, but the deity remained silent. Grim hazarded a look across West Tenth Avenue, where the prostitutes waited under the streetlamp. They ignored him. Over the last few days, the clothes Betty had gotten him had become dirty. Not as dirty as the others, but dirty enough to make other pedestrians studiously avoid him. He had been relegated back to bum stature.

That was fine with him. As long as everyone ignored him, he could move without notice. He could observe without concern. He could watch and wait without anyone caring.

Street Wise had to come back, he thought. He had to. These women were his meal ticket. He could not afford to leave them alone on the streets for too long. They might start thinking like Betty. They might start stealing from him. They might even try to escape. The pimp had to control them. It was his life. Sooner or later he would return. And Grim would be waiting.

The light sought to lure him away from vengeance and violence. But how many more would be hurt if he did not destroy this palpable evil?

The nausea winked out. Grim stood straight, wondering if he was too tired or hungry. But this did not feel the way it had before. His dictator was not screaming shut-down instructions to his body.

Grim shook his head. He could only continue waiting and watching. If his body was going to betray him, he could only hope it was after he tore Street Wise's heart out.

The nights were getting colder. Little clouds began to form outside the women's nostrils and lips. But Grim wouldn't allow even that to happen, just in case it might give him away. He slowed his breathing so there would be no telltale puff of white coming from the shadows inside the alley.

"Behind you," said his god. The words were quiet and calm. The dictator had given Grim's deity the message, and his god had passed it on.

There was no sense of surprise or threat in the presence. It simply moved closer to Grim, without the telltale hackles studding its aura. As Grim turned, he already knew the encroaching figure meant him no harm.

It was the same sort of bent, shambling figure Grim had seen in hundreds of places throughout the city. He had seen them stumbling on the subway platforms as he searched the tunnels. He saw them nestled over street grates and against exhaust ducts on the building walls. With the coming of autumn he saw them crawl out of gutters and into the foyers of apartment buildings.

Now one was moving slowly through the alley toward him. The derelict held his tattered clothes around him. He bowed his head, perhaps so Grim couldn't see his splotched, chipped face with the beard and moustache so greasy it looked like gray-and-black plastic.

Nathan grew near and held a shaking hand out toward the creature he had made his master. "My lord," he said. He still couldn't think of anything else to call him. Following the example of almost everyone else, he used television as his inspiration and titled Grim with the most familiar epithet.

Grim stared at the shaking hand hovering in mid-air between them. The two creatures looked at each other, already communicating. The expression on Nathan's face told Grim almost all he needed to know. Street Wise would not be coming back here, not tonight. The nausea had been a sign. The worst had happened.

Grim remembered well the slaughter of his homeless worshipers at the hands of Jeremy Bancroft. He wanted no more of that on his conscience, so he had sent his army to protect the angel, while he intended to capture the murderer of Betty.

They had done their job well, while he had not. The dozens of them stumbled and begged throughout the day, then searched, fed, gathered, and slept at night. Their eyes and ears were everywhere. Their minds were limited but fanatical. Nathan needed to tell only a few the descriptions of the woman, and they all knew. He needed to ask only a few about the pimp before descriptions of times and places came back to him.

Grim looked at Nathan with his wet black eyes. His top lip pulled back off his teeth. "Where?" he said.

Melanie awoke in pain. She lay where they had put her, on the thick, wide, solidly built bed in the small room upstairs. The one window looked out on the wall of the neighbor's house—but was now shuttered and had its shade drawn and curtains closed.

They had taken everything but the bed out of the room. There was no end table, lamp, or bureau. There were no chairs. There was a light fixture on the ceiling, but it was off. The only light came from the hallway.

The door had been closed, and no doubt locked. It was now open, and she squinted to see a silhouette framed in the doorway.

Melanie tried to speak, but the packing in her mouth and duct tape sealing her lips prevented anything but muffled mush from emerging. She tried to sit up or turn toward the figure, but that was also difficult. They had put handcuffs tightly around her wrists behind her, then also cuffed her arms just above the elbows. It was amazing how much that second pair of cuffs restricted her.

Another pair of steel cuffs bound her ankles, and the man had taped a pair of white shoes with four-inch-high heels to her feet.

"Try running in those," he had commented. "Try walking. Try even standing for a few minutes."

He was standing in front of her now. His head was down, and his hands were at his sides. He looked at her the way panthers look at deers. Melanie was astonished he hadn't already done something to her.

"Don't worry," he said, in a tone that told her just

the opposite. "I won't touch you. Under strict instructions. 'Don't touch.' You have to be, in common vernacular, untouched. Didn't say anything about looking, however. So I'll just stand here and look until I can figure a way around the instructions. . . ."

Melanie had awakened several times on the trip in. She never actually fell asleep, but the liquid tranquilizer disconnected her brain from her body. Each time the haze cleared, her eyelids fluttered, she groaned and tried to get up, but they splashed her with the liquid again.

The last time she regained consciousness, she was in the room, on the bed, and he was taping the high heels on her feet. She didn't know where she was or who her kidnappers were, but she remained quiet. If her dream monster's nightmares were any judge, they were sadists and murderers.

She had lain back, thought of her monster, and prayed for sleep.

Heaven had finally smiled. Her prayer was answered. Street Wise's prayers were not. Now he stood in the doorway, trying hard not to believe.

"Untouched," he said. "I wonder how that is defined. Not handled?" He took a step into the room. "Not explored?" He took another step. "Does that refer to just me, or anyone, before or after this moment?" He took another step, and another. "That is, if you have already been 'touched' in that use of the word, does that deny any subsequent touching?" He was beside the bed now, looking her up and down. "Or," he said, with a smile, "does it mean 'left in an intact state or condition'? Not damaged or injured? Not altered, treated, or influenced?"

He began to move his hand over her, sculpting her shape in the air. He brought his fingers just a few millimeters away from her, letting his palm hover

over her stomach and chest, as she tried not to breathe too deeply. She stayed as motionless as she possibly could.

"Who would know?" he said quietly. "That's the question. You couldn't tell anyone, even if we let you speak again. Who would believe you? You would say anything to get me in trouble, and I'm sure I lie a lot better than you. I've had a lifetime of practice."

He kept his hand over her chest, letting it rise and fall just below his skin. "Well, so has any beautiful woman," he reasoned. "Naturally you learn to lie at an early age since men act so stupidly so quickly. 'I don't mind,' you say. 'Not at all,' you say. 'Of course I don't hate you, don't think you're stupid, don't think you're ugly, don't think you're too fat, too thin, too short, too tall, too poor, too rich.'" Street Wise looked into her blue eyes. "Oh, I'm sorry. We're never too rich, are we?"

She thought he'd strike her then. Instead, he stood straight, his hand returning to his side. "Who would know?" he asked quietly. "Who would, really?"

Melanie watched as he struggled with something. She saw his expression go from pensive to concerned to disbelieving to nothing.

"They're all fools," he finally said. "She tricked them all. They believe what they need to believe. I've seen nothing. No miracles ever happened to me. There is no one watching. No one cares."

He leaned over and started to undo the buttons on her shirt.

Melanie tried to turn away, but he rolled her back, placed his hand inside her shirt—just over her breasts—and pushed down. With his free hand he undid the rest of her buttons, down to her waist. She kicked and heaved and tried to shout, but he anchored her onto her bound, aching arms.

"I've had plenty of practice at this as well," he said

calmly. "Don't worry. I am not going to undo your legs. I'm not that stupid. Think of me as a blind man. I only want to memorize you as they would." He pulled the shirttail out of her jeans and undid the remaining buttons. He put his anchoring hand on her solar plexus and pushed once, hard.

He knocked the wind out of her. She almost sat up, her face reddening. The gag puffed and sweat beads dabbled her forehead. He pushed her back down and neatly unbuttoned her denims. He carefully took the zipper between his thumb and forefinger.

He pulled it just as the door downstairs exploded inward.

Street Wise was beside the bed as if yanked by a spring in the back of his head. Melanie saw the blood drop out of his face. His eyes were bulging and his mouth was hanging open.

"No," she heard him say, just before he ran to the room's door. "Must be Muriel . . ."

The pimp stepped into the hallway in time to see a figure race up the stairway, his back to him. Street Wise instantly knew it wasn't the social worker.

It felt as if pins were being pushed through every one of his pores from the inside. He had touched the girl and there was an answer. At least there was that, wasn't there? At least now he knew. All his fears were valid. There *were* greater powers.

The hallway light was dim, and in the pale yellow light, Street saw the figure reach the top of the stairs and turn toward him.

"God," said the pimp. Realizing what he had uttered, he quickly backed away, pointing. "You, I mean. You're my god."

They stared at each other. When nothing happened, the pimp rediscovered his voice after a moment.

"You must know that," he pleaded. "I never

doubted . . . no, that's not true . . . I doubted, but
you know I followed you . . . your teachings, your
desires. I wouldn't have changed, even if He had
responded. That's the truth. You must know that!"

Street had backed all the way to the wall. He
pushed himself against it. The man with the chewed,
horrible face took a step toward him.

"She's all right!" Street insisted. "I didn't touch
her. Not in that way. I only touched the skin above
her chest. I swear! You must have seen . . . you
know, right? What are you going to do? What are you
going to do to me?" By the final word he was
screeching.

Grim got within two feet and tried to push his fist
through the man's face.

Street Wise was best at one thing: survival. From
the moment he was born, his brain was trained for it.
His will to survive overrode any emotion he had.
From the moment the monster attacked, the vicious
pimp's *own* dictator took over. He yanked his head
to the left, shrieking. Grim's fist went into the handsome, sedate wallpaper and the plaster behind it.

Grim's knee shot up as Street dropped. But the
pimp had already protected himself, with one hand
cupping his genitals and the other pushing on the
knee. That was also instinctive. Always after a failed
punch, the knee is the next thing any street fighter
would use. It was what the pimp would have done.

Street Wise fell to his left, rolled, and came up on
his feet, running. He charged for Muriel's bedroom,
at the end of the hall. Grim went right after him.

The pimp touched the doorknob and felt a shock.
The electricity filled his entire body. In that one split
second, Street Wise stood in eternity. In the blink of
an eye, he saw all time and space. He stood in the
center of the universe and looked into the eye of the
serpent.

"I will protect you," it said.

Strength and certainty filled him. Then he was back in the darkened hall, panic powering his muscles.

The pimp almost turned the doorknob as he slammed against the thick wood obstruction, forcing it open. Just inside was an oak entertainment console, facing the bed on the left wall. Street pulled it down as he passed, trying to hit Grim with it.

The television, VCR, and tape players crashed on the carpet as Grim froze just inside the doorway, then leaped at Street over the fallen furniture. The pimp was too fast, too scared, and too slippery even then. He dodged, leaped onto the bed, bounced, and bounded to the top of the bureau.

He kept his head down so he wouldn't hit the ceiling, then jumped for the hall doorway again. Grim was already twisting his own body and using the very base of the mattress for a trampoline. He dived through the air, almost slamming into the right bedpost.

His fingers just grabbed the hem of Street's suit jacket. The pimp's dive was cut off in midflight and the two went crashing to the floor, shaking the house.

Street screamed, sprang up, and tore his jacket free—sending himself into Muriel's bathroom. He landed on the marble sink counter, his back smashing the mirror. All he saw was Grim leaping after him, his arms out.

Street kicked the bathroom door closed, but Grim's body slammed it back open. Street grabbed a handful of whatever was next to him, ignoring the sudden pain, and hurled it at the oncoming creature.

Makeup, perfume, and broken reflective glass smashed into Grim's face. The powder, stinging liquid, and biting glass made a cloud around the creature's head.

Street slid off the counter and planted a side kick directly into Grim's stomach. The creature slammed back into the bathroom door, which had finally closed. The force of the blow splintered it, but Grim didn't break through. Instead he bounced back into Street's fists.

Street slammed his right fist into what was left of Grim's nose. He shot his left into Grim's jaw. Grim's head shook, eyes still blinded.

"Go down, idiot!" screamed his god. His dictator, however, was unimpressed.

Street put both his fists together and swung them at the side of Grim's head. Finally Grim ducked, the strike just missing him. He grabbed the pimp around the waist and pushed him into the closed door. The splinter grew larger but still didn't break.

Street Wise came back, clawing, punching, and kicking. Grim couldn't get his footing on the slippery broken glass.

The kicks were ineffectual, but one punch pushed against Grim's ear. He stumbled to the side, his legs going out from under him. His hand went into the toilet. He rolled away, falling backward into the tub.

Street planted a foot in Grim's stomach. He tromped on the creature's torso. He grabbed the hot water spigot and turned it on full.

A torrent of water smashed into Grim's face. Of course it was cold . . . but only for five seconds.

Street Wise got both feet into the tub. He jumped up and down savagely on the flailing figure trapped there.

"You're not him!" the pimp screeched at him. "You're not him! Come on, look at this, you fucker! How about this?"

Grim felt the water heat up. He felt the torrent of

liquid almost scald his face. Only then did he reach
up and pull the button over the faucet.

The steaming hot water blasted into Street's face
from the shower massager.

It was like a fist that sent him back, out of the tub.
Grim erupted from the water, leaping with both feet
aimed for the pimp's spine.

Street grabbed the side of the door and pulled
himself away. The feet hit him in the hip, causing
Grim to crash into the towel rack. Street got hold of
the bathroom doorknob, yanked open the cracked
door, and tried to crush Grim between it and the
wall.

Grim erupted through the crack, his fist shooting
for Street's nose.

Street dodged again, the knuckles grazing his ear.
He was already moving, back out into the hall. Grim
grabbed for his hair, his suit, and finally his feet.

He just managed to get his hand on one shoe. The
pimp stumbled. Grim was immediately on the man's
back, trying to bring him down. Once he had him on
the floor, he would smash the snake until poison ran
out of every orifice.

For a moment Grim was blinded by the memory
of the crying children. Street chose that moment to
do the unexpected.

Springing up from all fours, he propelled both of
them to the left, over the hallway banister, down
onto the stairway.

Grim landed on his back, Street Wise on top of
him. Both of them toppled forward. As long as Grim
held on, Street used him like a turtle shell. He
twisted his body this way and that, smashing Grim
into the wall, the banister, and the steps.

"Let go!" Grim's god shouted.

Grim soared off the pimp and slammed onto the

teakwood floor between the living room and the dining room.

The image of Street landing square on his back with both feet was fresh in Grim's mind. It seemed as if his god's and dictator's voices mingled as one, but his own inner voice was still the loudest.

"Get out of the way!"

He spun over, ready to catch Street Wise between the legs, in the stomach, or in the throat.

The pimp was not there. There was no one on the stairs. Grim was alone in the front hall.

He saw his angel in his mind, falling, her wings in flames.

He vaulted to his feet and raced up the steps a second time. He was fast but mindful. He knew Street Wise could be anywhere, doing anything.

The hall light was off. The door to the other bathroom at the end of the hall was closed. The guest room door was open. Light from it spilled into the hall. Inside Grim could see the figure on the bed.

He vaulted over the banister and landed in front of the door. He recognized his angel. The ceiling fixture splashed his face with white light. He could see the recognition and agony in her eyes as well. He saw the pimp, standing on the other side of the bed, holding a strange gun to her head.

It was rose colored and it gleamed. It was unlike any weapon he had ever seen or his god had ever shown him.

Melanie tried to talk to him through the gag. She tried to "think" things at him. She silently begged Street Wise to knock her out . . . so she could dream again. Dream and warn him.

Grim stood in the doorway. He appreciated that she was trying to talk to him. He knew she would never simply babble apologies or inane orders to save himself. He knew she was trying to tell him something specific. But all he knew for sure was that she had a gun at her head. And leaving would not save or help her.

"Come on," grunted Street, obviously in pain. "This the best you can do?" He grimaced, then stood straight, ignoring his aches and bruises. "You wanted her untouched, right? That's what my old lady said. She had to be untouched or you wouldn't take her." He smiled . . . grimly.

"But you're not the one, are you? You're not the grand Pooh-Bah, the big cheese, the head honcho, are you?" He looked the creature up and down with disgust. "You're just an errand boy, aren't you? Strictly lower-class stock. What's going on? You trying to earn your horns?"

He shoved the gun barrel tighter against Melanie's head. "What are you waiting for?" he demanded. "Want to grab her soul before she's offed? Or will her lily-white spirit go in the wrong direction for you? Come on, you stupid zombie, get your dead ass in here."

Grim stepped inside. Street smiled and crooked a finger at him. "Closer, cretin. She won't bite." Melanie groaned, her head sinking to the pillow. Grim finally stood at the near end of the wide bed, looking down at his angel.

No wings. No halo. When he had seen her in the flesh the last time he had actually thought she had merely landed to show him where the evil he wanted to stop was. He had imagined she had then spread her wings, leaving the immemorial world behind.

But now she was captured, in flesh. Like him.

Unlike him, she might actually be human.

She searched his face for any sign. She had called the name before. She called it again, even through the gag.

"Geoffrey?"

No answer.

Only Grim heard his god cry.

"Greater powers," Street Wise scoffed. "You couldn't even beat me."

He lifted the water pistol and shot it into Grim's face.

For the next three minutes, Street Wise alternately sprayed him and beat him until he finally lay motionless on the guest bedroom floor.

17

When Grim awoke, Betty was by his side again.

Street Wise had wanted to blow the creature's brains out as soon as he was helpless on the guest bedroom floor, but Muriel never allowed him to bring anything but the water pistol into her house. He argued until he was red in the mouth, but Muriel had remained serene and always said the same thing.

"Lucifer will watch over us."

Street Wise thought about getting some knives from the kitchen and plunging them into the creature's head. He wondered what would happen to a demon who died twice. Where would he go then? Was there a hell for hell?

But finally he realized the body would have to be moved before he could dissect the creature. Muriel would not appreciate his goring up the guest room (the upstairs was already destroyed enough), nor should he leave any evidence that might tie the social worker to his activities.

Street knew he was the rational, practical one. Despite Muriel's insistence that tonight all would be changed, he had been hearing penny-ante prophets all his life. Each one had set a date for the apocalypse and each day had come and gone. Like the others, Muriel would probably go back and recalculate.

In the meantime, Street decided to do the dirty someplace else. Of all the locations possible, the pimp could think of only one truly suitable. But he had to hurry. It would be dawn soon, and with it would come the cleansing.

The creature was muscular and his skin was tough, but his limp body wasn't particularly heavy. And the pimp wasn't particularly careful with it. He dragged it to the top of the stairs and let it fall down under its own power.

From the front hall, Street dragged it to the back door. Quickly he ran back upstairs, taped Melanie's bound feet to the bed's baseboard, ran down to his van, and drove it all the way up the driveway. Getting the creature from the kitchen to the front seat took ten seconds.

Getting from the house to the sewer entrance took ten minutes. He figured he was truly blessed since the lights were with him, and the Henry Hudson Bridge was fairly clear. Shafts of sunlight were just beginning to be visible on the horizon as Street pulled his van into a parking space near Two Hundred and Fifth Street.

Here the road was wide, the sidewalk narrow, and the wall around the Broadway–Dyckman Park low. Street stood beside the driver's door and inhaled deeply. The early-morning air was crisp and cool. The pimp was invigorated.

He checked both ways, seeing no one down the

long boulevard. Here the stoplights regulated the flow of traffic in easily discernible rhythms. There would be thirty seconds of vehicular activity, followed by thirty seconds of empty silence.

In the motionless moments, Street Wise got his "drunk" friend out of the passenger seat. The pimp was thankful he hadn't stirred, though he would have simply doused the creature's head with liquid trank again.

Street dumped Grim over the low wall, then hopped after him. They landed near a small circular section cut out of the ground, just inside the small park. Street pulled a small crowbar from his jacket pocket and jammed the end into one of the holes in the thick metal lid in the center of the circle.

He pried off the manhole cover, lifted the creature, held him over the hole, and let go. Grim dropped twelve feet, landing on a concrete walkway beside the sewer canal. He collapsed like a rag doll, on his side, his flopping arms luckily cushioning his head.

Street climbed down the ladder set in the wall—careful to pull the lid closed after him. Once he was beside his enemy, he grabbed one ankle and dragged the creature to his "room."

Grim awoke and looked into the eye of the woman he had been searching for. Her other eye was a torn, drooling socket. Once she was dead, the starving, trapped rats had used her for sustenance. One had even accidentally punctured her left eye.

She sat on the steel mesh floor, her legs bent, her arms wide. She seemed to be smiling because of the way the rats had gnawed at her lips. Her smile was like Grim's now.

Her clothes were soaked and torn. In the holes Grim could see where the rats had feasted on her arms, stomach, and legs. Part of her face was missing.

Her earlobes had been gnawed. She was no more than two feet from the man who had once saved her.

He quickly pulled his head forward as something crashed into the mesh behind him.

"Hey!" said Street Wise. He was punching the steel ball where Grim's head had been. "Hey, aren't you going to scream? Shout? Even say hello?" The pimp had to cover his nose with the scented handkerchief in his breast pocket just to get close enough.

He stood beside the chained-down prison, shaking his head in mock disappointment. "No one's shocked by anything anymore," he complained. "First a priest rapes a nun without a whimper, now you wake up next to a dream girl and don't even tip your hat. What's the world coming to?"

He checked his watch, then quickly scrambled back onto the walkway. He surveyed the scene while carefully replacing the handkerchief in the breast pocket of his suit.

"Damn," he said. "I wanted the rats to chew on you while you slept, but it appears you stink worse than them. Or maybe it's professional courtesy. No matter. Say hello to your boss for me." He turned and walked back toward the ladder. "Unless I see him first." He laughed and started climbing.

Grim watched him go. He waited until he had disappeared. He listened until he heard the manhole cover get scraped aside, then slide back into place. Only then did he turn back toward Betty. The rats had clawed their way beside and behind her. As usual, they wanted nothing to do with him. The death stench of their brethren was still on his hands and feet.

"Keys," said his god.

Grim saw the silver metal hooks hanging around the vermin's necks. When he reached toward them, they scattered, but there were a few that lay motion-

less on the mesh grating—their tiny mouths open
and airless. Grim took one by the tail and held it up
to his face.

It dripped as it hung there.

"Drowned," said his god.

Grim tried the key around the dead rat's neck in
the lock affixing the small steel mesh door. It didn't
work. He looked back at the other scurrying animals.
He couldn't afford to be confused. So he jammed the
key into the mesh above his head.

The dead rat hung there. Grim reached for another.

Nathan waited until the van drove away. Then he
cautiously came out from behind the tree and made
his way over to the manhole cover.

He had told his master where the pimp was hiding. One of the worshipers had seen Street Wise
going in and out of the house before. Nathan had
told the man to find a place to lie nearby. When the
worshiper had seen Street help Grim's angel into the
house, he sent word.

Nathan had tried to follow his master, but his king
had gone too quickly. The derelict had little choice
but to follow far behind. He had been crossing the
park when he saw the lone van going the other way.
Nathan was afraid it was the one the worshiper had
described. His fears were justified.

"My lord?" he called. He looked both ways, then
tried again, a little louder. There was no answer.
Nathan put his raw, cracked fingers into the manhole cover and tried lifting. He could hardly budge
it. He tried again. It made a small scraping sound,
then settled even deeper into the hole.

Nathan pulled with all his might, his back straight-
ening. Arm muscles he hadn't used in years
stretched and groaned. Nathan didn't rest. He just

kept pulling and pulling until he could feel the manhole cover begin to give.

Just then he felt a powerful kick in his side.

Nathan fell, propelled by the sudden, vicious attack. He hit the rocky ground on his back and slid a few inches. He stared through the brown mist at the man who towered above him.

"You're about as inconspicuous as a cockroach on a cake," Street Wise sneered, kicking him again. "You didn't think I saw you hiding behind that tree? What the fuck's going on, old man?"

Nathan cringed, trying to recover from the pain. He had curled up on his side. He knew he had to do something. The next kick would be in the head or between the legs.

"My master . . ." he grunted, trying to get to his knees, trying to crawl toward the manhole.

Street Wise kicked him down, in the shoulder (as Nathan had hoped). "What are you talking about, you old bastard? That . . . demon . . . is your master?" The pimp actually looked fearful for a moment. "Who are you?"

"I am . . . his friend," Nathan said with more pride than he intended. The pimp considered it, then smirked.

"A follower, huh? This guy must be real low-grade if you're the only one following him. Just another cultist gone to seed." He kicked at Nathan again, catching him in the chest. "Like Igor or something. Nothing. Nobody."

Nathan fell on his back, his hands held pleadingly in front of him. "Yes, yes," he gasped. "No more, please. What . . . what did you do to him?"

"Sent him to my room," Street said absently. He suddenly remembered Muriel's instructions.

"I am going away to prepare," she had said. "Make sure the girl is not harmed. She has to remain untouched and undrugged for the ceremony. We'll need someone else, but we can pick a least likely suspect from one of our club members. . . ."

But if they needed all the energy they could muster, it wouldn't be wise to waste one of their own people. Street Wise looked at Nathan in a whole new light.

Nathan recognized the expression. He already knew this man had taken the angel and trapped his master. He would do anything to hurt King Grim.

The pimp smiled, putting his hand out. With his other, he reached into his pocket for the water pistol. "Sorry about that, old man. I think I made a mistake. Here, let me help you up—"

Nathan leaped off the ground and slammed into the pimp. He swung his fists at Street Wise's head, his legs kicking feebly. When his fingers only bounced off the pimp's skull, the derelict tried to scratch.

Street was surprised by the attack, but only for a second. The old man's punches had no strength and his kicks no power or precision. It was like a cripple having a fit on top of you. He swept the derelict's arms aside and chopped down.

Nathan fell on all fours. He heard Street Wise laughing. He leaped up and tried again. The pimp explosively pushed him away.

"Hey, man!" he exclaimed. "Watch the suit."

Nathan charged again. Street just pivoted and tripped him. The pimp laughed again. "Hey, old man, nice one."

The derelict was on his feet, trying to grab him. Street batted the arms away, his expression darkening. "Hey, hey, hey, take it easy, you old bastard. Watch the fucking wardrobe, will you?"

Nathan managed to hook one chipped fingernail under Street's lip. When the pimp shoved him away, the nail tore the soft underside, drawing blood.

The two men stood three feet from each other. Nathan was gasping for breath. Street's shoulders were hunched as he gingerly touched his lower lip. He saw a small red smear on his index finger. He looked sharply up at Nathan.

"You miserable bastard," he said. He stepped forward and slammed his fist into the center of Nathan's jaw.

The derelict went down, but Street wouldn't let him lie. He was already above him, his fingers twisted in the bum's lapels, dragging him upright.

"You could have AIDS or something!" the pimp squealed, and hit him again. The roundhouse right sent Nathan into the park wall. Street still wouldn't let him lie. He kicked him in the side twice more as Nathan tried to stand and face him.

Street looked the blank-faced derelict straight in the eye, hauled off, and slammed his fist into Nathan's nose. The derelict somersaulted backward, over the low wall, and crashed on the sidewalk face first.

Nathan lay on his elbows. He could hear the pimp sucking in breath from the other side of the wall. He could hear the roar in his own ears. He waited until the swirls and starbursts disappeared from his vision.

He looked down to see a crimson sun exploding on the sidewalk. It was a fat circle of scarlet, already soaking into the grit-covered concrete. Nathan watched it merge and mutate until he knew that no amount of water, soap, or scrubbing could remove all traces of it from the sidewalk.

Nathan watched as a red planet appeared in orbit near the sun. Then a crimson moon. Then the gray sky was flecked with ruby stars. Nathan felt the blood pouring out of his nose. He heard the pimp scramble over the low wall. He felt hands gripping the soiled clothes along his back.

Nathan knew what was going to happen next. The pimp was going to drag him away, throw him in the van, and drive to where he kept the angel. Once there, he would discover how the pimp planned to kill him.

Nathan was right. But before that could happen, the derelict did two things. He stared intently at the galaxy of blood he had created on the sidewalk. And he smiled . . . the rust-colored liquid staining his chipped yellow teeth.

It was seven o'clock in the morning. The streets were filling with pedestrians, cars, vans, buses, and trucks. Beneath the street, the rats were hanging from the steel mesh ceiling, rocking gently as Betty's one dead eye watched them. She smiled and smiled and smiled.

Grim just kept reaching for the others as they desperately tried to escape. He was almost as fast as they were, however. He grabbed their bodies, pulled them up, twisted their little heads until their spines snapped, then tried the key in the lock.

When it didn't work, he hung them from the ceiling so he wouldn't try the same key twice.

Sometimes the terrified rodents would turn and try to bite him. Sometimes they were successful. Grim ignored the bleeding and just kept twisting their heads off and trying the keys.

"Plague," his god warned.

"Suggestions?" Grim silently replied.

His god said no more.

Grim stopped. He looked up. The dead rats had begun to ripple. They started to wave like a really perverse wind chime. Grim looked over his shoulder. There was a wind coming through the tunnel. It riffled his long, dirty hair. He felt it on his face and across his body. He heard the distant roar.

He turned back and kept grabbing the rats, twisting their necks faster. He kept grabbing, twisting, trying the key, and hanging them faster and faster until the first drops of water dotted the back of his neck. He kept grabbing, twisting, and hanging them as he heard the water rumbling closer and closer, louder and louder.

He kept killing the rats until the tunnel started to shake and he could no longer aim properly. He waited until the water crashed into the curve of the tunnel the mesh ball sat in. Then he leaped onto Betty, pressing himself beside her.

The water slammed into the ball, trying to hurl it down the tunnel. As it had hundreds of times before, the chain affixing it to the tunnel floor held. The cage was pulled into midair and hung there, shaking in the torrent.

Grim stepped on Betty's torso, keeping her from floating to the top. There was only enough room for his head between the water's surface and the steel ceiling. He broke the surface amid another dozen rats, all clawing to stay alive. Grim stared into the face of one, already trying to gnaw his lip and nostril.

Some of the dead rats had been knocked loose. They floated on the water's surface like a furry oil slick. But many still hung there, bouncing off their swimming brethren or hitting Grim's head.

Grim took a deep breath and submerged. He held himself down with his arms. He looked up, looking for the tiny swimming arms and legs of the remaining vermin.

Grim pulled at their tails with one hand, dragging them under the water. He snapped their necks and pulled off the keys. He kept doing it, killing them and putting the keys on his wrist by the collars Street Wise had fashioned. He kept himself amused with his god's warnings.

"There might be no key that works," he heard. "It might be another example of the pimp's sadism."

Fine, Grim thought. He accepted that. And kept pulling, twisting, and collecting the remaining keys.

Ten blocks away, where the Harlem and Hudson rivers met, two city workers opened the second sluice gate.

18

Muriel Holford swept into her home, only momentarily concerned by the condition of the front door. She closed it as best she could. It would never be locked again. Still holding on to the packages she carried, Muriel went immediately to the spare bedroom. She clicked on the overhead light.

Seeing her guest still carefully secured (with the buttons of her shirt and jeans done back up), all the tenseness went out of Muriel's shoulders. Her lips formed a wide, tranquil smile. "What on earth happened here?" she asked, putting the two bag-wrapped boxes on the floor.

She went to the other side of the bed, sat next to Melanie, and started pulling the thick, sticky tape from her lips. "My dear," she admonished, "you've been crying. Whatever for? What did you see?"

Melanie couldn't help gasping when she was finally able to get breath. The metal handcuffs were

still completely unyielding, and the way her elbows
were pulled back made it difficult to lie, sit up, or
even breathe. Her arms were all but dead to her.
Her legs had been slightly raised when Street Wise
had tied them to the baseboard, so those limbs were
tingling as well.

"The creature," she gasped. "A . . . wraith came
here."

"A wraith? Whatever are you talking about,
dear?"

"A monster," said Melanie painfully. "A demon in
human form. He broke in the door, came up here!"
She was surprised and impressed by Muriel's reaction. The middle-aged woman watched her carefully, with the same placid expression. "If you don't
believe me," Melanie exclaimed, "look at the room
down the hall!"

Muriel's eyes flickered in that direction only momentarily. "Where's the young man who was watching you?"

"Gone," said Melanie, looking away.

Muriel grabbed the blonde's chin and pulled her
face back. She didn't want to lose eye contact. "What
do you mean?"

"The creature took him away," Melanie lied.

Muriel smiled without humor, released Melanie's
chin, and got up. "Well, we'll just wait for one of
them to return, won't we?" She went over to the
packages.

"You don't believe me?" Melanie asked incredulously, trying to sit up—despite the cuffs. The pain
lanced up both arms and across her shoulders. Sweat
reappeared on her forehead.

"Need you ask?" Muriel answered pleasantly.
"This house is protected by Satan, my dear. If anything, our friend Mr. Wise had to take care of some
personal problem on my property." She pulled out

one long, rectangular, white box from a shopping bag. "That is the more accurate description, isn't it?"

Melanie's expression told the social worker almost all she needed to know. She came back to the near side of the bed, laying the box beside Melanie.

"You're special, my dear," she told the blonde. "I know that. I can see that. You know more than you're telling. Perhaps a lot more." She waved a hand. "No matter. I have my own plans for you, that will not encroach upon your knowledge. If anything, your suffering will only enhance my triumph."

"What are you talking about?" Melanie demanded.

"You see?" Muriel replied. "Any other woman would be begging for her life—if she could talk at all. Most would be trying to gather the air and courage to scream. But not you. You ask questions. You tell stories. You still have the strength to think. You are indeed special. I'm glad. That makes me very happy."

The woman opened the box and pulled out a beautiful white dress.

It was satin, trimmed in lace, decorated with white pearls. It had a deep V neck and a long skirt made almost entirely of lace. The satin bodice was joined to the skirt just above the hip in a zigzag pattern. It was a wedding dress.

"This," Muriel said, "is for you. It will fit perfectly. I know. My eyes have never failed me."

Melanie was astonished. Her middle-aged captor behaved rationally. Only her actions were insane. "You . . . you want me to marry that young man?"

Muriel's laughter was girlish and heartfelt. She laid the wedding dress beside the blonde and leaned over her. "No, my dear, of course not. This is where you will need all your strength, to understand. You will not be Mrs. Wise. You are to be a bride of Lucifer."

Melanie was dumbstruck. Even after what she had been through, she could only begin to accept the statement.

"You see?" said Muriel, standing by the headboard. "You need your intelligence simply to comprehend it. It's simple. I intend to bring the Devil to Earth in human form."

Melanie lay back, looking at the ceiling. She bit her lower lip. When she spoke, her voice was sad. "And to do that, you have to kill me."

Muriel shook her head. "That's up to him."

Now Melanie laughed, bitterly. "Your friend? The man who was guarding me?"

"No, no, no," Muriel fussed. "Satan."

"Stop," said Melanie. "You don't honestly believe that, do you? You can't! The Devil? Tell the truth. If you're going to kill me, or torture me, or whatever, at least tell the truth. *You* decide what happens to me. Maybe you're trying to do it in Lucifer's name, but you, or your 'Mr. Wise,' are going to decide."

The social worker shook her head sadly, looking at the floor. "The more things change," she said, "the more they stay the same. Lucifer still requires, and deserves, ecstasy. Unlike those who would submerge their lust, he craves it. He understands the hormonal, genetic effect of a gorgeous woman. He knows and enjoys the power of sex."

"Stop it!" Melanie gasped. "If I'm raped, if I'm sacrificed, you'll make that decision. You! Admit it!"

Muriel looked at the girl with smug pity. "Just like the others. Just like Mr. Wise, in fact. So strong, but willing to believe nothing unless you see it. That is understandable. That is why you will be his slave." The social worker sat on the bed, by Melanie's head, and brought her face in close.

"But remember what you have seen, my dear. Manhattan's greatest mass murderer tried to kill you. You were involved in the violence at the crib. I know. I saw you on the news. And now, you say a monster came in here. You believe *that*, don't you? You've seen the sons, and daughters, of Satan, haven't you? So why don't you believe in the Devil himself?"

She gripped Melanie by the chin, making her look deep into her eyes. "Think of the evil you've already seen, my dear. Think of the evil you have felt. Take responsibility for your own thoughts!"

Melanie studied the plain woman's composed, seemingly benign face for any hint of fanaticism or insanity. She saw only calm, quiet, total belief.

Muriel got up and took the wedding dress carefully by the shoulders. She walked over to the opposite wall and opened a small closet. "It is forgivable, I suppose," she said absently. "In fact, it is entirely logical. Satan is not of this world. He is not even of this physical plane. It is little wonder that humans are unwilling to give him substance. And I mean that in both the literal and figurative sense."

She carefully hung up the wedding dress. "They cannot comprehend him, so they don't." She closed the door and faced the bed. "But Lucifer *does* exist, my dear. And you *will* be his bride."

Using most of her remaining strength, Melanie hauled her torso up. She groaned loudly, smacking her back against the headboard so she could face her captor. "So," she said. "What are you doing? Following a menu? What is this, some sort of prophecy handed down in your family for generations?"

Muriel smiled. "Good," she said. "I'm glad you're getting into the spirit of the thing." She reapproached the bed. "No, of course not. What are prophecies but human fears written down? All prophecies eventually come true because they're written that way. They are designed to fit any disaster that comes up."

She stood at the end of the bed, both her hands on the baseboard. "We make them come true," she continued. "No, what I'm doing is a matter of common sense. This is a matter of fulfilling my own destiny as a human being. This is a matter of knowing all human fears and finding the truth inside them. The gate to hell is different in every country, but it is always there. In China, it is three doors. In Italy, it's a crack in the wall." Muriel became thoughtful. "Who writes those prophecies, anyway?"

"So which one do you have?" Melanie asked sarcastically. "A sewer grate? How will you prepare the way? Click your heels three times and say, 'There's no place like hell'?"

Muriel burst out laughing, holding on to the bedpost. "Boy, you think you're one tough broad, don't you? You think that after everything you've seen, nothing can scare you, right?" The social worker became very still. "But I've got news for you, my dear. Even you haven't accepted the power of your own mind. You're still scared of that, aren't you? You're still scared of the truth."

"What truth?" Melanie retorted, fighting down the fear that stirred her stomach. "Whose truth?"

"Your own truth," Muriel said intently. "Whatever you're hiding. Whatever you're afraid of. Whatever you won't admit to yourself. It's just the human way of avoiding the acceptance of their own power. The power of their own minds." Muriel pointed at her forehead, then opened her arms as if to embrace the world.

"Every prophecy comes true because we make them come true. Every prophecy comes true because they are powered by the human mind. They come from our deepest thoughts. The ones that harness, channel, but do not control the power that is all around us, waiting to be tapped."

The social worker came quickly around the bed and put her arms on either side of Melanie's head. "But I will control that power," she promised. "If even for a second. I will control it—and build a bridge for Lucifer to cross."

Melanie grinned and cocked her head. "You were doing good until the bridge part," she said. "Everything was going great until you dragged Satan into this."

Muriel stood up. "Still don't believe, eh? Well, that is all right. You don't have to. It will happen, with or without your belief."

Melanie shrugged. "Fine. I hope it does. The way I look at it, I'm set. I'm the bride. My only worry is if you don't succeed. That's when you'll take it out on me."

Only then did it look as though Muriel would strike the captive. Instead she controlled herself and stood by the bed. "Stupid girl. You're just the flame. You will be just another fire to attract the Devil's attention. We are the lamp, you are the lure. All we need now is someone to create from."

"What?"

"I told you, stupid girl. Satan is from the spiritual world. He cannot rule this one unless he is made material. For that, we need raw material to create him from."

"I heard that." Both women turned toward the doorway at the sound of the voice. Street Wise stood there, his suit torn and dirty. "And I got him," he said.

The pimp and the social worker sat in the remnants of the main bedroom. Melanie was still in the guest room, her mouth packed and re-covered with new strips of tape. The same handcuffs restricted her wrists, elbows, and feet. When Muriel suggested her position be changed, Street maintained that the weaker she was when the bonds were removed, the better.

"The sooner we get her out of here, the better," Muriel told him, ignoring the rubble. "Channel Six News is already asking for any information on her whereabouts. Now, what about this derelict?"

"I remembered what you said," Street told her. "So when the bum showed up, I took him."

"Where is he?" Muriel asked, worried he was right outside, in the van.

"Don't worry," Street said, reading her mind. "I'm not that stupid. He's secured in the storeroom at the mall."

"Did he give you any trouble?"

"None after I showed him who's boss. He just lay, curled up near the door. I had to clean him up when we got there, though. His hand was nearly torn in two and his nose was still bleeding. I figured you might want all his blood."

Muriel nodded, impressed by his quick thinking. Obviously some of her intelligence was rubbing off on him. "Good," she said.

"Now just who was this guy in here?" the pimp asked.

"Me? I was just going to ask you the same thing!"

Street looked surprised. "I thought he was from you. You said you were going to prepare yourself. I thought he was a sign you had succeeded!"

Muriel was delighted. She laughed merrily, clapping her hands. "So now you *do* believe!"

"I saw him," said Street. "Seeing is believing."

His remark made Muriel serious again. It reminded her of Melanie's attitude. "My darling,

Hasn't it occurred to you that this . . . creature was the one who trashed your shack and crib?"

When the social worker talked, Street listened. He thought back to the one glimpse he had of that attack. "Wait a moment. He could have been the one I shot at on the fire escape. . . ."

Muriel nodded with satisfaction. "You see?"

"But who *is* he?" Street said.

"Who are any of the people who hate you? A vice cop, disfigured in a raid. A father, lover, brother, fresh out of the hospital . . ."

"You didn't see this guy," he told her. "That's why I thought he might be one of Satan's minions. . . ."

"He could have been this secret friend of that prostitute you punished," Muriel said.

Street thought about it. "Possibly," he finally reasoned. "That would explain why she didn't run off with him right away. If he was handsome or rich, she would have left like that." He snapped his fingers. Then he rubbed the corners of his lips. "But why didn't he scream?"

"What?"

"I put him in my room with her. When he woke up, he didn't even react."

Muriel looked disappointed. "That was very foolish, my love," she said. "What if he picks the right key?"

Street was still rubbing his lower lip. "I put him in very close to seven," he said defensively. "There's hardly any space in the room left with the dead girl there. And believe me, she was plenty raw and pungent." He thought again about the creature's lack of reaction.

"I didn't tell him what was going on," Street mused. "Even the rats seemed frightened of him. . . ." He lowered his hand, looking back at Muriel. "Even if he did find the right key, he could never get out of there. The water was coming any second."

Holford just looked at him with patience and forgiveness.

"And . . . and . . . even if he *did* get out, there's no way he could find us at the mall!"

"He found you here," Muriel said quietly.

Street blanched for a second, then his skin reddened with angry passion. "Fine," said the pimp. "I've already beat him once. If he comes back, I'll kill him this time." He stood up, already planning. He straightened the suit as best he could. "But I don't think I'll have to bother," he scoffed. "There's no way he's coming out of that sewer."

The cage door opened. Grim surged out, thrusting toward the surface as hard as he could. The keys were pulled off his wrist and swirled through the liquid and sewage. They blinked gold and silver as Grim tore through the water.

The second blast had come a half minute after Grim went underwater. The rats had been hurled to one side of the cage, then all of them struggled under the surface. The vermin, the corpse, and Grim were in a horrible brown, airless, free-fall.

Grim had pulled Betty's body behind him and anchored his feet on the bottom of the cage and his head on the top. Then he just kept grabbing the swimming rats, twisting their heads, and getting the keys. He had to keep killing them, because the live ones, even without the keys, would get in his way. The dead ones simply floated to the top of the cage.

His dictator shouted orders to his body as he dug his way through the floating and hanging rodents, all collected at the top of the cage. He tried the keys one after the other until one finally worked.

Street Wise probably would have tried to cheat

him if he had time to organize. As it was, he had simply dumped Grim inside. But now that Grim was out, he still had to get above water. Every second he stayed submerged he was closer to death and farther from the park sewer entrance.

Grim clawed and kicked toward the top.

"Don't fight," said his god. "Use the current."

Grim made his body an arrow. He used his arms and legs as scissors. He shot up through the garbage-filled liquid in a northwest direction.

His head slammed against the tunnel top. It bounced, then scraped along the coarse metal.

"Float!" his god yelled.

Grim let his body go lax. He shot down the tunnel, carried by the current, as he slowly, painfully rose to the surface again.

The tunnel top scraped his nose and chin. The brown water washed across his eyes and lips. He sucked in air and filth.

Grim moved his head back, spitting out the refuse. He looked through the liquid and saw the circular shadow just in front of him. He threw his arm wide, his fingertips just catching the edge of the tunnel going up to the street.

His body snapped around as he held on. But then the current was too strong and he was pulled away.

He whipped around a corner still tossing and tumbling. He forced himself upright and surged for the surface again. Another tunnel went by, just above his head. He nearly broke his skull on the edge. He tried to grab on but couldn't.

He didn't have much time left. The farther he went, the faster he went.

"Down," commanded his god.

Grim twisted his body around and forced himself lower.

"Aim," said his god.

He could see the open holes far above. They were small dots in the ceiling of the tunnel.

"Fire."

Grim calculated his speed and forced himself up. He used all the strength he had. If he missed, his skull would split.

His body erupted from the water, his torso slamming into the wall of the passage going up to the street. The current tore at his legs, trying to drag him back down, but his fingers clawed at the passage wall.

"Behind you!"

Grim threw one hand back, finding steel ladder rungs. His fingers gripped them tightly. He started to pull himself up.

Something slammed into his legs. He looked down.

Betty stared up at him, one-eyed, smiling.

Grim screamed and reached for her.

But then she was gone.

Grim huddled on the passageway ladder, crying.

The cars, buses, and trucks rumbled down Broadway shaking the sidewalks. They covered the asphalt for thirty seconds, and then they stopped.

In the middle of the street a manhole cover popped up. Like a flipped coin, it jumped three feet in the air and then crashed back to the roadway.

The pedestrians cringed and ducked. The manhole cover had gone only a few yards. They were in no danger. They straightened to look.

A wet, dirty, diseased man climbed out of the hole. His hair was long and stringy. His clothes were soaked and ripped. He was covered in a brownish ooze.

His head was down so they couldn't see his face.

Grim looked down the street at the oncoming line

of vehicles. He sneered at them, then walked slowly toward the sidewalk. The pedestrians scattered, holding their noses and covering their mouths, as he approached.

Grim looked around. He was on the east side of the park. He had gone into the sewer on the west side. Grim climbed over the low stone fence and marched across the grass—not bothering to go around the small lake. He walked right into it and through it, letting the relatively clean water wash away the excrement that covered him. Whoever was in the park that early was careful not to notice him.

By the time he found the manhole he had been dropped down originally, he looked almost the same as he had the previous night. When his clothes dried, there would be no reason for anyone to notice him. His hat was long gone, but as long as he kept his head down, no one should be unduly fascinated by his livid, rent scalp.

All Grim's anger was spent. All it had gotten him was traps and trouble. His punches had missed. His attacks were defeated. Now he would have to rise to another plane. He would have to give Street the respect he deserved. . . .

Grim stood, his sodden shoes on either side of the bloodstains on the sidewalk. Water dripped from his nose onto the concrete. It beaded, then soaked into the crimson.

Grim looked to his left. There were no red dots. He looked to his right. There was broken glass, crumpled paper, torn cloth, crushed cans, and another red dot.

A little, dark red—almost black—circle near the wall. It looked like a tiny painting of a sun going nova. Look, there's another one, seven feet down the street.

Grim hunched over and started to connect the dots. He had all day. He would follow the miraculous bloodstains . . . and the distant echo of his angel's cries.

19

It was midnight at the Riverdale mini-mall. The stores had closed at nine. In this part of the city, some distance from the very last subway station, the streets were quiet and empty.

Inside the mall it was even quieter. The fountain was dry, its colored lights turned off. Only the emergency lights were on, creating pools of white that illuminated small parts of the stores. The night breeze riffled the flowers, bushes, and small trees that were set in the tile around the rectangular courtyard.

Suddenly the three-hour silence was broken. The security grates and steel fences that covered the inside windows of the stores began to roll up with loud clicks, hums, and rattling.

First the metal bars that crisscrossed in front of the Rest Inn diner began to rise, then the large grate in front of the Fullmer Ford dealership, then the steel slats of O'Neill's Nu-Music shop, then the big fence of the Palmers Department Store. As they rose, people began to emerge from the hall between the stores.

They wandered around, already feeling the special new energy. They looked in wonder at their surroundings, as if seeing them for the first time. Each brick, each leaf, each crack in the wall held special significance for them. They looked in fascination, seeing things they had never seen before.

It had started that afternoon. All had considered not going, somehow escaping. But one look at their loved ones kept them prisoners. Some even considered taking their children or loved ones and making a run for it. But they didn't—and not because they were afraid of the social worker. What they were afraid of was seeing their loved ones disintegrate before their eyes.

That was what they had worried about in the morning, and by afternoon the fear was fully grown. By four o'clock they could no longer deny the situation. It began with strange thoughts. They had been preparing dinner or shopping or watching television or even going to the bathroom. But in each case, they noticed something.

Maybe it was the way dust filtered through a shaft of sunlight. Maybe it was the way a multicolored leaf fell outside a window. Maybe it was the way sudden interference crackled on the radio or disturbed the television image. Or maybe they suddenly became aware of the way their hands moved.

All of the club members started to realize the miracle of their lives and the world they lived in. It was as if a dam that had been built between their minds and bodies started slowly to open. At first it was a mere trickle of sensation. They stared at their hands or the air. But as they watched, the electric flow from their minds grew stronger.

They started to see how nature interconnected.
And it scared them.

At first they were terribly frightened. It was the
harbinger of change, and all were deathly afraid how
it would affect them. But soon the current was too
strong. It overwhelmed their senses, filling and
flooding them. Each was exhilarated. Each could
barely contain feelings of wonder and happiness.

They became aware of their individual existence.
They stopped taking everything for granted. All
things were astonishing, amazing. Now, at midnight,
they looked around at one another—delighted and
saddened by what humanity was capable of, and
what it had wrought.

They murmured greetings to one another. They
were deliriously happy to be alive. Street Wise
watched them from the storeroom doorway, tragedy
etched in his features. He looked back at Muriel,
who smiled benignly on him.

"You see?" she said. "You believe now?"

Street tried to talk, but couldn't find the words.
"You mean . . . this is what it always could have
been like?" he finally choked out. She nodded. "Why
. . . why didn't you tell me?"

"You had to be prepared," she said. "You had to be
ready to accept it."

Street Wise wanted to argue, to tell her that he
hadn't been prepared today either. But he wanted
this feeling to continue even more. He swallowed
and looked out at the night sky.

Melanie thought they were drugged. She sat on a
crate, her mouth still taped, her wrists and ankles
still cuffed. She wore the wedding dress. Muriel herself had stripped and dressed her. Any help from Mr.
Wise might have "soiled" her.

Her face was flushed. Her head was pounding.
Sweat ran down her brow and into her eyes. She

could see her chest heaving in the tight satin bodice. She could see the creamy flesh of her legs through the sheer, gossamer white lace. On her feet were pure white, satin-covered high heels. Muriel had even gone so far as to pour glue inside so she couldn't kick them off. Beneath the gown, she was naked.

She looked over to where the derelict lay. Nathan didn't return her gaze. He lay on his side, facing the storeroom wall, staring at his hand. It was the hand that Jeremy Bancroft had stabbed through. It was the hand with the wound he had torn open and let drip out the van door.

It had scabbed over again but was still wet and livid. Nathan stared at it with religious zeal. He was weak and giddy from loss of blood, but more than that, he was happy. He shared these people's Nirvana. They too had given everything to their lord.

Street Wise looked back at the hell mother. "Please . . ." he begged.

Her smile got wider. She was wearing a simple but elegant dress. Not for her the robes of false worship or traditional stupidity. She knew Satan wasn't concerned with wardrobe. Only with action.

"It's twelve o'clock . . ." Street reminded her.

Muriel laughed, feeling the power growing inside her. She saw an image of yeast rising. She felt it filling her. She had to stand, lest she burst. "Time is immaterial. So what if it's twelve? It could be one, or two, or three! Time doesn't exist where Lucifer is."

"It isn't the time," Street said wonderingly. "I feel it . . . inside . . . coming to a fever pitch."

She strode over, touching his cheek. "You will not believe what feelings you're capable of." She nodded toward the blonde and the bum. "Bring them out on my word."

Muriel swept by him and strode out among her people. They reacted entirely different this time.

They took her hand. Some kissed it. They treated
her with reverence and adulation. They murmured
appreciation, often incoherently. Even Willis Farmington nodded at her with total respect, his eyes wet.

All she had to do was motion for them to follow
her. They quickly gathered in the padded amphitheater seat-steps—near the dry, colorless fountain, lit
only by the emergency lights and the rays of a pale
quarter moon.

Muriel Holford sat before them, on the edge of the
fountain, and crossed her legs demurely. She leaned
in and spoke quietly but clearly. "I have felt it for
years," she told them. "As soon as I gave myself unto
Lucifer, I began to feel the power—my own power
—the power of the energy around all of us.

"I was not afraid of it. I was not frightened by
death. Death is natural, part of life, so I experi-
mented with this feeling. I sought to gather this
power. My husband had tried all his life, but failed.
He had tried collecting the power of God, but that is
impossible. Good can only be shared; it can only be
spent.

"So I turned to the other great power in this reality. For every light, there is dark. For every day,
there is night. But is dark and night inherently evil?
No, of course not. So I was not frightened of worshiping Satan. He is merely opposite. He is different. His
power is personal. It can be . . . gathered.

"I have shown you how. You have reaped the re-
wards. Now it is time for us to go further. We have to.
Why else would we be put here except to solve the
mystery of life? If we have purpose, then we must
understand and fulfill our destiny. I say we *do* have
purpose. You have already seen that we can control
our fates. We know we can use the power Satan . . .
and God . . . give us. I tell you it is now time to go
beyond . . . and collect our reward.

"It has pleased me to be your leader. But now you must all know that I am not. I am merely the vessel of Lucifer's love. He wanted me to discover others who could understand that only in the harnessing and use of our own power can we truly be happy. God wanted us to share our power equally. Satan argued that humanity consisted of the weak and strong. Why lower everyone to the same weak level, when the strong could excel and bring wonder and glory to this planet the likes of which we have never known?

"You feel it now, don't you? Believe me when I say that this is just the beginning. You can feel this power, this wonderment, this pure joy always. It is just a matter of accepting your responsibility as a human being. It is time to fulfill our destiny. Mine . . . and yours."

Every eye was on her. There was no doubt in any of their minds. Their loved ones were safe and happy. They were filled with emotions that they had never felt. A presence was here. They could see that the social worker was even more aware of the force.

Muriel turned to nod at Street. He went quickly over to the two captives. He grabbed the derelict by the arm and started to pull him up. By chance his eyes met Melanie's.

She recoiled. His eyes were bright with awe.

"I'm not sorry," he whispered. "You won't believe it. It's . . ."

He couldn't go on. He pulled Nathan's arm over his shoulder and hustled him toward the door.

"Be right back," said Street. "Please . . ." And then he was gone.

Melanie heard Nathan's feet sliding on the concrete hall floor, and then on the courtyard tile. She was alone for the first time since she had been brought here. She tried the cuffs at her wrists, but they were as unyielding as ever. She pulled at her ankles. There was a space about three inches between them. Since her elbows were no longer cuffed, she might just have the balance to attempt escape.

She tried to push the shoes off, but the glue adhered to her feet. It was like trying to tear off her own flesh. She didn't have time to waste. She placed her feet flat and pulled herself up. She had to lean forward to keep from falling. The cumbersome wedding dress was certainly no help.

She checked the distance to the door. She checked the give in her arms and legs. She might even be able to reach around and tear off part of the gag. If she hopped and slid her feet quickly, she might be able to find a way out or hide in one of the stores.

She took her first step. That wasn't so bad. Ignoring her throbbing head, she was about to surge forward.

She heard one word. It was quiet, but it still seemed to fill the space. It certainly filled her head. It sounded as if someone had spoken directly into her ear.

"Sit."

Melanie looked around. There was no one but her in the room. She listened carefully for any echo or sound from outside. She vaguely heard Muriel speaking, but she couldn't make out the words.

She was frozen in place. She knew she had heard it, but already the memory of the voice tone was disappearing. It could have been anyone . . . or anything.

Melanie was more afraid than she had ever been in her entire life. She sat.

"It is not enough to renounce God anymore," Muriel was saying as Street laid Nathan by the fountain.

"It is not enough to insult him. Lucifer is no longer interested in what you do to the Lord. He is interested in what you do for him.

"Do you ever wonder why God or his vaunted Son do not return? His worshipers always fail because they follow the dictates of false religion. They follow the words of men who worship God rather than follow God Himself. They adhere to false rituals, ones they make up based on arcane lies created not just to inspire the people, but to control them."

Street went to get the blonde.

"The same is true with the Devil," Muriel went on. "They think they can call him by preparing this planet. But the planet is already prepared. They think they will find him by spitting on God, by perverting the rites of religion. These rites are already perverted. They think they will show their worthiness by slaughtering animals and children. But that only shows their stupidity, cowardice, and weakness.

"Satan is attracted by strength, imagination, and power. It is true that the gods only help those who help themselves. They are only interested in those who are worthy. Those who are willing to accept their powers over others, and those who use powers with intelligence. . . ."

Muriel saw their eyes move. One by the one they looked beyond her, to the storeroom entrance. Muriel followed their gaze.

Street Wise was walking toward them, holding the beautiful bound and gagged woman in his arms. The social worker continued to speak.

"Satan must be impressed, enticed, and prepared for. It is not the world that must be prepared, it is the deity himself."

Street placed Melanie on a bench, transforming it into a padded altar.

"He is not of our world," Muriel explained. "He

exists in spiritual form. In order to walk among us, to lead us, he must be given corporeal existence. He must be given a human form."

She motioned toward Nathan. "That is what he is for. Raw material with which to work." She motioned toward Melanie. "She is the surviving victim of the city's greatest serial killer. Her husband was brutally murdered. She is undeniably beautiful. Her lovely eyes have witnessed untold horror. She is the enticement. Satan can do what he wishes with her. We will not be so bold as to suggest her use."

Muriel stretched her arms out to them. "And you . . . you are the channel through which he can travel. From the moment you spoke your greatest evil aloud, I have felt the power growing inside me. As each evil was born, the power in me grew. I am certain that I can be no greater. I am certain Satan can perceive my strength and desire. I know he is waiting."

Street stood by Melanie. He watched the social worker with his legs wide and anchored, his hands folded behind him. Nathan lay cringing on the ground beside the fountain.

Muriel Holford finally stood. "We are ready. Listen to me, children. You must think. You must concentrate. Remember your greatest evil. Close your eyes, lower your heads, and picture it with all the clarity you can. Remember, your loved ones' lives are at stake. If we fail now, all the good work that has gone before will be in vain. Think hard. Think now."

"There he is!" screamed Mr. Barker.

The social worker and the pimp had been just about to close their eyes when the man screamed. Their heads snapped in his direction. They saw him pointing toward the roof. They looked.

Grim the Undead stood there, watching them. He had searched until he found them. His worshipers had gathered, following him, some directing him, but he had sent them away. No more would be slaughtered for loving him. He demanded that they stay back. He demanded that they only witness.

"It's him!" screamed the Beaumonts. "It's really him!"

"No!" boomed Muriel, surprising them all. Street was already pulling the silver-plated .357 revolver from its shoulder holster.

"No!" Muriel said again as the pimp ran to the far wall and aimed. "It's a demon from the other side! He's been sent to stop us!"

Grim crouched, slid sideways over the roof wall, and dropped to the second-story floor. Street blasted at him, the bullets smashing the window behind him. Grim landed and stayed low, using the second-floor banister as cover.

"Get him!" Muriel screeched at Street. The pimp felt power he never dreamed he possessed. His prostitutes had been nothing. They had been a sign of his weakness and cowardice. But this, this was a creature who was worthy of control and destruction. The pimp was inspired.

He raced toward the one stairway on the west side of the courtyard—opposite the elevator. Melanie started to struggle and shout, but Muriel whipped her head around, pinning the captive with a paralyzing glare.

As Street raced up the steps, Grim stood, looking over the banister, directly at his angel. The club members gasped at his face.

"I tell you it's a trick!" Muriel shouted. "He is trying to stop us! If we fail, your loved ones will die in torment! You will live your lives in pain and horror. You will be cursed . . . by God!"

Grim ducked and turned to face Street.

The pimp was gone.

Suddenly the mall was quiet. The club members had screwed their eyes shut, bowed their heads, and were concentrating intently. Muriel Holford was standing in front of them, her arms wide. Nathan had begun to shake. Melanie lay motionless, as if exhausted.

Grim surveyed the entire second floor, staying low and balanced, ready to move in any direction. The pimp had a gun, but a .357 wasn't very accurate unless fired close to a stationary target. Grim was determined that the man would not catch him by surprise.

He checked behind him to make sure Street couldn't sneak through the stores. Grim backed against the front window of a small sports shop. There was no door between it and the bookstore on one side and the clothes store on the other.

Grim waited, but nothing happened. He looked through the banister bars. The members were still praying. Nathan was still shaking. Grim could see Melanie's eyes moving desperately, but her body remained completely still, as if pressed down.

Grim considered jumping to the main floor and taking his chances with the small mob. But he knew Street wouldn't think twice about shooting his angel. And he had little doubt she would bleed and die just like any other human.

Grim squatted, suddenly confused and afraid. What was going on here? Why did waiting fill him with such panic?

Grim started to run for the stairs.

A Ford Fiesta roared to life in the Fullmer second-floor showroom. Its lights went on like a monster's eyes opening, and it leaped through the glass.

It was already moving parallel to the second-story floor, so all it had to do was come out of the showroom sideways. It snaked onto the tile and tore toward Grim.

He tried to leap out of the way, to vault over the banister, but the bumper caught him on the shin. He was hurled against the windshield. Street braked. Grim was thrown back, directly through the window of the music store.

Street had the gun up, firing through his already cracked windshield. The bullets smashed the car glass and the store glass. To the pimp's eyes it looked as if his quarry was being swallowed by a stone beast with sharp crystal teeth.

Grim crashed through the shop window. He felt the steel-reinforced doorframe scrape across his skull. He flew over the racks of albums. He knew that pain would come eventually.

He shot across the store, feeling nothing but calm. He felt as though he was floating in place.

"Rise," he heard his god whisper.

Grim relaxed totally. He hit the back wall, which was cushioned by posters. He fell onto a pile of T-shirts and rolled off. He lay behind the counter, on his face.

Street jumped into the store. He stayed low, his gun ready.

It was Grim's turn to disappear.

The dark shop seemed empty. The car's gritted metal mouth filled the opening. Street stood by it, letting his cunning take over.

The creature had gone through the left section of glass, straight back. The pimp's eyes traced his flight. He saw the broken soundproof board on the back wall. He saw the torn posters, practically pointing down behind the counter.

Street stepped in, aimed, and pulled the trigger four times. The bullets smashed low into the counter, digging wood and carpet along the floor.

Street snapped open the gun's cylinder, dropped the spent shells with one hand, and pulled the speed loader from his jacket pocket with the other.

He clicked the six new rounds and closed the cylinder. It had taken only two seconds. He was about to bring the gun up when the first videotape hit him in the face.

It had been thrown like a tomahawk. The edge smashed into the bridge of his nose. The next slammed into the side of his head. He rocked in place, bouncing off the side of the car. A plastic compact disc sliced into his ear. The entire package had been thrown like a Frisbee, only much faster, much more wickedly. Another hit him in the neck. A third went into his left eye.

Street screamed, covering his eye with both hands. He tried to bring his gun arm down, but it was too late. A videotape hit his wrist. A compact disc package cut at his fingers. The pimp reeled, the gun going off into the ceiling.

Grim stood, one arm inside the counter to the left. He popped out the six-by-three-foot sheet of glass and threw the quarter-inch-thick countertop like a lance.

It had to travel only a few feet but the wind already took it, twisting it so it hit Street flat across the head and chest. It rammed him against the car and smashed all around him.

Street covered his head with his arms, screaming, as the glass shards tore at him. Grim grabbed a T-shirt stand by the base. He charged out between counters and caught the blinded pimp in the chest.

The tip of the metal stand caught Street just under the sternum. It lifted him off the ground and over the car roof. The pimp crashed to the second-story tile on the back of his head and shoulders.

The gun skittered away. Grim slid over the car roof. Street was trying to get up.

Grim hit him in the center of his torn face. He felt the nose breaking and flattening under the wall of his hand. Street rocked back, more blood splashing onto his tailored suit.

Grim hit him in the throat, trying to push the man's Adam's apple through his spine. Street's body undulated like a wave. But incredibly, he remained standing.

Grim kicked him between the legs. Street fell against the second-story railing.

Grim moved in before the pimp could collapse. He slammed his fists into Street's stomach, rupturing his spleen. He held the pimp up by the throat. He brought his fist back.

He felt an electric shock.

Street Wise stood in eternity again, the serpent smiling on him. He opened his split and mashed lips, blood bubbles popping as he tried to get the words out.

"Help me . . . Satan . . ."

Grim couldn't have paused more than a nanosecond, but in that time, Street somehow made his arms and legs propel him backward, over the railing, away from Grim's final strike. He slithered out from under Grim's hand, fell, and disappeared from sight.

Grim followed him, vaulting over the railing. He saw Street twisting his body around so he could land on his feet. He slammed forward. Grim was right behind him, also landing on his feet, but falling back.

Street tried to get up. He couldn't quite make it. He dragged himself toward the social worker, his hand out.

"Mama!" he screamed at her pitifully. "Mama!"

Muriel wasn't listening. She didn't look at him. She didn't move.

Street Wise crawled toward the center of the courtyard. He stared wildly at the club members. Their heads were still down. Their eyes were still closed. He tried to scream at them, but all that emerged from his throat was a rattling groan.

He looked back. Grim was getting closer, looming over him.

This time Street did scream. It gave him the strength to tear forward, just managing to get to his feet at the edge of the tiny amphitheater.

Grim leaped, feet first, smashing into Street's side. Whatever the pimp was going to say was mingled with his cry of agony and fear as he flew over the seats and smashed onto the fountain.

He landed on his back, directly on top of the main water nozzle.

Grim jumped after him. He landed on the edge of the fountain, then jumped in, slamming both fists down on Street's chest.

He felt the pimp sink onto the open metal tube. He saw the pimp's eyes roll around in his head. He felt his body convulse.

Street Wise was screaming and crying like a child, his wails filling the night air. He tried to reach out. "Mama," he whispered as he died.

Grim didn't care. He was already turning, already going to grab his angel and carry her away.

"No!"

He stopped dead in the fountain, looking up at Muriel Holford. She had turned to face him. Her eyes were wider than was possible and her mouth was completely off her teeth. Her muscles were clenched, bunched tightly under the skin on her face. "No," she snapped again. "It's working. . . ."

"My lord!" The words were agony itself. Nathan had stood on the other side of Grim's angel.

"I've failed you!" he cried. His arms were moving

spasmodically. The muscles behind every inch of his skin were dancing. "Forgive me," he said just as all the muscles stretched, paralyzing him.

Grim watched as he changed.

20

The Imp erupted from the Hudson River, invisible to everything but itself.

It had felt the disruption in human reality even under the water, where it had lain since its last failure to put the Undead creature under its control. The Imp had every intention of staying there until it came up with another plan to control Grim's power.

Then this happened. It was like an alarm inside its thoughts. Everything was the same, but everything was different. It was like looking at a one-dimensional image that had suddenly become 3-D.

The Imp shot over the city, its gem-worms coming off its skin like dandruff. It paused for a moment, watching the quivering, crystalline impulses float slowly toward the ground.

Incredible, it thought. Nothing but the Imp itself seemed to be aware of the tear in dimensions. The cars below drove as fast as they ever had. The people walked along the streets, ran for the buses, taxis, and subways as if it were just another night.

They didn't know, the Imp realized. They were completely ignorant of the massive change about to take place. The Imp concentrated on locating the source of the disruption. It wasn't hard to do. Van Cortlandt Park practically had lightning bolts and neon arrows pointing to it. The neighborhood stood out in bas-relief from the rest of Riverdale.

The Imp sped in that direction, trying to gather perceptions from all around itself. More than ever, it wanted to see what it had never seen before. It wanted to *be* perceived by those who had never seen it.

The Imp knew there had to be more to its existence. It knew there had to be more beyond its own senses. This was mere logic: if the humans weren't aware of the Imp, there had to be things the Imp couldn't see. It imagined the sky clogged with creatures being dragged toward the change like metal filings toward an electromagnet.

Damn the Undead man anyway, the Imp caught himself thinking. *Who needs him?* Reality was about to explode open, and the Imp was going to be there to pick up the pieces.

Nathan changed. The muscles beneath the skin moved. His skull had become opaque, and just below the surface another face was rising to meld with the features already there.

The horror of it pushed Grim back. He was almost on his knees, beside Street Wise's body. Nathan's mouth opened and loud, agonized sounds came out. He was barking at his deity, saliva and mucus flying.

Grim, unable to look away from the tortured Nathan, instinctively grabbed at the dead pimp's pockets, trying to find the gun. He felt a weapon's shape in the suit's right jacket pocket. Grim's hand dug into the flap.

Muriel had stepped back and to the side, her arms still wide, her face infused with glory. The derelict's beard grew longer, the hairs forced out from the inside. The club members gasped as the air was filled with snapping, popping, cracking noises.

Nathan made one last howl, then the derelict was no more. The beast's eyes bulged. Its knees smacked against the fountain's edge.

Grim ripped the rose-colored water pistol from Street's pocket. He aimed it directly at the center of the beast's changing face.

"No!" his god warned.

Nathan wasn't responsible. The woman was doing this. The power was coming through her. Grim pulled the water pistol around until the barrel obscured Muriel Holford's face.

The beast leaped, its tormented cries deafening Grim. It dived over the fountain lip, directly at the pimp's corpse. It slammed on top of Street, pushing his body even deeper onto the water pipe cutting into his back.

The beast's body knocked Grim aside. The water pistol fell under the two writhing forms. Grim grabbed for it just as the beast looked toward him.

They were face to face, their heads separated by inches. Nathan was gone. The new face was covered with brown hair and shone red beneath the strange beard. The eyes were white, with red orbs swimming deep inside them, as if covered in rancid cream. The nose had darkened, oozing pus from every pore. Phlegm was pouring out of its nostrils.

Grim fell back. The water pistol clanked on two water pipes and was knocked out of his hand. The beast looked away, both arms shooting down, both hands grabbing the round metal spigots.

The beast twisted the faucets open. The water spurted from the pipe openings. The liquid shot upward, obscuring the beast and the corpse from view.

But just before the curtain of water shot up . . . just before everyone was blinded by the fountain and its colored lights . . . Grim saw the beast put all its weight on the corpse. Grim saw the main water pipe start coming through the front of Street Wise's chest.

They all stepped back. Muriel leaped off the fountain ledge. Grim jumped out from the other side. Melanie rolled off the bench, unable to get her footing in the glued high heels. She lay beside the bench, sobbing and trying to breathe.

The club members gasped as the water roared skyward. They looked up as the seven nozzles shot the liquid twelve feet in the air. Their cries were choked off into shrieks as the water was laced with red.

Grim started to move in. He stopped when the water parted for a second. Inside he saw the beast. It was no longer on top of Street. It was becoming *part* of Street.

They were joined like Siamese twins: at the arms, at the hips, along the legs. . . .

Then the florid crimson water covered them again —the blood being recycled with the rest of the liquid.

Grim stepped away, unable to comprehend what he was seeing. Neither his god nor his dictator could explain. Instead they shut down the part of his mind that sought to understand.

They ordered him to do whatever was practical. Get her, and get out! Grim raced for his angel. Her altar was empty. He had just located her beside the bench when the beast emerged from the fountain.

Its head was up, crying at the moon. Its arms were

wide, spraying the gathered flock with stained water. It rose above them, twice as large as the hell mother.

There were horns coming from its temples.

It stepped out of the water, standing near the edge of the fountain. It had cloven hooves. Its legs were twisted, the bones altering to hold its weight. It was covered with bulbous wads of thick gelatinous flesh. It shook them off, the gore slapping the tiles.

Its expression was confused, disoriented. It looked over the petrified mass until its red, almond-shaped eyes settled on the social worker. It opened its mouth to speak. Its voice was raw and wounded.

"Mother?"

The miracle had happened. All Muriel's desires, dreams, hope, and work had paid off. She had not been afraid of her power. This was what she had achieved. She had been willing to accept the impossible. It stood before her.

She opened her arms to her creation. "Yes, my love," she cried. "Yes!"

No one could believe it, but they all had to accept it. The horned, cloven-hoofed creature was before them. They could only follow Muriel's bold example. They watched in awe as the woman and the beast embraced.

Melanie could see only her dream monster. He held her, pulling her off the floor. He wanted to look only at her, but could not. He looked above and beyond her, at the beast. He knew this was a creation of evils. He saw it, and he could feel it. He knew he couldn't just collect his angel and run. With this thing here, there was nowhere for them to go.

He had to lay his angel down again. He dived into the fountain. He reached wildly for the pistol, but couldn't find it. He had to turn off the spigots. When the water died, the beast and hell mother turned.

Grim stood, holding the weapon, pointing it at the woman.

He pulled the trigger. The beast lowered its large hand. The liquid tranquilizer splattered in his palm. His face became quizzical, then mirthful. He looked directly at Grim and smiled with infinite knowledge.

Then he swung his arm around, catching Grim full in the face with the back of his hand. Grim was thrown from the pit. He spun completely around in the air before hitting the tiles of the first level on his back. He slid all the way across the floor, his head slamming into the window of the Rest Inn.

Grim lay crumpled in the corner.

The mall was deathly silent. Even the crickets didn't chirp. The Ford Fiesta smoked in the upstairs window of the Nu-Music shop. A piece of glass fell from the bullet-riddled sports store above them. The water was slowly draining out of the fountain.

The beast stepped over to Muriel and placed a hand on her shoulder. He smiled down at his minions.

"My dears," said Muriel, indicating the beast, "my darlings, your master."

They didn't know what to do. They sat there, afraid to move. The beast admired their expressions.

"Where is she?" he asked.

Muriel started in surprise. "The woman!" she cried. "Of course!" She pointed quickly at the empty bench and the cringing blonde in the wedding dress beside it.

The beast waved his free hand curtly. "Release her."

"Yes," said Muriel, rushing to do his bidding. She took a handcuff key from her dress pocket and undid Melanie's ankles. She had to pull her up by the arms so the blonde could stand on her glued shoes and weak legs.

Muriel held her facing the beast. Melanie looked into the leering face, his expression containing untold wisdom . . . and sadism. It was as if every Muriel Holford and every Street Wise had been gathered in one form.

"Beautiful," breathed the beast.

Melanie tried to pull free of the restraining arms. She couldn't stop screaming.

The beast flicked his hand again in a regal motion of dismissal. "Sit," he said.

Melanie stopped screaming as if her throat had been clamped shut. She sat on the bench.

She had heard that voice before.

"My love," Muriel said, oblivious to the blonde's actions. She naturally thought that anyone would follow the beast's orders implicitly. "We have done it," she explained, approaching him. "You are here. We await your bidding. Claim this world for your own!"

The beast looked at her patiently. "What for?" he asked. His voice was getting smoother from use.

Muriel stopped in her tracks. He wasn't commanding now. He was talking to her, calmly and reasonably. "Uh . . . what?"

The beast spoke again, his tones unequivocally civilized. "Why?"

Muriel's expression began to quiver. It was a test, she realized. He was seeing if she was worthy to be his consort. She would not fail him. "It is yours!" she cried.

The beast seemed to think about it. He frowned and shook his head. "No, it isn't."

"It can be!" Muriel immediately shot back. "It shall be!"

The beast smiled again, like a patient teacher. "How?"

Muriel was flabbergasted. "Take it! Make it yours.

You have worshipers! They will follow you! The army of darkness!"

"What?" the beast interrupted sharply.

Muriel blinked. "The army of darkness," she repeated. "They can cover the earth. . . ."

The beast shook his hand and head. Muriel choked off her words, her mouth opening and closing. "Think," he said. He smiled at her when she was unable to respond.

Muriel Holford started to back away.

"Oh no, no, no," said the horned, cloven-hoofed creature. "Yes, I have followers, but what about those who don't follow me? They will gather armies. They will lay traps. They will shoot me. I will have to get a succession of human forms to remain whole."

Muriel held her ground, shaking her fist. "You can. You will! Crush them! Rule us!"

The beast looked pained. "Yes, I could kill them, but I would have to destroy this world. I would have to raze it to the ground. Remember, I don't strike you down. I only influence you to strike each other down."

"Do it, my lord!" Muriel cried. "Do it!"

The beast stepped back, facing the club members. "From the open?" he complained.

Muriel stood straight, her arms at her sides. Her brain was beginning to unravel.

"Lucifer!" she chastised.

He whipped his head around, looking straight at her. "What do I do for a living?"

Muriel babbled incoherently for a second, then leaned in. "You are the Prince of Darkness, ruler of hell!"

"Stop it!" he interrupted. "What do I do for a living?"

Muriel's thoughts were frozen. She stood, her concentration drifting.

"I'll make it easy," the beast said as if talking to a three-year-old. "Say you've been bad. Say you die. Where do you go?"

Muriel stared at him. Her thoughts began to click back in place. "Hell?" she said.

"Good," said the beast. "Yes, hell. Now tell me"— he bent down, putting his face directly in front of hers—*"do I reward you?"*

Muriel's mouth opened but nothing came out. She saw the truth in her mind before it raced away, burying itself in her subconscious. Then all she could hear were the words: *I knew it all along. I knew all along. I knew the truth, but I wouldn't admit it. I knew it. I knew . . .*

The beast turned toward the club members. He towered over them, his fingers curled into fists, his eyes burning, his facial muscles bunching. They saw acidic liquid covering his skin. The stench of death stung their nostrils.

"No," said the beast, his words becoming coarse and enraged. *"I punish you . . . in hellfire . . . forever!"*

The club members went crazy. Some turned and ran. Some collapsed. Some buried their heads in their hands and sobbed. Some had fits.

The beast stood straight up, smiling down on his worshipers. "You wanted me?" he said to no one in particular. "You got me. . . ."

The beast raised his arms. The mall shook as if bounced. The club members were thrown up, then slammed down. The tiles cracked and broke along their seams. Flames belched out, their orange tongues flickering.

The club members screamed and tried to regain their balance, but the fire was alive. It ripped open the ground, tore through the tile, and grabbed at them. It leaped onto their flesh and clothes, spreading, chewing. . . .

The beast raised his arms again. A second tremor shook the ground. Entire ditches blasted out of the ground, filled with boiling liquid flame. The beast started to move, pushing the fleeing members into the trenches.

"Yes," he said. "You attracted me, you enticed me. You gave me what I wanted. Now is the time to be who I want *you* to be."

"No!" Muriel Holford had found her voice. The beast stopped and looked toward her. She was standing on the edge of the fountain at attention, her arms at her sides. "You can't do this!" she sputtered. "You're Satan . . . you're evil!"

The others continued to scream and writhe, the flames getting higher, as the beast marched back to his hell mother. "Evil?" he echoed, getting closer. "You don't even know what evil is."

He stood before his maker, looking down on her with interest. In the midst of the flames and the screams of the tortured and damned, Muriel Holford was crying.

"I brought you here." She sobbed. "I gave you this world. Why don't you take it?"

The beast smiled with infinite sympathy. "Mommy," he said. "I don't need this world. I already have it, remember?" He took her arms gently and leaned down to look into her eyes. "It's true. Think. You all come to me eventually. If I plunged this world into darkness, who would I play with?"

Then he nonchalantly tore her arms off.

He threw them aside. Muriel Holford collapsed, unable even to scream. The beast bent and retrieved the handcuff key from her pocket. He looked down on her with a little less than pity.

"You've got to take responsibility for your

thoughts," he said, then stepped on her head as if grinding out a cigarette.

The beast gently, carefully, undid the handcuffs around Melanie's wrists. He stood back as she pulled the tape from her mouth. She looked up at him, licking her lips and gulping in air.

"You're lucky," he said. "You will forget. Your brain will not let you remember. The moment you no longer see me, I will be relegated back to your subconscious fears." He grinned. "I might be fading already."

Melanie had no choice but to accept his existence and his words. "You're . . . a nightmare?"

"Really." The beast sighed. "With all the other demons in this world, with all the other sins . . . am I really so unbelievable?"

"Why not," she choked out, trying not to cry, "kill me?"

He looked down his nose at her, seemingly considering his options. He wagged a finger at her. "You can do me a favor."

He swung around, his arm pointing through the Palmers Department Store. Hellfire erupted in a line, blowing open a path in the floor, hurling back kitchen appliances. A huge hole blew out of the opposite window, tearing apart the steel bars crossing it.

Almost as soon as it appeared, the flames puffed out, leaving just the path and the gateway back to Earth.

"Go," he told her. "Tell them what evil is."

Melanie Merrick stood. She glanced at the beast's calm face, then started to walk. She walked as if she were on a high wire. She put one foot carefully in front of the other, moving amid the flames and the screaming people.

One man ran at her, trying to use her as protection, but a three-foot-wide wall of flame erupted out of the ground between them. He smashed into it face first. She saw his hands on either side of the red-and-orange wall. It wrapped over him like a tongue. When it disappeared, he was gone.

Melanie only flinched, steeling herself for a second, then walked carefully on. She looked around her, trying to capture the sights, sounds, and smells in her mind. To capture them, to help explain the pain. She felt the tears hot on her cheeks and chin. She couldn't believe these memories would fade.

But she felt them already dissolving. They were like burning paper. The edges crumpled, then the image darkened and faded. *Her* dictator was already protecting her sanity.

There *were* powers greater than humans. One was inside each of their heads.

Melanie stopped just inside the front window of the department store. She looked back at the flames and the writhing humanity. In the distance, a small disfigured form lay huddled in a corner. Standing in the middle of it all was the horned, hooved, twelve-foot-tall figure.

"Go," he said, pointing away from all it represented. "Let them know what evil is."

Melanie stepped outside. A wall of flame blasted up, forcing her forward. It covered the opening, latched on to the building, and started to burn.

The beast within turned away from the beautiful woman. He looked over the tormented forms in a professional way, judging the degree of torture. He walked up to the top of the tiny amphitheater and gauged how long it would take the fire to consume every inch of the mall.

Finally he turned to look at the man lying in front of the diner.

"Now what," the beast said, "am I going to do with you?"

EPILOGUE

One is always wrong to open a conversation with
   the devil,
for, however he goes about it,
he always insists upon having the last word.

—André Gide

"Get up," said the beast.

Grim had little choice but to do what he said. He opened his eyes and got slowly to his feet. He stood in front of the Rest Inn diner, trying to take it all in.

"Well, what do you know?" said the beast, standing about ten feet in front of him. "Something new." He noticed the disfigured man was looking him up and down repeatedly.

"Oh . . . this old thing?" the beast said, referring to his horns and hooves. "Give the people what they want; you can never go wrong. How long have you been listening?"

Grim shrugged. Once he knew that Melanie was safe, he had been playing possum—hoping the beast would ignore him. He was not afraid now that he knew this beast wouldn't harm an angel. He looked up at the horned creature with respect.

"What is death?" Grim groaned, almost yearningly.

It was the beast's turn to shrug. "A lot like life," he
answered easily. "Made in His image and all, you
know . . ." The beast cocked his head to the side,
listening. Soon Grim could also hear the wail of distant sirens.

"Have to be going soon," said the beast. "But I
have something for you."

Suddenly Grim's mind was filled with the image of
a tall, muscular Hispanic man planting a bomb. He
saw the car explode.

He reeled back, hitting the cracked diner window
again. It shattered behind him.

"Think of it as a gift," said the beast. "From hell."
He started to turn away.

"Wait!" Grim cried, stepping forward, his hand
out. He willed the memory of the Central American
assassin from his mind's eye. He had to remain fully
aware for one last question.

The beast turned back, both curious and annoyed.
It had to be important for this miserable Undead
creature to delay him.

Grim took another step. He had heard it when he
was lying there. He had to know. "What *is* evil?" he
asked.

The beast smiled, almost laughing, in honest appreciation. "My dear boy," he said. Then he leaned
down and whispered directly into Grim's face. "Evil
. . . is something you pay for."

Then, with a flourish, he blasted a cannon of hellfire through the diner window, across the interior,
and out the back wall. The flames pushed Grim forward, bore him through the restaurant, and hurled
him into the parking lot.

To his dozens of followers, it looked as if the mall
had spit Grim out.

Inside the burning square, the beast turned back. He watched as the bodies of the club members quivered and stilled, the flames still feasting on them. He watched the fire lick up the store walls, covering the mall like a tidal wave. He turned his head, listening to a symphony inside the darkness of his own mind.

Somewhere children were screaming in terrible pain, wracked with renewed disease, crying for their parents. Somewhere, in many places, the children of very successful satanists were dying.

The beast didn't smile, but he took what pleasure he could. After all, having mercy on stupid, misguided, evil humans was not exactly high on his list of priorities. Neither was ignoring other supernatural creatures.

Suddenly the twelve-foot beast pivoted to the right and lashed out. The Imp was kicked all the way across the courtyard.

The flames parted to allow the Imp to slam straight into a wall. It bounced off with a satisfying smack, then rolled across the broken tiles, its gem-worms shattering.

It regained its balance and twisted into a shape of astonishment. "You knew!" it bleated, floating upward, its shape changing from surprise, through fear, to joy. "You can perceive me!"

The beast swung his head toward the Imp, paralyzing it with just his expression. The gem-worms inside the Imp turned pure white and dissolved into ectoplasmic ash. The Imp's shape almost melted, but before it could, the Imp snapped straight up through the air. It shot away from the mall like a wiggling bullet.

The Imp exulted in terror. The beast had acknowledged its presence. There *was* more to its existence

than it perceived. This was proof! Now nothing
would stop it. If Grim could make a bridge for the
beast, he could make one for the Imp.

The Imp curled into a shape of satisfaction as it
sped away to make plans. It swore King Grim would
tear a hole in the world big enough for the Imp to get
through. And it would happen soon.

The beast watched the bulbous creature retreat.
He was tempted to rip it out of the sky, but resisted
the prank. The Imp's desires might even teach him
something new about the depths of human deprav-
ity.

"Keep up the good work," the beast whispered
toward it sardonically. Then he looked around, motioning to the flames as if they were pets. "Come, my
children," he said. "Time to take it home."

Grim rolled across the parking lot, the asphalt
tearing at his clothes. It ripped and peeled the cloth
from his elbows, knees, thighs, and forearms. He
somersaulted and spun until a line of worshipers
caught him. They went down like tenpins.

More followers went to help King Grim as he tried
to get his breath back. He turned toward the mall
just as a huge wing of hellfire blasted out the east and
west walls. As they all watched, another gigantic
torrent shot straight up into the air.

For a moment, the mall was pierced by a huge
inverted cross of flame. Then the fire shot back,
seemingly sucked into the earth. The light was so
bright that Grim and his followers had to shield their
eyes.

When they could see again, the mall was gone. In
its place was only blackened rubble. In the distance
they could see fire trucks, police cars, and ambulances racing down the streets.

There, all the way on the other side of the wreckage, was a tiny figure in white. . . .

Grim struggled to his feet, trying to get to the cover of the park woods bordering the parking lot. But his followers were not just holding on to him. They were holding him back.

The panic suddenly left him, as if switched off. He stared into the silent, staring faces around him. In them he read accusation, doubt, disappointment, and fear. He looked behind him. Nathan was no longer there. He had been swallowed up into a beast's human form, his spirit finally released to whatever reward was waiting. But without him, Grim had no diplomat, no organizer, and no translator.

Nathan had been used by a power who couldn't care less about humans. A power that collected human evil. A power that studied humans just to see how it could screw them up.

Grim called to his god for help. Like all gods, he didn't answer. He was merely an umpire. He could only observe, advise, and, occasionally, throw you out of the game.

But King Grim was no god. That much his worshipers had witnessed. And like all betrayed followers, they had decided. One by one, they turned away from their paper emperor. They trudged away on their own feet of clay.

Grim watched the crowd spread, and thin out, as the sirens got louder. He saw the branches of the trees sprayed with the vehicles' white, blue, and red lights. The derelicts' bodies were strobed as they walked past the thick, brown, bark-covered tree trunks. Then, one by one once more, they disappeared—winking out in the flash between the flashing colored lights.

Within seconds, Grim stood alone in the parking lot, forsaken. He felt shallow relief, and a deep loss.

He didn't run after them, nor did he fall to his bleeding knees. Instead, he turned to look after his fallen angel. She walked on the other side of the blackened, smoking pit, her arms out, her lips already forming the hollow words. But by the time she turned to face the wreckage, he was gone.

"Let me tell you what evil is," she said to the emptiness. "I want you to know what evil is. . . ."

Hell hath no limits, nor is circumscribed
In one self place; where we are is hell,
And where hell is there must we ever be.
                              —Christopher Marlowe,
                                Doctor Faustus